Cruise Control

"So who decided to chain off the area around the crime scene?" I asked.

Tilly laid her walking stick on her lap. "It seems logical to assume that the chief security officer and the ship's captain were probably instructed to do that by either the Coast Guard, the FBI, or some other mainland law enforcement agency."

Nana nodded agreement. "Cruise ships got the right to ask help from any law enforcement agency they want."

"Did you learn that on your A&E special, too?" I asked.

Nana shook her head. "Reruns of *The Love Boat*."

"I suspect that's why they cordoned off the crime scene," said Tilly. "To preserve the area as much as possible for the island police, though I'm not sure how much evidence can be preserved on a windswept deck. This is a cruise line's worst nightmare. They're in the business of selling fantasy, and crime scene tape and evidence kits are not part of the *Aloha Princess* fantasy package. Can you imagine the panic aboard ship if word leaks out that there could be a killer prowling the decks?"

"But there *is* a killer prowling the decks!"

Top O' the Mournin'

"Hilarious and delightful. . . . I found myself laughing out loud and wiping away tears (of joy) as I quickly flipped the pages. I can't wait for the next trip!"

—*Old Book Barn Gazette*

"A delightful cozy that is low on gore but rich in plot and characterizations. There is plenty of slapstick humor. . . . The mystery is well constructed and the supporting cast yields a number of suspects. . . ."

—*TheBestReviews.com*

"No sophmore jinx here . . . very funny and full of suspense."
—*Romantic Times Bookclub Magazine*

"WARNING: Do not munch on Triscuits or anything covered in powdered sugar while reading this book! I nearly choked from laughing so hard. . . . There was belly laughter, or at least a chuckle, on each page. This is the most fun I've had in a while."

—*The Mystery Company newsletter*

Alpine for You

"I found myself laughing out loud. . . . The word 'hoot' comes to mind."

—*Deadly Pleasures*

"Light and witty. . . . While we're all waiting for the next Janet Evanovich, this one will do perfectly."
—Sleuth of Baker Street (Ontario, Canada)

Also by Maddy Hunter

PASTA IMPERFECT
ALPINE FOR YOU
TOP O' THE MOURNIN'

maddy
HUNTER

A *Passport to Peril* mystery

Hula Done It?

POCKET BOOKS
New York   London   Toronto   Sydney

An *Original* Publication of POCKET BOOKS

POCKET BOOKS, a division of Simon & Schuster, Inc.
1230 Avenue of the Americas, New York, NY 10020

Copyright © 2005 by Mary Mayer Holmes

ISBN-13: 978-0-7434-8292-9
ISBN-10:   0-7434-8292-1

This Pocket Books paperback edition November 2005

10 9 8 7 6 5 4 3 2 1

Cover illustration by Jeff Fitz-Maurice
Interior design by Davina Mock

Manufactured in the United States of America

For information regarding special discounts for bulk purchases, please contact Simon & Schuster Special Sales at 1-800-456-6798 or business@simonandschuster.com.

DEDICATION

To Mum—
Everything I am, or ever will be, I owe to you.
I love you!

—mmh

Hula Done It?

CHAPTER 1

Aboard the cruise ship, *Aloha Princess*
En route to Kauai, Hawaii—October 28

"The Hawaiian islanders weren't as predictable as the English, and it was this unpredictability that Captain Cook and his crew found so confounding. There was no rhyme or reason behind the natives' gift giving one day and their hostility the next. History places blame for Cook's death and dismemberment on the shoulders of the islanders, but I prefer to blame the era. Cook needed the assistance of a behavioral psychologist, and unfortunately, psychology was hardly even a fledgling science in 1779."

Professor Dorian Smoker glanced toward the back of the lecture room for the umpteenth time, his pale blue eyes flickering with an uneasiness that seemed unwarranted for a man recognized as the world's leading authority on Captain James Cook. What in the heck was back there that he found so disturbing?

I glanced subtly over my shoulder to find people packed into the room like proverbial sardines. I wasn't surprised to find standing room only. Professor Smoker was the academic headliner for our cruise, which advertised excursions to the sites visited by Captain Cook on his fateful third sea voyage, so the audience was filled with bespectacled, erudite types with name tags that identified them as members of organizations I'd never of: the Sandwich Island Society, the World Navigators Club, Haute Cuisine International.

I wasn't sure why the Haute Cuisine people were here, but intuition told me they'd probably confused Captain Cook with Mr. Food and were expecting a guy in an apron and chef's hat to wow them with food preparation and tasty free samples. Instead, a man in a navy cardigan and baggy Dockers had mesmerized them with tales of an eighteenth-century English explorer.

And I do mean "mesmerized." Even the guests who were obviously sitting in on the wrong lecture made no attempt to leave. As physically unremarkable as Professor Smoker was, once he started speaking, he oozed such magnetism that he held all of us spellbound. His knowledge gave him an intellectual swagger and confidence that elevated him from dowdy to dazzling, from Mr. Rogers to Buck Rogers. Without having to rely on artificial creams, costly implants, or media hype, Professor Dorian Smoker suddenly became the sexiest man on the planet—not bad for a fiftysomething academic with a slight paunch, bad posture, scruffy beard, and thinning gray hair.

But I still wondered about the odd glint in his eyes. Was it alarm or a piece of fuzz caught behind a contact lens?

I'm Emily Andrew, full-time coordinator of global excursions for a senior travel club and person most likely to misinterpret a lot of things related to life, death, romance, and spastic eye movements. I'm aboard the *Aloha Princess* as the official escort for a group of eleven Iowans who've lived in my hometown most of their lives. I'm a longtime resident, too, except for a few years when I worked the New York City theater scene and was married to Jack Potter. I refer to that phase in my life as my "preannulment period." I was hoping my "postannulment period" would show marked improvement, but I keep running into glitches, most especially with a certain Swiss police inspector by the name of Etienne Miceli.

Professor Smoker cleared his throat. "Five days after the Captain was slain in the surf of Kealakekua Bay, one of King Terreeoboo's chiefs returned a jumble of bones to the crew of the *Resolution*—Cook's hands, skull, legs, lower jaw, and feet. His thigh bones and arms were never recovered."

My grandmother—whose name tag was crammed with microscopic text that read *Marion Sippel—Windsor City Bank Travel Club, Windsor City, Iowa, Birthplace of America's First Pork Fritter Fingers—*

looked up from the ragged sheet of paper she was studying and leaned over to whisper in my ear. "If they'd waked him at Heavenly Host, there wouldn't a been no public viewin'. It's one a them rules a thumb. You gotta have a body to be eligible for the open casket option."

A man with a high-tech camera around his neck slipped through the door at the front of the room. He snapped a few shots of the professor and the audience, then disappeared unobtrusively out the door again. Ship's photographer. The same man who'd snapped individual and group photos of us as we'd boarded and showed up to take candid shots during the lifeboat drill. I had a sneaking suspicion this guy's camera was going to be in our faces a lot during the cruise, whether we wanted it there or not. Our own personal *paparazzi*.

Professor Smoker sipped a mouthful of water before allowing his gaze to drift slowly over his audience. "Captain Cook's remains were committed to the deep on February 22, 1779, and on the following day, under the command of Warrant Officer William Bligh, who would gain infamy years later aboard the mutinous ship, *Bounty*, the *Resolution* set sail for England. Eight months later the ship arrived back in the Thames, having suffered the deaths of a score of crew members, and the ship's surgeon, as well. As a note to any actuaries who may be sitting in the audience, Cook's wife, Elizabeth, survived him by fifty-six years."

"I hope I don't survive your grampa by fifty-six

years," Nana whispered. "That'd make me"—she pinched her eyes shut in a quick calculation—"a hundred and thirty-two. We're talkin' brain cells like leaf lettuce."

Nana had switched from cable to Direct TV after our Italian trip, so her always impressive store of mindless trivia had increased exponentially over the last four months.

Professor Smoker smiled with pride and conviction. "Let there be no mistake. Captain James Cook's accomplishments were both extraordinary and unparalleled—distinctions that have earned him the title of the greatest explorer of all time."

Applause. Whistles. More applause.

Followed by a voice that bristled with animosity. "Your praise completely ignores the darker side of Cook's explorations. How do you answer those who charge that he and his crewmen spread incurable diseases and precipitated the collapse of countless native cultures?"

Smoker's pale blue eyes hardened like magma. "I call the charges ignorant and unfounded. Next question."

"The great explorers sailed without instruments," another man shouted out. "Cook's ships boasted the finest navigational equipment of the era. That fact alone diminishes his achievements and sets other explorers far above him. This is not new to you. When will you admit that you've misled the public about—"

"I've never misled the public about anything,"

Smoker cut him off, obviously annoyed. "Are there any more questions?"

Wow. The last time I'd heard people get so hot under the collar about an historical figure was during my senior year at the UW, when the Memorial Union sponsored a panel of experts who rabidly debated the burning question: Was Attila the Hun a midget, or was he just short? I'm always surprised how fanatical people can get about obscure details. I mean, what *difference* would it make if Attila had charged into battle on a miniature pony instead of a stallion? He'd gotten the job done, hadn't he?

"Excuse me, Professor." Tilly Hovick raised her walking stick in the air to attract his attention. Tilly was a retired university professor who'd become fast friends with Nana on our trip to Ireland. She stood nearly six feet tall in her stocking feet, was thin as a torchlight, and had an affinity for pleated woolen skirts with matching berets, though as a concession to the tropical climate, she'd switched to Madras plaids with coordinating visors. "You're familiar with the *Resolution*'s crew roster. Was there a seaman aboard by the name of Griffin Ring?"

Dorian Smoker lifted his brow in surprise and a curious smile touched his lips. "There was indeed a crewman by that name aboard the *Resolution*. Ordinary Seaman, Griffin Ring. A taciturn fellow with a dubious background that scholars later discovered may have involved the suspicious death of a relative and the theft of a family heirloom before he embarked on the expedition. But no formal charges were ever drawn up because he died shortly after returning to England. His name is absent from most primary sources, so he remains something of a mystery in the annals of navigational history." Smoker's eyebrow arched further upward at Tilly. "Do you mind my asking what interest you have in Ring? He's mentioned so sparingly in the literature. How do you know his name?"

Tilly extracted a plastic storage bag from her canvas tote. Inside was a book the size of a paperback novel, which she removed from the plastic and held up for Smoker's observation. Bound in discolored leather, it was as thick as a deck of playing cards and looked like something straight out of the *Old Curiosity Shop.* "I found this in a hidden compartment of an antique chest I recently inherited. It appears to be the handwritten journal of Griffin Ring, Ordinary Seaman aboard the sloop, *Resolution.* From what I've read, it documents the events of Cook's last journey of discovery in the South Pacific. You're the expert, Professor. How would you determine if this journal is authentic or a masterful hoax?"

The room erupted in a low-level buzz. Heads turned. Chairs creaked. All eyes riveted on Tilly and the slim book she clutched in her hand. Professor Smoker inhaled a deep breath, then nodded meaningfully to a young woman in the front row, who stood up to address us.

"Professor Smoker thanks you for attending today's lecture." Her voice projected into every corner of the room without effort. Good lungs. Great diaphragm. I suspected she'd had professional voice-training instruction, or lived in a big family. She was in her midtwenties with a foot of coarse brown hair caught in a scrunchie at the base of her skull and no visible jewelry other than a glimmer of a chain peeking beneath the open collar of her blouse. She wore a straight skirt that hit her just above the knee and a pale yellow knit vest that I'd seen in the latest Lands' End catalogue. Her smile was subdued, her tone no-nonsense, and she wore serious, elliptical eyeglasses that appeared to add ten years to her age and twenty points to her IQ. My instincts told me she was probably Phi Beta Kappa, Phi Kappa Phi, and the quintessential type-A personality—the kind who experienced total meltdown when she wasn't in control.

"Please check the schedule in tomorrow's *Compass* for the time and location of our next session," she continued. "Apparently we're going to be a moveable feast. And if you have questions about—"

"I've got a question," a woman at the back of the room called out. "Where's the Coconut Palms Cafe? The ice-cream social begins in ten minutes, and they're serving thirty-two different flavors. That's one more than Baskin-Robbins!"

"I know where it is," another woman replied. "Five decks up. And it's all you can eat!"

That led to serial chair-scraping and a mass exodus through the two exit doors. Who could blame them— one more flavor than Baskin-Robbins? Even I was curious.

Nana tugged on my arm. "I need two M&M's for the scavenger hunt. You think they might have M&M's at the ice-cream social?"

"What kind do you need? Peanut, almond, crispy, peanut butter, or plain?"

She consulted her list. "Blue."

Professor Smoker left his podium and sauntered in our direction. "Would you mind if I took a closer look at your journal, Mrs."—he eyed Tilly's name tag—"Hovick?"

"Professor Hovick," she corrected, giving his hand a firm shake. "Iowa State University. Retired."

The degree of respect in his eyes inched upward, like water on the indicator level of a twelve cup coffee maker. "History?"

"Anthropology. And these are my traveling companions, Marion Sippel and her granddaughter, Emily."

Smoker nodded to each of us before beckoning to the young woman who had announced the end of the lecture. "Let me introduce you to Bailey Howard." He gave her an appreciative smile as she joined us. "My brilliant graduate assistant who has single-handedly rescued me from drowning in a sea of memoranda, email, and otherwise useless bureaucratic spam. It'll be a sad day when she graduates. I'll be lost without her organizational skills."

Bailey angled her mouth into a crooked smile, looking uncomfortable with the compliment. She shrugged one shoulder. "I'm a Virgo. We have an obsessive need to create order out of chaos."

If she alphabetized her soup cans and spices, I'd have to bring her home with me. My mom would love her.

Smoker laughed. "Bailey knows nearly as much about Captain Cook as I do. In a few years, I suspect she'll be applying for my position. But in the meantime"—he extended a polite hand toward Tilly's book—"I should very much like to peruse your journal. You found it in an antique chest, you say?"

Tilly handed over the journal. "An antique bachelor's chest willed to me from a cousin who lived in England for many years. Marion's grandson found the hidden compartment quite by accident when they were visiting last week. He was pretending the chest was the control panel for the Starship *Enterprise*, and when he turned a knob to reverse engines, the compartment opened up. A charming youngster, young David," she said stiffly. "So"—she searched for the right adjective—"energetic."

Nana shook her head. "In the last year he's went from action figures to farm machinery to spaceships. His mother thinks he's got Attention Deficit Disorder. Or Hyperactivity Disorder. Or Attention Deficit Hyperactivity Disorder. They sure got a lot a names for normal five-year-olds these days. You got grandkids, Professor?"

Smoker opened the journal, his eyes skimming the first page. "I've never married," he said offhandedly. "I'm afraid I've made my career my life. This journal is in extraordinary condition for a book that's over two hundred years old. Excellent ink pigment.

Minimal deterioration of the paper. Legible handwriting. It's almost too good to be true."

"My sentiments entirely," Tilly agreed. "Not to mention that your typical seaman in the eighteenth century couldn't write." She cocked her head. "Yet if you read a few pages, you find a certain element of authenticity about it."

"The twentieth century gave rise to forgers who knew their profession well," Smoker asserted. "I'd need to read the complete journal before I could make any kind of determination, but at first blush, Professor Hovick, I'd deem it a well-crafted hoax." He closed the book and attempted to hand it back.

"I feared as much. But still . . ." Tilly leaned on her walking stick, her eyes registering a sudden decision. "I invite you to read the complete journal, then."

The book seemed to weigh more heavily in Smoker's hand. "It could take days. Are you comfortable entrusting it to me for that long?"

She nodded assent. "However long it takes, Professor. If you're able to resolve its true origin, I expect it will be well worth the wait."

"I can't promise any startling results, but please consider it on my front burner. What's your cabin number, Professor Hovick? I'll get back to you as soon as possible."

While Tilly and Dorian Smoker exchanged cabin numbers, I observed two young women standing by the door at the back of the room, watching us and each other with icy glares. One was a statuesque brunette with a milk white complexion that looked as if it had never been zapped by an ultraviolet ray. She wore a skimpy pink halter top and belted white short-shorts that bared a pierced navel and abdominal muscles so flat, you could probably bounce quarters off them. The other woman had long blond hair the texture of straw, a too-dark tan that screamed of a tanning bed, and a colorful tattoo that hugged her shoulder. She was dressed in a skintight tank top enhanced by a push-up bra and wore a black micro-miniskirt that was the size of a candy wrapper. They looked like Dallas Cowboy cheerleaders waiting for a football game to break out someplace.

"You don't got a business card I can have, do you, Professor?" Nana asked Smoker as she eyed her crumpled list again. "It's on account a the scavenger hunt. We're s'posed to ask perfect strangers to give us really stupid stuff, and that's s'posed to break the ice."

He smiled as he slipped the journal back into the plastic storage bag that Tilly handed him. "You're in luck, Mrs. Sippel." He reached into the pocket of his shirt and removed a small case. "I always carry extras when I'm lecturing. You never know who might want to visit my website, or make a contribution to the university." He plucked a white card from the stack and offered it to Nana. "Will that do?"

Nana gave it a quick glance before stashing it in the oversized leather pocketbook that was her signature piece. "Penn State, hunh? Go Nittany Lions! You don't happen to have a couple a blue M&M's on you, do you?"

"Afraid not. You might try a vending machine."

"I haven't seen none on board, but then, I haven't been lookin'. Good idea." She looked suddenly worried. "I only got a few more hours before the hunt ends, and if I can find a few more things, I got a good chance a winnin' the grand prize."

"Which is?" asked Smoker.

Nana read from her paper. " 'A priceless memento that celebrates the uniqueness of the Hawaiian Islands.' I'm thinkin' maybe a free ticket to that luau they're offerin' on Maui."

Better that than a book contract with a five-figure advance. A little chill tickled my spine. Been there, done that.

Bailey Howard tapped her watch to catch Smoker's attention. "It's about that time, Professor. We're supposed to vacate the room by four."

Smoker gave us a devilish wink. "You see what I mean about her being organized and efficient? She'll be dean of the College of the Liberal Arts before long. Ladies, it's been a pleasure meeting you." He graciously shook hands with all of us, which, I figured, was our cue to leave.

As we ambled toward the exit, the two cheerleaders charged toward us, eyes locked, teeth set, like early-bird Wal-Mart shoppers the day after Thanksgiving. "I bet the professor's celebratin' a birthday today," Nana said as they brushed by.

"You think?" I peeked over my shoulder, watching the duo greet Smoker in the same way cannibals might greet a wayward traveler.

"Yup. Them two gals are dressed like they just

popped outta one a them X-rated surprise birthday cakes. You s'pose they got a naughty bakery on board?" She paused in thought. "I wonder if they do special orders?"

Whether it was his birthday or not, the good professor certainly looked surprised, but not in a good way.

In the corridor, Tilly nodded back toward the lecture room, a knowing look in her eye. "I saw this all the time when I was teaching. Sexual misconduct is rampant in academia, especially with the more high-profile professors. He's probably slept with both those young women."

"No," exclaimed Nana.

"Yes," assured Tilly.

Nana peeked back into the room, stunned. "He sure don't look like no studmuffin."

"A man doesn't have to be good-looking for a woman to find him sexually attractive," Tilly maintained. "They've conducted studies. Position, authority, knowledge—to a woman, these are much more powerful aphrodisiacs than good looks."

"Who done that study?" asked Nana. "Someone at Iowa State?"

"I read it in *Cosmo*. The sad thing is, those girls probably signed up for the cruise hoping to surprise Smoker, and instead they ended up surprising each other. Did you see their faces? The shock? The anger? The humiliation? Classic reactions for women who learn they've been deceived by a philandering lover." Tilly shook her head. "Smoker had better be prepared to do some fast talking. You know what they say, 'Hell hath no fury . . .' "

"Blue M&M's," said Nana, spinning in a bewildered circle. "Which way to the Coconut Palms Cafe? It's located aft, but I don't know if that's left or right."

I didn't know either, but I did know one thing. If what Tilly said was true, I was glad not to be in Dorian Smoker's shoes right then.

The *Aloha Princess* boasted thirteen decks, three swimming pools, two five-star restaurants, a miniature golf course, a climbing wall, a world-class fitness center, an exotic spa, and thirty-two kinds of ice cream—but nowhere within its luxurious chrome-and-glass interior was there a blue M&M to be found. Striking out at the Coconut Palms Cafe, we ventured to the casino on deck six, where we ran into the rest of the scavenger-hunting Iowa contingent, their voices raised in complaint as they brandished their lists.

"They don't have vending machines on this boat," whined Bernice Zwerg in a voice that scratched like coarse-grade steel wool. "How are we supposed to get our hands on those over-priced packets of M&M's without vending machines?" Bernice had undergone emergency bunion surgery on both feet last June, but she'd bounced back in time to book a last-minute reservation on our cruise. Lucky me.

We were gathered near the front of the casino, opposite the glassed-in cashiers' windows, where a coin-counting machine rattled like a faulty race-car engine. Reflective disco balls hung from the ceiling. Slot machines hunkered in military formation on the floor. Gaming tables flanked the perimeter. Digital sound effects rang out like a chorus of off-key kazoos, joined by the hoots, hollers, screams, and laughter of the casino's patrons.

"Did anyone try the General Store on deck five?" asked Dick Teig, hitching up the belt of his size 52 waist Italian knit trousers. I'd discovered a killer in Italy; Dick had discovered couture. "They should have M&M's in the candy section."

"Osmond and I checked," announced Alice Tjarks in her KORN radio voice. "All they have is Skittles." She waved into the lens of Osmond Chelsvig's camcorder, then gave him a big 'I'm on vacation' smile.

"Skittles?" crowed Helen Teig, Dick's wife. "I love Skittles. Did you buy any?"

"At three dollars a bag?" Alice shot back. "Who's got money like that?"

"I do," said Nana. Nana had won millions in the Minnesota lottery, so she had money to burn. "But I'd rather spend it on them midget Tootsie Rolls. The fresh ones don't even stick to my dentures."

Ding ding ding ding ding. A victorious shriek echoed out from the depths of the casino.

Helen Teig rubbed her eye, accidentally wiping her left eyebrow off her face. "So what else are we missing besides M&M's?"

Lucille Rassmuson raised her hand. "I can't find a balloon. I even checked the florist shop. They don't do balloons, only flowers."

"I found a balloon!" enthused Margi Swanson. This was Margi's first trip with us. She worked part-time as an RN at the medical clinic in Windsor City, but she said she was reaching the age where she needed to start spending some of the money she'd spent a lifetime earning. She'd recently lost seventy-five pounds on the "Eat Everything in Sight and Still Lose Weight" diet, so as a reward to herself, she'd signed up for the cruise.

"Where'd you find a balloon?" Lucille asked suspiciously. She was wearing her favorite piece of jewelry pinned to her sweater today—a quarter-size campaign button with her deceased husband's cigar-smoking face stamped on it. Her good friends, the Teigs and Stolees, had surprised her with matching earrings for her birthday. I guessed next would come coffee mugs and calendars. In today's marketplace, the possibilities were endless.

"It's not actually a real balloon," Margi said in a stage whisper. "I'm using a condom."

Gasps. Wheezing. Choking.

"What size?" asked Nana.

"Jumbo. It blows up to the size of a beach ball."

Nana's eyes lit up. "You got any more?"

"Plenty. I stocked up at the clinic. If rampant hanky-panky breaks out aboard ship, I can hand them out to the masses."

Suppressing a grin, I turned toward Nana. "Why do you need condoms? George isn't even here."

"Them jumbos are hard to find, dear. I'm stock-pilin'."

Nana's boyfriend, George Farkas, Windsor City's only resident with both a prosthetic leg and hardware the size of a SCUD missile, had planned on cruising with us, but he'd come down with a sudden case of shingles and been forced to cancel. His doctor didn't know what had triggered the episode, but there was mention of stress. I figured the thought of being the focus of Nana's romantic notions for ten days had finally gotten to him. I mean, he'd barely escaped with his life in Italy, where the beds had been stationary—he'd probably been plagued by nightmares about what could happen on the high seas. No wonder he'd gotten stressed.

"Did anyone find a rock?" asked Osmond as he adjusted one of his double hearing aids.

"I did," said Bernice, pulling it out of her *Aloha Princess* tote. "In the spa. There was a whole bunch in one of the rooms I toured, so I borrowed one."

A cocktail waitress with a tray of tall, icy beverages skirted around us, offering free drinks to the people camped before the dollar slots.

"Which way is the spa?" asked Lucille.

"That way," said Bernice, pointing right.

"That way," said Dick Teig, pointing left.

"Three decks up," attested Alice.

"One deck down," corrected Margi.

Uff da. What was happening here? Iowans never got lost. Ever. Since the beginning of time, no Iowan had even taken a wrong turn! The fact that no one knew how to get anywhere revealed an incredible phenomenon: Everyone's natural directional system apparently stopped functioning near large bodies of water. Either that, or the new souped-up metal detectors at the Des Moines airport had caused the first incidence of group dementia ever recorded.

"Show of hands," Osmond shouted. When there was a vote to be taken, eighty-eight-year-old Osmond always did the honors. "How many of you found a paper clip?" All hands went up. "A map without advertising?" Five hands went up. "An eraser?" Nine hands went up.

"Mine's attached to a number two pencil," confessed Margi. "That won't get me disqualified, will it?"

Ding ding ding ding ding.

Seated on a high stool before a shiny one-armed bandit behind us, Grace Stolee let out a scream and pointed to the circular white light atop her machine. If the *dings* and flashing indicated a winning jackpot, Grace had just hit it big.

"Don't move!" instructed her husband as he leaped off an adjacent stool and aimed his camcorder at her. "This is Grace winning a big jackpot aboard the *Aloha Princess.*" He shot a close-up of the coins pouring into her tray. "Quarters." He panned higher. "Flashing light." Then lower. "Three winning sevens." Dick Stolee kind of had a thing for stating the obvious.

"What's the payout, Grace?" he asked, zeroing in on the payoff chart below the window.

Osmond Chelsvig abandoned the group to film Dick Stolee filming Grace. Alice Tjarks dug her camcorder out of her tote and positioned herself to film

Osmond, filming Dick, filming Grace. What *was* it with these guys and the infinity shots?

Grace stabbed her finger at the payoff chart. "Three sevens, three quarters, that's—" She screamed again. "TWENTY THOUSAND QUARTERS!"

"How much is that in real money?" asked Dick Teig.

While the majority of the group hurried over to surround Grace, I nodded to Nana and Tilly, indicating that I was ready to head out and explore some more. I'd had enough of the casino's gaming tables and slot machines. Gaming tables reminded me of *chemin de fer*. *Chemin de fer* reminded me of Italy. And Italy reminded me of Etienne, who'd won an unexpected fortune while visiting his family and had gotten his memory jogged enough to ask me . . .

My heart started thumping in my ears.

. . . to have the gall to ask me . . .

My face grew hot.

. . . to have the absolute *effrontery* to ask me . . .

Nuts. I was *not* going to think about Etienne right now. I refused to let him spoil my holiday. But I needed to get out of the casino, and fast.

Inhaling a calming breath, I headed out the door, with Nana and Tilly hot on my heels. "Where to, ladies?" I asked, digging a floor plan of the ship out of my shoulder bag. "A spin around the Promenade deck, which is . . . let's see . . . one deck down? Or would you prefer a round of miniature golf on the putting green on deck thirteen?"

"I've never played miniature golf," Tilly admitted.

"The closest I've come to it is playing croquet with a tribe of Pygmies in the Andaman Islands."

"I'd like to hit the spa and borrow a rock like Bernice done," Nana said. "And while I'm there, I'm gonna sign up for one a them Ionithermie treatments. It costs a hundred and twenty dollars, but the flyer promises you can lose up to eight inches a ugly cellulite in the first session. And it's not real complicated. They plaster you in seaweed and wire you up like the Frankenstein monster, and that detoxifies your fat cells and firms you up real good."

"I underwent a similar ritual in New Guinea," Tilly recalled, as we approached the elevator. "Only they plastered me in jungle foliage instead of sea vegetation, and I wasn't sure if their goal was to cleanse me or eat me. Cannibals are oftentimes quite hard to read."

When the door to the elevator slid open, we stepped into a cylindrical glass tube that overlooked the atrium at the center of the ship—a huge column of open space between decks four and eleven that was rimmed by tiers of balconies and overhung by a crystal chandelier that looked like a giant upside-down sno-cone. I punched the button for deck eleven then clung to the safety rail as we glided upward on the barest whisper of air.

"I'll be," Nana marveled, her nose pressed to the elevator glass. "This is like bein' inside a hypodermic needle."

I looked down at the elegant champagne bar on deck four, where a staircase of illuminated acrylic risers spiraled toward the next floor. That would be the perfect place to have the group pose for pictures on Halloween night, when we were all expected to dress in costume for the masquerade gala. I hadn't decided on a costume yet, but I figured I could rent one at the clothing shop on deck five. They were supposed to have a good selection in a variety of sizes.

"It's breathtaking, isn't it?" mused Tilly, as we peered outward through the ship's glass walls. The gleaming waters of the Pacific Ocean appeared calm as bathwater. There was no land in sight, only blue sky and open sea. "Balboa first named this ocean the South Sea, but Magellan changed the name to the Pacific, no doubt for the calm waters that greeted him after a harrowing passage around the tip of South America. Can you feel the stillness, ladies? The wonderful calm? This must be the same calm that Magellan felt."

A bell *pinged*. The elevator door *shushed* open.

"MAN OVERBOARD!" shrieked a woman as she banged through the door from the outside deck. "Man overboard! Help me! Somebody help me! PLEASE!"

It was Bailey Howard.

CHAPTER 2

She ran straight at us and grabbed Nana's arm, screaming hysterically, "Tell the bridge! Please! They have to stop!" She choked on an agonized sob. "They can't let him die!"

"Where's the bridge?" I screamed back.

Nana pointed left.

Tilly pointed right.

I yanked out my floor plan and located the bridge one deck down at the bow of the ship. "Stay here! I'll be right back." While Nana and Tilly ministered to Bailey, I raced past the elevator, flew down the stairs, charged through an endlessly long corridor, and burst onto the bridge with a painful stitch in my side, and a breathless entreaty. "STOP THE ENGINES! MAN OVERBOARD!"

Heads turned. Eyes riveted on me. My ears pounded with the sudden silence until a uniformed officer with a well-trimmed white beard sang out, "Stop all engines," which prompted a chain reaction of activity. As I stood there panting, the bearded officer hurried across the room to me, scrutinizing my face with sober eyes.

"Who has fallen overboard?"

I opened my mouth to respond, only to realize, I didn't know.

"I still don't see no sign a him," Nana reported an hour later from her lookout at the ship's rail. The wind that buffeted the stern had exploded through her hair and snarled it like a cheap angora sweater, but she was far too interested in the activity in the sea below to notice. She readjusted her binoculars. "He seemed like a real nice man, even if he did get a little snippy with them fellas what disagreed with him. Be an awful shame if he missed the whole trip."

We were dead in the water as the ship's launches searched the immediate area for the body of Professor Dorian Smoker. Bailey had been carted off to the infirmary to be treated for symptoms of shock. Tilly and I were huddled in a sheltered spot away from the rail, where her visor would be less apt to fly away, and my short, sassy Italian 'do' wouldn't be whipped into a style worn only by rock stars and mythological creatures who sported more than one head.

"I don't mean to be the voice of doom," Tilly remarked as she cast a somber look toward the launches circling in the water, "but if they haven't found his body by now, they probably won't recover it until it floats to the surface in a few days. Tissue decomposition takes place rapidly in tropical waters. If this were an Alaskan cruise, they might not recover the body for months."

My knees went a little gimpy as I realized that at any moment, the mission to "search and rescue" might be downgraded to "find and retrieve."

I hunkered closer to the bulkhead as a trio of curious onlookers, clad in cargo shorts and hiking boots, lumbered past me to join Nana at the rail. One was a giant of a man whose red-gold hair and beard smacked of ancient Viking roots. I remembered seeing him in the second row at Professor Smoker's lecture, his head towering above everyone else's. Giant Vikings aren't exactly commonplace, unless it's Sunday afternoon and you're attending an NFL game in the dome in Minneapolis.

"Forgive me, madame," he asked Nana in English too perfect to be his native tongue. "Do you know what they're looking for?"

"They're lookin' for that nice Professor Smoker, on account a he fell off the ship. The men in them little boats fished a life buoy outta the water a little while ago, but I haven't seen 'em fish out the professor yet. You wanna borrow my binoculars and have a look-see?"

The giant translated Nana's spiel for his two male companions in a rapid-fire language that sounded a bit like "gangsta" rap minus the expletives. Only when one of the men muttered a thoughtful *"Uff da,"* did I realize it wasn't gansta rap. It was Norwegian! They really *were* Vikings! Or maybe distant relations.

The three stood conversing in curious undertones for a half minute before the giant handed the binoculars back to Nana. "The professor could not swim?" he asked.

Tilly thumped her walking stick on the deck for attention. "Swimming is one thing, young man. Getting sucked beneath the keel of a nine-hundred-and-sixty-two-foot ship is something else entirely."

He turned from the rail to face Tilly, eyes wary, lips stretched razor-thin. "A tragedy, yah. For us, too. We traveled many miles to hear the professor speak."

The ID dangling around his neck read *Nils— World Navigators Club,* and he looked as if circumnavigating the globe at the helm of a sailing ship would be second nature to him. His face was bronzed and leathery, his eyelashes bleached to pale gold. Crow's-feet slashed outward from his eyes as if he'd spent his entire life squinting into the sun. I suspected he probably knew everything there was to know about navigating, and absolutely nothing about the most important aspects of life at sea—SPF and sunblock.

He said something to his companions, who pushed away from the rail and turned around to face us. They were both half a head shorter than Nils. One was sandy-haired and solid, with tree trunks for legs, a broad chest, and a World Navigators Club name tag that identified him as Gjurd. The other boasted feathery white-blond hair, a lithe, wiry body, a wide gap between his front teeth, and a name that J. R. R. Tolkien might have given to one of his elves—Ansgar.

"You will excuse us, please?" Nils offered politely, nodding to each of us.

"Before you go——" Nana grasped Nils by the arm and looked far up into his face. "You're a tall one, aren't you? You oughta meet Emily's ex-husband sometime. She's tall, too. And it's even worse when she's wearin' them stiletto heels. She's fixin' to become a famous romance novelist. Isn't that somethin'? She woulda come on the cruise with us, but she come down with a bad case a writer's block, so she's in therapy instead."

Nils stared at Nana, stoic and confused. I clapped a hand over my eyes and shook my head. *Oh, God.*

"Do you happen to have any M&M's on you?" Nana inquired. "I only need two."

This prompted a boisterous discussion among the three men that ended when Ansgar asked a question that Nils translated. "Plain or peanut?"

Almond, crispy, and peanut butter obviously hadn't made their way to Norway yet.

"Don't matter what kind. They just gotta be blue."

Nils unzipped a pocket in his cargo shorts and pulled out a small crinkly bag. "Skittles are similar, yah?"

Nana shook her head. "They gotta be M&M's. But if you see a roly-poly gal with only one eyebrow walkin' around, offer her some a them Skittles. Her name's Helen, and you'll make her day."

Nils forced a cautious smile before he and his companions strode off in the direction in which they'd come. In bygone days, these guys would probably hop into their Viking ship and storm down the coast to plunder and burn. Civility had certainly altered their way of life. A bout of plundering these days probably meant hopping into the Anchor Bar and knocking back the entire bowl of beer nuts.

"Looks like they're throwin' in the towel," Nana reported from the rail. "The launches are headin' back to the ship, but they've left some markers in the water."

Tilly shook her head. "Considering the currents and tidal activity, his body will probably reappear nowhere near this area, but I suppose that's protocol."

I stepped out from my little cubbyhole near the bulkhead to eye the sleek contour of the two decks that rose above us. "Exactly where was he standing when he fell?"

Tilly pointed upward. "Deck twelve. One level up. Near the golf simulators on the port side."

I braved the wind to stand next to the rail, which was a mile-long beam of polished wood mounted atop slanted Plexiglas panels. It was pretty high, hitting me just below my collarbone, which meant it probably would have hit Professor Smoker about midchest. "How do you manage to fall off the deck of a ship when the guardrail is almost as tall as you are?"

Nana shuffled over to us in her spanking-white, size five sneakers. "After what happened on the Italy tour, I thought you said you was never gonna be suspicious about another freak accident, Emily."

I gnawed my lip thoughtfully. Yup. I remembered saying that. And meaning it . . . at the time. "But this is so bizarre. Look at this thing." I slid my hand along the guardrail. "It's built like an obstacle in a steeple-chase. You're not going over this thing unless you're on a horse." I frowned distractedly. "Not to jump to any conclusions or anything, but if you ask me, I think it's impossible for anyone to fall off this ship."

"I quite agree," Tilly said, "which leaves us no alter-native but one." She thrust her walking stick at my shoulder bag. "I believe the infirmary is on deck three, Emily, but you'd best dig out your map. I think we should pay Ms. Bailey Howard a sick call."

"Emily figured out in no time flat why so many guests ended up dead in Florence, didn't you, dear?" Nana leaned over to pat my knee as we sat in the wait-ing room.

I slid down a notch in my chair. Florence. Not to belabor the point or anything, but I DIDN'T WANT TO THINK ABOUT FLORENCE!

"She wowed the group so much with her fancy theories, there was even talk a someone interviewin' her for one a them early-mornin' programs on KORN, or a human interest story for the *Register*." Nana framed her hands in the air around an imagi-nary headline. TOUR ESCORT CRACKS TUSCAN CRIME-WAVE."

The last big human-interest story in our local paper had been entitled, UNDEFEATED FIVE-YARD DASH CHAMP VOWS "I'LL BE BACK!" It was a gripping account of Bernice Zwerg's bunion surgery and had kept readers on the edge of their seats until the very end. The buzz at the local Farm and Fleet was, Pulitizer.

Tilly's brow lifted in admiration. "A feature article about Emily? I must have missed it. When did it appear?"

Nana shrugged. "It didn't. Folks decided she ruined her credibility with all her second-guessin', so they interviewed Dick Teig and done an article on Italian couture for the plus-size male instead."

We were in the bowels of the ship, in a twelve-foot-by-twelve-foot room painted igloo white and lit by overhead pillow lights so glaringly bright that I was glad I was wearing sunblock. Chairs of chrome and white leather lined the walls. A tidy reception desk dominated the room. Pamphlets on seasickness, respiratory illnesses, and UV rays hung in plastic pockets on the wall, right next to dozens of heavy-duty white paper bags that looked suspiciously like the ones the airlines stash in their seat pockets for motion sickness. Geesch. There certainly were a lot of them.

"Is there candy in that dish?" Nana asked, nodding toward a glass bowl on the reception desk. She pinched her eyes shut. "You look, dear. I can't handle the suspense."

I wandered over. "Skittles," I called back to her.

She sighed her disappointment. "They got any blue ones?"

"I'm so sorry to have kept you waiting!" A middle-aged woman dressed in nurse's whites rushed

through the door from the treatment area. "We usually only get this backed up when the seas are high
and the decks are awash." Folding her hands at her
waist, she took a deep breath, tilted her head to the
side, and gave us a benevolent smile. "Now, what
seems to be the problem today?"

I mimicked the head tilt and returned her smile.
"Would it be possible for us to see Bailey Howard?"

"Are you family?"

"We're part of her . . . cruise family," I improvised.
"We're the people who helped her right after the incident happened. We're pretty concerned about her."

"The good Samaritans. I'm so happy to meet you."
She clasped each of our hands in a warm welcome.
"I've given Bailey a mild sedative to calm her down,
but no one feels calm in a health facility. I expect the
best medicine for her right now would be some sym-
pathetic company who'd sit down and hold her hand
for a while." She wagged her forefinger at us. "You
wait right here. I'll see if she's up for visitors."

As I waited, my attention kept drifting to the
motion sickness bags hanging on the wall. Unlike the
lifeboat situation on the *Titanic*, there looked to be
more than enough bags for everyone, but I certainly
hoped we didn't have to use them. Two thousand sick
people would never fit into this infirmary.

Nana pulled out her cruise ship itinerary. "You
s'pose this incident with the professor is gonna affect
our schedule? If we don't get to Kauai in time to do
that zodiac raft ride along the Na Pali coast tomorrow, that'd be a real shame, 'cause they say it's like

ridin' the waves on a waterbed. I always wanted to try out one a them waterbeds. But I s'pose we can sign up for somethin' else."

The cruise line offered so many island excursions that my group hadn't been able to agree on just one or two, so we'd decided to split up to sample a wide range of what was being offered. I suggested that when we returned to Iowa, we all write short articles describing our individual adventures, which I could use in a travel newsletter I'd distribute to all the bank's customers as a promotional tool. Everyone had thought it was a great idea except Bernice, who threatened to hold out until we talked "royalties."

"What are you signed up for tomorrow, dear?" Nana inquired.

"The kayak adventure." I'd kayaked on Lake Mendota when I'd attended the UW, and I was looking forward to wielding a paddle again.

After a few minutes the nurse returned and motioned us into the inner sanctum. "Bailey wants to thank you for your help. Follow me, would you?"

We trooped down a whitewashed corridor ablaze with incandescent light. Muffled voices floated out to us from behind examining rooms to our left and right, and at the end of the corridor, in a room opposite one labeled X-RAY, we found Bailey Howard lying in a standard-size hospital cot, her eyes red and puffy behind her designer frames.

"Have they found him yet?" she asked without preamble.

I opened my mouth to reply, surprised when nothing came out. Bailey took one look at my face and dissolved into tears. "He's gone, isn't he? He's really gone."

I scurried to her cot and sat down on the edge. Nana poured water. Tilly yanked a tissue out of the box and held it at the ready. "I'm so sorry," I said, squeezing her hand.

She bowed her head, tears streaming down her cheeks and onto her chin. The nurse gave me the eye and quietly retreated. Bailey squeezed my hand tightly. "This isn't real. It can't be. How do I go back to school and tell them Professor Smoker is dead?"

Chances were the wire services would pick up the story and spread it worldwide before Bailey ever got the chance, but that's not what she needed to hear right now. "The cruise staff may have asked you this already, but is there someone you'd like us to contact for you? Your parents? Boyfriend?"

She slipped off her glasses and swiped tears from her face. "I don't have a boyfriend. And my parents are a joke. They're both off finding their 'inner child'—with new spouses half their ages. I don't even know where they are right now."

"Tissue?" asked Tilly.

Bailey dried her eyes on the tissue and slid her glasses back on. "Thanks. The three of you have been so nice to me. You've been nicer than people who know me." She sniffled, looking suddenly guilty. "But that's my own fault, I guess. When you're working on a dissertation, you become pretty self-absorbed. Since I've been in grad school, I've shut out everyone except

Professor Smoker . . . and . . . and the members of my major committee." She bowed her head. "He was everything to me. Mentor. Cheerleader. Coauthor of a half dozen critically acclaimed papers that appeared in some of the most prestigious refereed journals in the academic world. What am I going to do without him?"

When her bottom lip began to quiver, Nana pressed the water glass into her hand and encouraged her to drink. Nana visited hospital patients every week as part of her Legion of Mary duties, so her bedside manner had become the stuff of legend.

"We've all lost people who's dear to us," Nana empathized. "When I lost my Sam, I didn't know how I'd go on. Fifty-three years, we was married. We'd pretty much turned into each other, except for he had more hair growin' out his ears, so when I lost him, I lost a big piece a myself."

"I'm sorry." Bailey sniffled again. "Was he ill for very long?"

Nana shook her head. "It happened real sudden-like."

"Heart attack?"

"Ice shanty. And Tilly here lost her brother a few months back, didn't you, Til?"

"A tragic accident," Tilly said glumly. "He fell from his saddle during an ostrich race in Kuwait and was trampled by the rest of the pack. It was sad he couldn't have held on. He'd been in first place until then, and the grand prize was an oil well."

Bailey stared at Tilly, her breathing shallow.

"Even Emily's lost someone," Nana continued.

Bailey turned her soulful gaze on me and sniffed loudly. "Who did you lose?"

I whipped my head around at Nana. "Who did I lose?"

"Your young man, dear."

Bailey sucked in her breath. "You lost someone in a tragic accident, too?"

Why was it that the subject you wanted to talk about the least was the subject everyone else wanted to talk about the most? "I didn't lose anyone," I defended, but my halfhearted denial tipped Bailey off immediately.

"That's okay," she rasped through her grief. "You can tell me. What happened? Did your guy find another woman?" When I winced, she clapped her hand over her mouth. "Another man?"

"That woulda been her first husband," Nana said.

"ALL RIGHT!" I sputtered. "You want to know what happened? I'll tell you. But first you tell me: when a man tells you he loves you, what usually happens after that?"

"In what society?" asked Tilly.

"Great sex," said Nana.

"He asks you to marry him," said Bailey.

I pointed my finger at Bailey. "Exactly. He proposes marriage. And when he tells you he has an important question to ask, you expect him to say, 'Will you marry me?' Right?"

The three women nodded.

"Well, not Etienne Miceli. *Nooo*. A marriage

proposal from my black-haired, blue-eyed Swiss/
German/Italian police inspector with the washboard
stomach and one percent body fat? Huh!"

"Are you going to mention the thong?" Tilly asked.

I rolled my eyes and plunged on. "After nine long
months of phone calls, separation anxiety, and cybersex, after an agonizing month dealing with his short-
term memory loss, do you know what he finally
remembers to ask me?"

Nana raised her hand. "I know, but I don't wanna
spoil it for no one else."

"HE INVITES ME TO THE MICELI FAMILY
REUNION NEXT MAY! Next *May!* It might as well
be the next millennium. And why does he invite me
to his family's reunion?" I gave Nana a take-it-away
gesture.

She sucked on her dentures and offered a little
shrug. "You're goin' a little fast for me, dear. I'm still
back at the part where you done the cybersex."

I threw my hands into the air. "Because I have to
meet his grandmother! It's mandatory. Before you
can entertain even a fleeting thought about marrying
into the Miceli family, you need to pass muster with
Nonna Annunziata. And her appointment book is
filled until next May because the family has grown so
large. Just my luck—Micelis are serial breeders."

Tilly thwacked her walking stick on the leg of
the cot. "Old world culture, Emily. These Swiss/
German/Italians aren't the kind of people who frequent Las Vegas wedding chapels."

"I don't think they do weddings, period."

"They love weddings," Tilly corrected. "But they're also known to have engagements that last forever. Italian men don't believe in rushing into anything when they have the rest of their lives to plan the details."

"Well, I have no intention of being engaged for the rest of my life! I'm thirty years old. I have better things to do than wait for Etienne Miceli to parade me past all the relatives for their 'old world' approval. If he can't decide on his own that I'm the woman he wants to grow old with, then . . . then . . ."

I heaved an anguished sigh, feeling like a Mylar balloon with a helium deficiency. "What is it with me? All the men in the world, and I have to fall in love with an old-world European."

"You're thirty?" Bailey asked, awestruck. "I never would have guessed you were that old."

Oh, yeah. That made me feel a whole lot better.

Bailey tightened her hand around her tissue, her emotions unraveling. "This . . . this is the worst day of my life. You might have lost your boyfriend," she sobbed, "but I lost the man who's the head of my graduate committee. He was supposed to sign off on my dissertation! How am I supposed to finish my Ph.D. without him? I'm in debt up to my eyeteeth to pay for my education, and I could be left with nothing! No degree, no title. No nothing!"

She stuck her hand out for another tissue. Tilly obliged.

"Was Professor Smoker in good health?" I asked gently, trying to redirect the conversation. "I mean, did he suffer from vertigo, or motion sickness, or some other kind of condition that might have caused him to lose his balance and fall over a five-foot-high rail?"

Bailey removed the tissue from her face and stared at me wide-eyed. "Fall? He didn't fall. He was pushed!"

CHAPTER 3

"**W**HAT?"

Fresh tears scalded Bailey's cheeks. "It was horrible. I saw the professor struggling with someone near the aft rail. I screamed at them to stop. I yelled for help, but"—her voice cracked—"no one heard me! The deck was deserted! Two thousand passengers on this ship, and not one of them was within earshot to help me!"

I stared at her, too numbed to say anything but, "He was pushed?"

"He was murdered!" Her tone grew screechy as she battled a rising sob. "The . . . the two of them disappeared behind the bulkhead when I was running toward them. I thought I could reach him in time to help, but . . . I wasn't fast enough." She sucked in her breath, then let it out again in a rush of words. "By the time I reached the stern, Professor

Smoker was in the water and the man who pushed him was gone!"

"Fella musta run around the other side a the deck," Nana speculated. "Did you run after 'im?"

"No! I had to help Professor Smoker. I . . . I ripped a life ring from its box and tossed it over the side, but"—her face grew crimped and red as she wailed out—"but his head had already disappeared! I couldn't see him anymore!"

She buried her face in her hands, shoulders shaking, chest heaving. I wrapped my arms around her and patted her back. "You can't blame yourself."

"Yes, I can! If I'd run a little faster, Professor Smoker might not be dead!"

"If you'd run a little faster, *you* might be dead," I said gently. "Think about it. After taking care of the professor, the killer might have turned his sights on you."

"I wish I *was* dead," Bailey sobbed. "Everything I've worked for—without Professor Smoker's imprimatur, it's not worth spit."

Nana retreated into the bathroom and returned with a paper towel compress. She placed it on Bailey's forehead. "At least you got a good look at the fella."

"But I didn't," she whimpered. "He was wearing a hooded sweatshirt and sweatpants. I didn't see his face. I couldn't see his hair. I think it was a man, but I was so far away, I'm not even sure about that. For all I know, it could have been a woman! The captain asked me for a description when he looked in on me a little while ago, and all I could tell him was that the person was wearing a hooded gray warm-up outfit." Sobs. Tears. Nose blowing. "What good am I as an eyewitness? If they never catch Professor Smoker's killer, it'll be all my fault!"

I'd be more apt to fault the fashion industry for encouraging the unisex look in athletic attire, but that was just a personal opinion.

"Why was Professor Smoker on deck twelve in the first place?" Tilly inquired.

"He wanted to check out the golf simulators." Bailey gave an indulgent eye roll. "He loved golf. He claimed it was his only vice. Well, that, and Indian cuisine. So while he drooled over the simulators, I searched out a quiet lounge where we could look over the Ring journal. And I found one on the top deck, overlooking the bow. So I took the stairs back down to deck twelve and"—her voice caught in her throat—"and that's when I saw the commotion at the rail. I ran to help him. I ran as fast as I could, but I was half a city block away from him! Why do they make these ships so big?"

"Economics, dear," Nana piped up. "The bigger they are, the more guests they pack in, the more money they make. I seen that on an A&E special that took an inside look at the cruise industry. But it don't make no sense to me about the professor. He seemed like a nice enough fella. Who'd wanna kill 'im?"

"Everyone wanted to kill him!" Bailey cried.

Oh yeah, that's what I wanted to hear. "Excuse me?"

"Did you see who showed up at the lecture?" she

choked out. "The World Navigators? The Sandwich Islanders? Do you know who those people are?"

I recalled the three World Navigators we'd met earlier. "Umm . . . if I tossed out the phrase 'Viking look-alikes,' would I be close?"

Her face whitened with the kind of shock people experience just before cardiac arrest. "You've never heard of them, have you? How could you not have heard of them?"

"We're from Iowa," Nana explained.

Bailey's shock continued to parade across her face. "I'm sorry. It's just that we run into their anti-Cook literature so much at the university that I naturally assume everyone has heard of them. Both groups set forth ideas that are radically opposed to Professor Smoker's theories about Cook, and they've been vicious in their attempts to discredit him. Scathing papers. Hateful articles. Threatening emails. In the week before we left, some of their emails became so extreme that I begged the professor to consider canceling the cruise. But he wouldn't. He could be so stubborn. He said he wasn't going to let a bunch of miscreants ruin his holiday in paradise." She rubbed her nose and sniffed. "Besides, he enjoyed lecturing too much to miss an opportunity to influence a new audience."

"I should think the chancellor's office would have forbidden him to lecture anyplace where his life might have been in jeopardy," Tilly theorized.

Bailey heaved a guilty sigh. "He didn't report it to the chancellor's office. He didn't tell anyone. He considered the threats to be quackery; acknowledging them would have been beneath his contempt."

"Did he realize both groups were going to show up for the cruise?" I asked.

"Not until he walked into the lecture room and saw them all sitting there with their society affiliations pinned to their chests."

Aha! So that's what he'd looked so unsettled about. Receiving threatening emails was one thing, but knowing you were in the same room with the people who might have sent them had to be downright scary. "Had the professor met any member of either group before he stepped into that room today?"

Bailey shrugged. "I'd have no way of knowing that."

"He didn't mention that he recognized anyone?"

"Not to me. But when you're as successful as Professor Smoker was in academia, you inspire professional jealousy, and everyone starts gunning for you. You make more enemies than you know what to do with." She slanted a hard look at me and sniffed. "Dorian Smoker had enemies crawling out of the woodwork on this ship, and you saw the end result. One of them killed him."

I sighed to myself. Another vacation, another body. This was getting *really* old.

"You mentioned you and the professor were going to peruse my journal," Tilly spoke up. "Do you have the journal with you?"

All color drained from Bailey's face as she stared at Tilly. "Oh, my God. I forgot about . . ." She cast a frantic look about the room before squeezing her eyes shut and patting the left side of her chest. "Professor Smoker had it with him. He . . . he didn't want to let it out of his sight, so he put it in the inside pocket of his jacket to keep it safe."

"And the jacket is . . . where?" Tilly inquired.

"He was wearing it when he was pushed overboard." Bailey swallowed slowly, like a boa constrictor trying to digest a house. "Oh, my God. I'm so sorry! I've lost Professor Smoker. I've lost your journal. I'm sorry. I'm so sorry!" The floodgates finally opened. Sobs. Tears. Wailing.

I heard a rush of footsteps in the corridor and looked over my shoulder to find the nurse scurrying into the room. "I think visiting hours are over for now, ladies," she said quietly, circling the bed to tend to Bailey. We offered apologies and nods of sympathy before shuffling dutifully out the door, embarrassed that our visit had obviously made Bailey feel worse rather than better.

"You was right about the professor not fallin' on his own," Nana whispered to me. "Might be you'll be back in contention for that human-interest story in the *Register*. Awful shame about that poor Howard girl, though. Last time I seen someone cry that much was twenty years back, when our NBC affiliate preempted the Lake Winnibigoshish ice-fishin' championships for the local bowlin' league quarterfinals. Your grampa was awful upset about that."

Tilly leaned heavily on her walking stick, looking too dazed to put one foot in front of the other. "What if the journal wasn't a hoax? What if it was the real McCoy? Good Lord, I may have single-handedly robbed the academic world of its most significant historical document in decades."

Nana looped her arm around Tilly in a comforting gesture. "Don't you go frettin' now, Til. You put it in one a them zippered bags. Them things are real rugged. That's why we pay the big bucks for 'em. Probably keep your book dry as a bone."

Hope entered Tilly's face. "That's right. Ziploc bags lock in freshness like no other storage bag can." She squared her shoulders and stiffened her spine. "All is not lost, then. Thank you for reminding me of that, Marion. What do you say, ladies? Is it time to regroup in the cabin?"

"Before I forget, dear." Nana looked over both shoulders before motioning me closer, and saying in an undertone, "About that cybersex you and your young man was havin'. You mind if I take a peek at the instruction manual?"

We wended our way back through a maze of narrow passageways to the midship elevators. "Isn't this somethin'?" Nana remarked as we waited for one of the upper directional arrows to turn green. "Lookit how level the floor is. Would you ever guess we was in the middle of an ocean? How come we're not tiltin'?"

"Stabilizers," said Tilly. "These modern cruise ships are built to remain steady even in the most brutal seas. Given the improvements in naval technology, seasickness may soon go the way of the dinosaur, much to the dismay of the makers of Dramamine, Bonine, and Queasy Pops."

The elevator *pinged* to a stop. Nana and Tilly stood aside to let a couple of passengers off, then bustled forward to get the best places by the floor selection panel. Nana punched in a number before looking out the door at me. "You comin' with us, dear?"

"I gained a pound just sniffing the air in the Coconut Palms Cafe," I confessed, "so for the sake of my hips and thighs, I better take the stairs. I'll meet you back in your cabin in a few minutes." *After I made a slight detour to deck twelve.* I knew Bailey Howard was so emotionally distraught that her perception might be a little off, but something she'd said hadn't rung true. I needed to check it out for myself.

I trudged up nine flights of stairs, staggered out the bulkhead door into the open air of deck twelve, and collapsed against the rail, starved for oxygen. Oh yeah, taking the stairs was a great idea. Maybe I'd try it again sometime . . . on my next vacation.

When I was able to breathe again, I cast a long look toward the stern, trying to picture what Bailey might have seen a little over two hours ago. She'd been right about one thing. The stern did seem half a city block away, but from this vantage point, you'd have a clear shot of anything that was happening at the port rail, though the details might be a little fuzzy.

I began walking aft, the open ocean to my right, the bulkhead to my left. The deck was too narrow at this point for deck chairs, but as I passed beyond the curve of the bulkhead, the space expanded into a sports area that boasted a regulation-size basketball court enclosed within a flexible mesh cage, kind of like an aviary for amateur athletes. Adjacent to it, on the starboard side, a tangle of aquamarine waterslides corkscrewed like the L.A. highway system, spiraling down toward an elevated pool that looked much more geared toward children than the large, kidney-shaped pool on deck eleven.

But there were no giggles or splashing from the pool area. No hoopsters slam-dunking the ball on the basketball court. Two thousand guests on this cruise ship, and not one of them was using the sports area. The place was quieter than a Tuesday night at the Windsor City Drive-in Theater.

Which is exactly what Bailey had said.

But I hadn't believed her.

I skirted around the basketball court, slowing my steps as I approached the golf simulators. I popped inside a little foyer cut into the bulkhead and noted two doors on the interior, one labeled SIMULATOR 1 and the other SIMULATOR 2, with a sign-up sheet posted on the wall. I checked the sheet and found Dorian Smoker's name printed in block letters beneath a list of a half dozen other names, his assigned time for simulator two being eight o'clock this evening.

A little chill lifted the down on my arms. Was this evidence? Shouldn't someone bag this and dust it for fingerprints or something? I looked around help-lessly. *Uff da.* I didn't even know who had authority over criminal investigations at sea.

I returned to the deck and as I rounded the stern, found my progress halted by a chain that extended from the rail to a hook on the bulkhead. Beneath the chain were several plastic cones stamped with the words, DANGER—WET—KEEP OFF. I guessed chains and cones were the cruise liner's version of crime scene tape.

I regarded the narrow space between the rail and the bulkhead, a sour taste creeping into my mouth as I realized this was where someone had pushed Dorian Smoker to his death. I walked to the rail and in the stunning silence of the moment, peered down at the froth of whitecaps rippling the water below. Bailey had obviously been telling the truth.

There was a killer walking the decks of the *Aloha Princess*.

I propped my chin in my hands and sighed.

Déjà vu all over again.

"I could have donated it to the Smithsonian for future generations to study. They have a magnificent rare book collection." Tilly sat achingly stiff on the narrow sofa in her stateroom, pining over what might have been.

She and Nana were booked into a "Large Oceanview" cabin—the "large" referring to the size of the porthole rather than the size of the cabin. But all the amenities were there. Twin beds aligned in an L against the interior and exterior walls. Mirrored vanity with a bank of lights. Minibar and refrigerator, itty-bitty safe, and television stacked in a wall cabinet.

Sitting area complete with sofa and miniature coffee table.

"I could have donated it to the British Museum," Tilly continued, "or . . . or the Naval Museum in Portsmouth."

"Didn't you want no money for it?" Nana was perched next to me on the edge of her bed, removing her stash of scavenger hunt items from her pocketbook.

Tilly looked appalled. "Financial remuneration is the last thing I would ever want for a document that rightfully belongs in the public domain."

"Bet you coulda got millions for it at that famous auction place," Nana contended.

"Sotheby's?" I asked.

"Nope, eBay," said Nana. "You wouldn't believe what folks are sellin' these days. Some fella advertised an aircraft carrier a couple a months back. I thought about biddin' on it, but I chickened out."

I looked at Tilly. Tilly looked at me. We both looked at Nana. "No place to store it?" I teased.

Nana shook her head. "Didn't wanna pay the postage."

I laughed in disbelief. "Why would you bid on an aircraft carrier?"

"For your father's birthday, dear. By the time you reach my age, you run outta good gift ideas, so it was either that or a necktie." She eyed the articles she'd arranged on the bed, then opened her pocketbook wide and poked her head inside. "Osmond give me one a them rocks from the spa when I seen him in the

hallway, but I don't know what I done with it."
Sweeping her scavenger items to one side, she
dumped the contents of her pocketbook onto the bed
in a Mount Everest of a pile. I eyed it in amazement.
Wow. She'd really cut back on the nonessentials.

"They've chained off the area where Professor
Smoker was pushed overboard," I announced, as
Nana began the slow process of sorting through her
things.

Tilly nodded sagely. "The captain must be quite
shocked by this turn of events. Cruise ships are probably more secure than gated communities. I read that
being on a cruise ship is safer than virtually anywhere
else in the world, except the teacup ride in the Magic
Kingdom. Do you realize that in the last twenty years,
there hasn't been one cruise passenger death related
to a maritime accident? Twenty years. Can you imagine?"

"Quite a streak," I admitted uneasily. I had a streak
of my own going: largest number of dead bodies
found by a non-European while traveling abroad. At
least this time, someone else had found the body . . .
or not found it, as the case may be. "Do either of you
know who handles criminal investigations aboard
ship?"

"They explained that on the A&E special." Nana
waved a hair pick triumphantly in the air. "I been
lookin' for this for months! Musta been hidin' at the
bottom of my pocketbook." She leveled a severe look
on the gargantuan bag. "Your grampa always said I
should downsize. He mighta been right. Anyway, that

show was sayin' every cruise ship has a private security force aboard, kinda like them fellas what guard those fancy buildin's in New York City, but they're not law officers, so they don't know nothin' about police procedures."

"So who decided to chain off the area around the crime scene?" I asked.

Tilly laid her walking stick in her lap. "It seems logical to assume that the chief security officer and the ship's captain were probably instructed to do that by either the Coast Guard, the FBI, or some other mainland law enforcement agency."

Nana nodded agreement. "Cruise ships got the right to ask help from any law enforcement authority they want."

"Did you learn that on your A&E special, too?" I asked.

Nana shook her head. "Reruns a *The Love Boat.*"

"So do you think they'll ask the authorities to come aboard when we reach Kauai?" I persisted.

"I suspect that might be why they cordoned off the crime scene," said Tilly. "To preserve the area as much as possible for the island police, though I'm not sure how much evidence can be preserved on a windswept deck. This is a cruise line's worst nightmare. They're in the business of selling fantasy, and crime scene tape and evidence kits are not part of the *Aloha Princess* fantasy package. Can you imagine the panic aboard ship if word leaks out that there could be a killer prowling the decks?"

"But there *is* a killer prowling the decks!"

Nana tossed a collapsible cup and a package of tissue to the side. "Could be the killer's not interested in knockin' off no one else. Mabe his only target was the professor fella."

Tilly mulled that over. "That's a consideration, Marion. If Professor Smoker's death was a random killing, every guest on board is in danger. But if he was specifically targeted by one of his enemies, as Bailey suggested, then no one else's life is actually in jeopardy."

"Don't seem to me that Bailey's too safe," Nana argued. "What if the killer thinks she got a good lookit 'im? What if he decides his next step is to kill her before she can finger 'im?"

"How would the killer know it was Bailey who saw him?" I questioned. "As far as he knows, it could be any one of over a thousand woman aboard who screamed at him."

Nana shook her head. "Well, the police are gonna need a better physical description of the fella than a gray warm-up suit. Shoot, everyone on board's probably got one a them. You s'pose they're gonna go through everyone's grips?"

"They'll never do that," Tilly asserted. "Much too intrusive. Besides, I doubt they have probable cause. And they certainly want to avoid the publicity an official search would entail. Not to mention potential litigation should some disgruntled passenger take issue with what he might consider an unwarranted invasion of privacy."

"I don't get it," I sputtered. "Exactly what kind of

theories could a professor suggest that might get him killed?"

Tilly shook her head. "I'm embarrassed to say I haven't a clue. I know Professor Smoker was purported to be the world's leading authority on Cook, but I'm afraid I accepted the claim at face value. Perhaps when Bailey is feeling better, she could enlighten us about what made his theories so controversial. But remember, we're talking about academia. Academicians can spend entire careers arguing over whether it's best to crack an egg at the wide or the narrow end."

Nana gave a loud suck on her teeth. "Well, would you lookit that." She pulled a small plastic bag from the bottom of her pile and brandished it in the air. "It's a little care package, with all my favorite goodies! Midget Tootsie Rolls. Licorice Jelly Bellies. Cinnamon bears. And look! A bag a peanut M&M's!" Her eyes lit up like halogen lights. "This must be your mother's doin', Emily. Bless her little heart. She musta hid it in my pocketbook when she come to say good-bye." She clutched the bag to her breast and threw a contrite look toward heaven. "I take back every unkind word I ever said about Margaret."

I smiled. "I guess this means you'll be a shoo-in for the scavenger hunt prize, hunh?"

"If I can find all my stuff and get it to the Dolphin Room in time." She began sorting through the pile at warp speed. Denture cream to the left. Paper clip to the right. Antacid tablets to the left. Automatic pencil with removable eraser to the right. I eyed her lopsided collection of "stuff" for a moment, coming to sudden attention when a far-fetched thought seized my brain.

"Oh, my God! What if Professor Smoker wasn't killed for this theories at all? What if he was killed for his ... stuff?"

"What stuff?" asked Nana. Mini clothesline and clothespins to the left. Square of folded white paper to the right.

"The book! Tilly's journal! What if someone realized it could be priceless if it was authentic? What if the book was wrestled away from Professor Smoker before he was pushed over the side? What if it's now in the hands of his killer?"

Tilly's face turned the color of wallpaper paste and her eyes froze in sudden horror. "If what you're saying is true, Emily, then *I'm* the person responsible for Professor Smoker's death. Oh, my stars. I've as good as killed a man."

"C'mon now, Til," Nana chided as she pitched a flat rock into her scavenger hunt pile. "You're no killer. You had nothin' but good intentions when you give that journal to Smoker for a look-see."

"But my good intentions may have caused his death." She pinched her eyes shut and gave her head a woeful shake. "I never should have let that journal out of my sight. How could I have been so negligent? I have a Ph.D; I should know better. But the name 'Griffin Ring' is so historically obscure, I never thought anyone other than Professor Smoker would recognize it. Someone in that lecture room obviously did, however. And I suspect if they knew about Griffin Ring, they must have known about the treasure."

I lasered my attention on Tilly. "Treasure?"

She heaved a regretful sigh. "I only had time to skim the journal, mind you, but one entry in particular caught my eye. In it, he writes of being sent to search for freshwater and mentions burying something of great value amid an outcropping of rock near a waterfall in the interior of one of the islands. He doesn't hint at what the object is, but if you remember correctly, Professor Smoker said that Ring was suspected in the death of a relative and the theft of a family heirloom back in England. It could well be that what he buried was this family heirloom, and one can only guess what its value might be today."

Treasure? Euw. How Blackbeard the Pirate of him. "Did he say which island?"

"He did better than that," Tilly lamented. "He drew a map. That's what caught my eye in the first place. But I never took the time to study it, so I have no idea which island it might be. I was too convinced the book was a hoax to give the map serious attention." Her shoulders sagged miserably. "And now the journal and the map are both gone, so we'll never know if the treasure was truth or fiction. The find of the century, down the tubes."

Nana grabbed the folded white paper from her scavenger hunt pile, snapped it open, and regarded it briefly before holding it up for Tilly. "Is this the map you're talkin' about?"

Tilly's jaw dropped to her chest, recognition lighting her eyes. "That's it! That's the map! How . . . what . . . where did you get it?"

Nana shrugged. "Outta your book. You told me I oughta thumb through it while you was takin' your shower, and that's when I run into the map. See here?" She angled it toward me. "It don't have no advertisin', so I photocopied it for the scavenger hunt. The rules don't say nothin' about photocopies bein' ineligible."

"Bless you, Marion!" Tilly shot to her feet as if she'd been fuel-injected. "You've saved the day! Where's my guidebook?" She yanked open a drawer in the vanity, seized her *Frommer's*, and flipped through the pages. "William Bligh was a gifted cartographer and the officer Cook made responsible for charting the islands. I suspect Griffin Ring's map may be a fair rendering of Bligh's work, so we shouldn't have any difficulty identifying which of the islands it is."

She leaned over the book, observing the page from every angle. "We have five possible islands in the chain to choose from, each with a unique shape. Study the island on your map closely, ladies, and tell me. Does it resemble a Nez Perce spearhead, an Acheulean hand ax, a . . . hmm . . . a Baganda throwing stick, the remnants of a *Pithecanthropus erectus* skull, or a Pomo head basket?"

"It looks like a cow flop," said Nana.

"A cow flop. That would make it the equivalent of"— she paused, studying the *Frommer's* intently—

"the Pomo head basket. And that means Ring's map is the island of"—she stabbed the page with her index finger—"Kauai!" She flipped to another section of the book and skimmed the text. "Are there any other markings?"

Nana traced the map with her finger. "It's got a long crooked line what must be a river, and a big X by some squiggles what look like a waterfall."

"There's only one navigable river in the entire state of Hawaii, and that's the Wailua River on Kauai. So if Griffin Ring was searching for freshwater on the island of Kauai sometime in 1778 or '79, the river he used to reach the interior was most likely the Wailua."

"The Wailua River," I muttered, plucking my excursion itinerary out of my shoulder bag and eyeing the short description. "It says here I'll be kayaking tomorrow on 'the most scenic river in Kauai.' Do you suppose that's the Wailua? It also mentions that I'll be hiking to someplace called the Secret Falls. You think that might be the waterfall that's on the map?"

Nana shoved the paper at me. "If it is, how 'bout you root around for the treasure while you're there? It's s'posed to be right by that X."

With a determined look on her face, Tilly picked up the phone and punched in a number. "Yes. About the kayak adventure that's scheduled for tomorrow— what river does that take place on?" She paused, her face brightening. "The Wailua?" She flashed us a thumbs-up. "Excellent. This is Tilly Hovick. I'd like to reserve two tickets for—" Another pause. A frown creased her brow. "Then put my name and that of

Marion Sippel on the waiting list. We'll be down in a few minutes to turn in our tickets for the zodiac raft ride."

Tilly hung up, giving Nana a contrite look. "I hope I haven't overstepped my bounds, Marion. I know how much you were looking forward to that raft ride, but since you were the one who resurrected the map, I thought you might want to share in our quest for buried treasure."

"You bet," Nana said, plucking the map back out of my hands. "But what happens if we don't make it off the waitin' list?"

Tilly looked genuinely worried. "Then the burden of finding the treasure will fall into Emily's hands."

Oh, great. No pressure there.

"But I hope it won't come to that. Let's keep our fingers crossed that there will be enough cancellations to allow us to sign up. In the meantime, we need to be wiser this time, and more discreet. We mustn't tell anyone what we're doing. This needs to be our secret. Agreed?"

Nana and I nodded. We were both good at keeping secrets, so I wasn't concerned about spilling the beans to anyone.

What did worry me was the possibility that if Griffin Ring's journal wasn't at the bottom of the ocean right now, it was in the hands of someone who might be looking for the treasure, too. Which begged the question, if Dorian Smoker's attacker had killed to possess the book, to what lengths might he go to obtain the treasure?

CHAPTER 4

"If you please, I'll have the Strasbourg pâté, the prosciutto with melon, the breaded oysters, and the Nova Scotia smoked salmon."

I rolled my eyes as Nils the Viking followed the example of his friends, Gjurd and Ansgar, and placed an order for four out of the five appetizers that appeared on our dinner menu. Cruise lines allowed you to order everything on the menu if you wanted, but I preferred to leave some food for the passengers who were scheduled to dine at the second seating.

Dinner was being served in the South Seas dining room on deck four—an eye-popper of a room walled in glass, overhung with crystal chandeliers, dressed up with crisp white linen and velvet chairs, and gleaming with ornate silverware and long-stemmed goblets. I was dining with five other people who'd been assigned to my table for the duration of the trip—Margi Swanson, a man named Jonathan Pond, and the three World Navigators I had met earlier. I engaged in some idle chitchat with the Navigators and tried not to dwell on the fact that if what Bailey Howard had suggested was true, one of these guys could be a killer.

Our table was located at the far end of the room near the kitchen, where the sounds of crashing china, shouted orders, and clanging pots overpowered the piped-in notes of a familiar Debussy melody. The other Iowans in my group had signed up for a table for ten, so Margi and I had agreed to become dinner partners at a separate table. Margi was extremely social, so it didn't faze her to sit with total strangers. Her level of self-confidence had obviously been boosted by the fact that she'd spent most of her life telling people to strip down to their skivvies and pee into a cup.

Our tuxedoed waiter, Darko from Romania, executed a snappy bow to Nils before moving on to Margi, who sat to my left. "Madame?" he asked, paper and pencil in hand.

Margi hesitated, looking as if the final war between good and evil was waging inside her. She furrowed her brow, licked her lips, and in a flash of decisiveness said, "I'll have exactly what he's having." She flashed the waiter a self-satisfied smile before adding, "Except . . . I'll have the chopped madeira jelly and chunks of orange without the pâté. Pâté. That's like cat food, isn't it? I'm not really fond of cat food. And I'll have the melon without the prosciutto. That prosciutto sounds like it might be too spicy for me. I get a touch of acid reflux now and again. And I hope the melon is cantaloupe, because honeydew gives me cankers. I'll try the oyster breading without the oysters, with sweet sauce instead of hot sauce, and I'd like the lettuce and onion rings that accompany the smoked salmon without the salmon."

As Darko scribbled notes, Margi leaned toward me to whisper, "My sister accuses me of being afraid to try anything new. Well, I'll show her, and you're my witness, Emily. Can you believe she was telling folks at the clinic that I'd bypass all the exotic food in favor of everyday fruits and vegetables? I *so* want to see the look on her face when you tell her how daring I've become." She grimaced at her fingertips before extracting a small plastic bottle from her pocket and offering it up to the rest of the table. "Hand sanitizer, anyone?"

"Madame?" Darko stood above me, pencil poised midair.

I shivered as a waiter bounded past our table, stirring up a cyclone of cool air that chilled the back of my neck. "Fruit cup," I said, as a dozen more waiters converged into the aisle, to-ing and fro-ing like Olympic relay racers.

Darko clicked his heels. "I come back soon to take your entrée orders."

"Enjoy the peace and quiet while you can," Jonathan Pond advised me from across the table. "Wait until you see what happens when they get really busy."

"Spoken like a veteran cruiser," I said, smiling.

"How many trips does this make for you?" He looked like an aging computer geek in desperate need of a makeover—bad haircut with a fierce part down the middle, black-framed eyeglasses held together with a wad of duct tape at the bridge, round shoulders, and white Oxford shirt buttoned all the way to his Adam's apple. All he needed was a pocket protector crammed with leaky pens and number two pencils. The only feature about him that didn't scream Stereotype was the plaster cast and blue sling shackling his right arm.

"Actually, this is my first cruise," he replied, "but if I'm sitting here, something's bound to go wrong. It goes with the territory these days. I'm cursed."

Oh, my God! A kindred spirit! I nodded sympathy, feeling an instant bond with Jonathan Pond. "I know exactly what you mean. I've felt that way ever since I started this new job of mine."

From behind his Coke bottle lenses, he fixed me with a somber look. "I wasn't being flip. I really am cursed."

The three Vikings exchanged curious looks with each other before breaking out in disbelieving smiles. Margi regarded Jonathan's cast with the kind of lust dieters direct at double chocolate cake with extra frosting. "Excuse me, I hope you don't mind my asking, but how long have you been wearing that cast?"

Jonathan wiggled the fingers poking out the end. "Three weeks."

Duty hardened Margi's gaze. "Have you sanitized it yet? My clinic recommends weekly scourings with a nonabrasive cleaner. I have some with me; would you like to borrow it? It smells a little like lemon-scented hog manure, but it does a dandy job of getting rid of those nasty germs."

Margi's fanaticism in her battle against common household germs had earned her the nickname "Immaculate Margi." Her sister was even worse. We called her "Lysol Linda."

"How did you hurt your arm?" I leaped in before Jonathan could crush Margi's feelings by saying he'd rather be devoured by germs than smell like a pig.

He twisted his mouth self-consciously. "A surfing accident."

"You surf?" Wow. He sure didn't fit my image of your average surfer.

Nils's interest in Jonathan Pond escalated tenfold. "The three of us, we would like to learn this sport." He slapped his chest before nodding toward Gjurd and Ansgar. "The conditions in the fjords are not so good, not like in your Hawaiian Islands. Where do you do your surfing?"

"Mostly in my dining room," Jonathan said. "That's where the computer is set up." He paused to reconsider. "Where it used to be set up . . . before the accident. I was surfing the net when a pickup truck hit the house. Lost its brakes and plowed through the wall at sixty miles an hour. I'm lucky I escaped with only a broken arm. You should see what it did to my computer; it was really gruesome. I have a photo. You want to see?"

"That's okay," I said, as he started reaching for his wallet.

He stayed his hand. "Are you sure? I have pictures before the fire and after."

"Fire?"

"Yeah. The house burned down the next morning. Totally unrelated to the accident. Electrical short or something. Went up like a matchstick."

I stared at him in shock. "Was anyone hurt?"

"No one was home when it happened." He exhaled a painful sigh and with downcast eyes explained, "My wife left me last summer. Ran off with someone in her gourmet-cooking class. But who could blame her? Beth liked nice things. French copper cookware, Henckel cutlery—everything I couldn't afford to buy her anymore, even at online discount prices. I give her credit for sticking around as long as she did, after they outsourced my job to India. Beth is a real dish. I couldn't expect her to wait around forever while our finances improved. Anyone who's ever been unemployed knows that sending out résumés to potential employers and finding the right job can take months, sometimes years."

"How long did she stay after you lost your job?" Margi asked sympathetically.

"Longer than I ever expected. Four and a half days. Just goes to show you how tolerant she'd gotten over the years."

He'd lost his job? His wife had run off with another man? His house had burned down? He'd broken his arm? Geesch, this guy made my life look like an enchanted fairy tale. "You've had a healthy run of bad luck," I said, trying to lighten the mood.

He nodded. "But I've fully recovered from my broken leg. I don't even limp anymore."

I scanned the ceiling in search of hidden surveillance devices. We were on *Candid Camera,* right? But I had to ask. "When did you break your leg?"

"Just before I lost my job. Would you believe I blew a tire and accidentally rammed the Oscar Mayer Weinermobile on its cross-country trip to promote meatless hot dogs? My Chevy ended up in the scrap pile. The weiner never got a scratch. The police determined the bun gave it extra protection."

Margi clucked out a warning. "Broken bones are a very bad sign. I'd recommend a bone density test to check for osteoporosis. How's your daily milk consumption?"

The wine steward appeared at that moment to take our drink orders, followed by Darko, who scribbled down our main course orders before collecting our menus and merging back into the stream of foot traffic headed for the kitchen. How everyone managed to move so quickly and not collide with each other was beyond me.

"I approve of your choice of the New England clam chowder," Margi said, nodding to Jonathan. "Calcium helps build strong bones."

"It's the only thing on the menu I could eat one-handed." He sighed with disgust. "I was so stupid!"

"You're being too hard on yourself," Margi consoled. "Think about it. The king crab legs would have been impossible."

"No! I was stupid about my first trip to the islands

last year, when I pocketed a rock from the volcano
fields on the big island. Worst mistake of my life.
They don't post signs; they don't warn you in the
tourist brochures. But when your luck starts going
south and you try to figure out why, you discover
some dumb myth about the volcano goddess Pele
making your life a living hell if you steal any of her
precious lava rock. Volcano goddess. Right. Who
believes stuff like that? I'm a techie. Techies don't
believe in primitive superstitions; we're too firmly
grounded in virtual reality. But I took a rock the size
of a silver dollar and I've been paying for it ever since,
so the old girl made a believer out of me."

"Which island is the big island?" asked Margi.

"Hawaii!" Nils, Gjurd, and Ansgar shouted, like
game show contestants in lightning-round mode. I
suspected World Navigators probably had global
atlases tattooed onto their chests as part of some ini-
tiation rite.

"I'm not on this cruise to enjoy myself," Jonathan
continued. "I'm here for only one reason: to dump
that cussed rock back where it came from."

"You couldn't simply mail it?" I asked. "It would
have been cheaper."

"Entrust it to the Postal Service? Are you crazy?
Even if I sent it registered mail, return receipt
requested, there's no guarantee it wouldn't end up in
a dead letter office someplace. And then I'd be
doomed for the rest of my life."

Which could be dramatically brief if his streak of
bad luck continued at its present rate.

"I didn't even dare take a plane to the islands. I hopped a freighter out of L.A. to Honolulu. I didn't want to risk any kind of air disaster."

Nils raised a questioning finger. "When you return the rock to its rightful home, your luck will then be restored, yah?"

"According to the myth, everything should get back to normal . . . if I can manage to survive that long. I'm just thankful there aren't any icebergs in the vicinity."

Speaking on behalf of the other nineteen hundred and ninety-nine passengers aboard the *Aloha Princess,* I was thankful for that, too.

"Icebergs, yah," said Nils, looking wistful. "Many years ago, my ancestors battled icebergs."

Margi sucked in her breath. "Oh, my goodness. Was your family on the *Titanic?* That's my very favorite movie ever. I saw it sixty-three times. Did your family survive?" She flattened her palm against her chest as if to quell palpitations. "Did they ever mention Rose and Jack?"

"My ancestors were Norsemen. First to cross the North Atlantic in open boats. First to navigate iceberg-infested seas. First to discover the continent of North America."

Margi snorted amusement. "I beg your pardon, but Christopher Columbus discovered America. We even have a special day to honor him. It has a real catchy name; maybe you've heard of it. Columbus Day?"

Nils slammed his fist down, causing our silverware

to bounce across the table like aerial acrobats. "Christopher Columbus? Bah!" He whacked the table again, catapulting my salad fork into my lap. "Bjarni Herjulfsson discovered America!"

I squinted one eye at him. "Barney who?"

"Bjarni Herjulfsson."

"How do you say that in English?"

He squinted back at me. "B—jarrrni Herrrr—julfsson."

Oh, yeah. That was much better.

Jonathan looked perplexed. "How come I've never heard of him?"

Nils slapped his palm onto the table. Margi lunged for her flatware. "Because everyone has forgotten the sagas and the tales. They remember Columbus. They remember Magellan. No one remembers Herjulfsson!"

I suspected this oversight might have been corrected if the explorer in question had thought to change his name to something people could actually pronounce.

"Five hundred years before that imposter Columbus, Herjulfsson sailed through a fog when looking for Greenland and ended up finding North America."

"Oh, sure." Margi realigned her silverware. "Like our federal government closes banks and shuts down postal service to honor an imposter. I don't think so. Our national holidays are not venues to showcase phonies. What do you think shows like *Jerry Springer* are for?"

Gjurd and Ansgar spouted something at Nils in voices so loud and frenzied that people at neighboring tables pivoted in their seats to stare at us. Nils spouted something back, face red, eyes bulging, voice booming. Man, I could see what Bailey meant about these guys being a little testy. If you were smart, you wouldn't want to cross them. But, hey, now that we were on the subject . . .

"Do you have to be Norwegian to belong to the World Navigators Club?" I asked above the shouting.

Gjurd and Ansgar bit back what they were saying to stare first at Nils, then at me. Nils inhaled a deep breath before sitting back in his chair. "There is no requirement that members be Norwegian, but it helps. Beards are also welcome."

"So, what exactly do World Navigators do? I mean, do you have some kind of credo or something?"

"Credo. Yah." He hoisted his shirtsleeve to his shoulder and flexed his biceps to reveal a colorful tattoo of a Viking helmet accompanied by the words *Nils Nilsson, World Navigators Club.* "We all have credos," he said proudly.

Okay, no global atlases. I wondered if they'd nixed the idea because of the ever-changing geopolitcal situation, or problems with too much chest hair. Either way, I'd been close. "Credo," I corrected Nils. "Mission statement. Like the United Nations? The Campfire Girls? It states the purpose of why you get together."

"Why we get together? Yah. We drink good, strong beer. We sail in regattas. We discuss the greatest navigators in history—Bjarni Herjulfsson, Eric the Red, Leif Ericsson."

"Not James Cook?"

"Bah! Cook was a fraud. He followed in the wake of others more skillful than himself and accomplished nothing besides getting himself killed. Where was the challenge? He had bigger ships. Sturdier sails. Better supplies. Chronometers. Five chronometers on every voyage! Herjulfsson sailed without instruments in more treacherous waters. The so-called experts have made too much of Cook. That must change."

I shot him a puzzled look. "You said earlier that the reason you signed up for this cruise was to attend Professor Smoker's lectures. Why did you spend so much money to hear someone lecture about a fraud?"

He hesitated before offering me an odd half smile. "We are not narrow-minded. We understood Professor Smoker was a most influential and respected man. We wanted to hear his version of history, study him in person, and accompany him on his many island excursions before we decided what tack to take to prove his views wrong."

Hmm. Had they made their decision and acted upon it already? Euw, boy. Whether they were involved in Professor Smoker's death or not, though, the demise of the ship's academic headliner presented a scheduling nightmare for the guest relations people. "Do you suppose the entire Cook program will be canceled because of what happened? I imagine some of those excursions will lose their appeal without Professor Smoker there to provide the narrative."

"What of his assistant?" asked Nils. "She could take over at the helm, yah?"

Was it me, or was he having a hard time keeping the anticipation out of his voice at the prospect of Bailey's substituting for the professor?

"You can forget the assistant," Margi declared. "I heard it straight from Bernice. That girl will probably have to stay in the infirmary for the rest of the trip because she's on the brink of a nervous breakdown. She saw the person who pushed the professor overboard, and it's got her all upset."

Bernice? How had Bernice found out? She wasn't supposed to know that. No one was supposed to know that!

"Someone got pushed overboard?" Jonathan choked out.

Margi nodded. "They still haven't found the body."

A chorus line of waiters banged out of the kitchen and charged toward our table, trays of appetizers balanced on their palms and shoulders. Down went the trays onto serving tables. Up flew dishes artistically arranged with pink salmon, ripe melon, and something that resembled Meow Mix. Down went the plates before us, consuming every inch of table space available. Off sped the waiters again, all elegance and efficiency.

My gaze drifted over the array of food, dazzled by the color, the variety, the presentation. Even the Meow Mix looked appetizing.

"My lettuce looks tantalizing, doesn't it?" Margi commented.

"This is all my fault," Jonathan wailed. He buried his face behind his one good hand and shook his head. "If I wasn't aboard, that person might still be alive. I have to do something. I can't go on like this. Don't try to stop me, anyone." He shoved his chair away from the table and sprang to his feet. "I have to confess everything to the captain!"

As he bolted away, my fruit cup suddenly skated across the table after him, accompanied by colorful plates of pâté, prosciutto, oysters, salmon, and Margi's hunk of bib lettuce.

BOOM! *Tinkle*. CRASH! Splat.

Shrieks throughout the dining room. Gasps. Nils spat what sounded like a Norwegian cussword and leaped out of his chair, knocking it over with a *BOOM* that vibrated the floor. Gjurd let out a Viking yell. Ansgar glowered at the smorgasbord in his lap and growled something that needed no translation. Our appetizers lay splattered across the carpet like refuse from an all-you-can-eat buffet. Oh, my God. What just happened?

I glanced at Jonathan, who stood awkwardly in the aisle, yanking at the umbilical cord of tablecloth that was tucked into the waistband of his pants.

Oh, yeah. This guy was cursed big-time.

Margi fished a small packet out of her purse. "Moist towelette, anyone?"

* * *

The mess was cleared up and our meals reordered with polite enthusiasm if not speed. The Vikings ripped apart platters of Alaskan king crab with their bare hands and left without ordering dessert. Margi bypassed a main entrée in favor of sampling everything on the dessert menu, then left halfway through to stake out a good seat for the evening's entertainment in the Bali Ha'i Theater. My medium-rare prime sirloin arrived looking like a used engine part so I sent it back to the kitchen, and by the time they got it right, some early birds from the second seating were pacing beside the table, checking their watches and giving me dirty looks.

So much for leisurely dining.

I stood up, thanked Darko for all his trouble, apologized for leaving my meal uneaten, and knew I was doing the right thing when instead of looking disappointed, he looked relieved. I scooted down the aisle with my stomach growling from hunger, but the good news was, the dinner buffet in the Coconut Palms Cafe didn't close until midnight!

I skirted around the waterfall at the entrance of the dining room and as I made my way down the corridor to the elevators, spied a familiar face walking away from the desk in the guest relations cove, though considering the sluggishness of her gait, I questioned whether she should be on her feet at all.

"Bailey?" I caught up to her in a half dozen steps. "Shouldn't you be in the infirmary?"

She regarded me for a dazed moment before waving

the plastic card in her hand at me. "I had to replace my room key. It's so strange. I put it in my pocket earlier"—she poked two fingers into the shallow pocket of her knit vest—"but it's not there anymore. I must have lost it, but that's so unlike me. I never lose things. Ever."

"Can I walk you back to the infirmary?"

She gave her head a slow, loosey-goosey shake, as if it were attached to the rest of her body by a flimsy rubber band. "I'm not going back there. It was so noisy down there with people coming and going, I checked myself out. I told them I'd get a better night's sleep in my own cabin." She slapped her palm over her mouth and yawned. "I'm so sleepy. But I need to stay awake long enough to pack."

"Pack? Are you leaving?"

"Right after I give a statement to the Kauai police tomorrow. The only reason I was on this trip was to assist Professor Smoker. After what's happened"—she swallowed a sob—"I don't think I'm quite up for the carnival atmosphere on the *Aloha Princess*. Virgos have an almost compulsive need to plan ahead, so I guess I'll fly home and figure out where I go from here."

I couldn't fault her there. After my marriage ended, I'd gone home to regroup, too, but unlike Bailey, at least I'd had a family waiting to give me support.

"So I guess this is good-bye." She offered her hand in a formal handshake but looked uncomfortable when our palms made contact. "Hey, it was nice meeting you, Emily. I just wish it could have been under more pleasant circumstances. Hope you enjoy the rest of your cruise."

"Um—" I stood there awkwardly, caught between the classic rock and hard place. "I don't want to frighten you, but I think you should know that some people on board know you're the person who witnessed Professor Smoker's murder."

Bailey shrugged. "Doesn't surprise me. I suppose it was bound to get out."

"Yeah, but if that's the case, wouldn't you be safer sleeping in the infirmary tonight? I'm not implying that you're a target, but if you are, I'd think you'd be better off in a place where there are lots of other people around." People who were sick, lame, and drugged, but people nonetheless.

Her eyes narrowed pensively. "I actually gave that some thought while I was lying in my hospital bed. After what you implied this afternoon, every time someone passed by my door, I jumped a little, wondering if—" She paused. "Like I told you, there are way too many people down there, any one of whom could slip into a room undetected and take care of any business that needed finishing up. That's one of the reasons I decided to leave. Unlike my infirmary room, my cabin has a dead bolt, and I intend to use it. The only way anyone will get at me tonight is if they beat the door down."

That made me feel better. I loved it when people opted not to be stupid. "Do you need an escort to your door? It's my specialty."

"You're a professional escort?" She regarded my

scoopneck tee and walking shorts with a critical eye, looking confused and disillusioned. "Aren't escorts supposed to dress scandalously hot? You know—fishnet stockings? Stiletto heels? Sequins?"

"I *am* dressed hot, for Iowa." I smiled goodnaturedly. "Actually, I'm not that kind of escort."

She arched her brows, still skeptical. "If you say so. Anyway, thanks again for everything."

She disappeared amid the crowd of casually dressed couples who were queuing up to smile for the camera prior to their first dinner aboard the *Aloha Princess*. I envied her being able to escape the mandatory Kodak moment. Margi and I had tried to sneak into the dining room without having to pose for our official photo, but the photographer had turned into the "picture police" by corralling us near the doorway and posing us like manikins in front of an ugly clip art panel of the ship. "Say cheese," he'd instructed with drill sergeant exactness.

I'd looked into the camera and forced a smile, but the word I mouthed had nothing to do with "cheese."

With four hours to go until the buffet line closed, I maneuvered my way into the elevator and zipped up to the welcome quiet of deck eleven. To my left was a glassed-in area set up like a backyard patio where guests could dine at wrought-iron tables near windows that allowed them to experience both the warm Pacific breeze and the high humidity. To my right, beyond the glass partition that marked the gateway to the open deck, endless rows of adjustable chaise lounges flanked the adult swimming pool like vacant theater seats.

I heard a splash.

Banks of floodlights illuminated the pool and twin Jacuzzis, but I could see little beyond the phalanx of lounge chairs. Hunh. My curiosity piqued, I ventured through the sliding glass doors, wincing when a blast of humid night air and chlorine hit me in the face. As I skirted the perimeter of the pool area, I craned my neck to see who else was up there with me, but I continued to see nothing . . . until the solitary swimmer climbed out of the pool and stood up. He threw a towel over his head to dry his hair, so I couldn't see his face, but what I *could* see caused a little flutter in my tummy.

He was tall and broad-shouldered, with well-defined sinew snaking down his arms and across his chest. His skin was taut, his stomach flat, and as he dried his hair, I saw a flex of muscle that hinted of physical power. Water clung to his breastbone and ribs, then trickled down his bare flesh toward—

I lowered my gaze to the slash of spandex that rode daringly low on his hips and gave myself a quick mental slap. Whoa! What was I doing? I was in love. I shouldn't be ogling another man. Oh, my God—this could only mean one thing.

I failed the test. My wandering eye was proof that my love life was on the rocks, that Etienne and I were all washed up, that I was so deprived romantically that I could stoop to unabashed voyeurism without a twinge of conscience.

I angled my head to regard the stranger from another perspective and sighed my appreciation. Man, the last time I saw a body that ripped was during my nephews' Mutant Ninja Turtle action figure phase.

He whipped the towel off his head and tossed his hair back, then zeroed a look straight across the deck to find me gawking like a teenage groupie at a rock concert. His face was as beautiful as the rest of him, his smile shamelessly cocky, and as he strode toward me, I realized he was no stranger.

"Hello, pretty." He looped his wet towel around my neck and drew me close, covering my lips in a long, languid kiss before nuzzling the corner of my mouth and whispering, "I've missed you."

CHAPTER 5

I teetered off-balance as my legs unhinged at the knees. "Duncan?"

He seized my elbows to steady me. "Easy there." He gave me one of those piercing looks that bored through my skull like a dumdum bullet, then flashed me a slow, assessing smile. "You're looking good, Em."

As well as could be expected for someone whose lips had gone suddenly numb. Whoa! I tested my lips with my tongue, feeling as if they'd been injected with a lethal dose of Novocaine. I didn't even know if I could talk without slurring my words. "What . . . what are you doing here?"

A mischievous twinkle lit his coal dark eyes. "I thought that was obvious. I'm pursuing you."

Duncan Lazarus, the Oxford-educated tour director who'd guided us on our recent trip through Italy, had rolled into my life like a Sherman tank and been in hard pursuit ever since. According to Duncan, Lazarus men were doggedly single-minded about the women they wanted, and the woman Duncan wanted was . . . me.

He grasped my left hand. "Still no engagement ring, I see." He'd informed me that he considered me fair game until I had a ring on my finger, and over the past four months he'd been bombarding me with phone calls and emails from all parts of Italy in an effort to chip away at my resistance. "Are you sure your Inspector Miceli is part Italian? From what I've observed of Italian men, they're much more fervent in their pursuit of the women they love."

"Etienne is fervent," I defended. Unfortunately he was also Swiss, which diluted the fervency thing to some miniscule part per million.

"Etienne is clueless." Duncan trailed a lazy thumb along the curve of my jaw. "God, you're beautiful."

"Duncan!" I wiggled away from him, ducking under his towel and inching a safe distance backward. "I . . . You . . . We . . ."

His mouth curved in a slow grin. "Take a deep breath. It'll help you get something out of your mouth other than pronouns."

"What are you doing here?"

"You mean, in addition to pursuing you?" He sluiced water from his shoulder and chest with a careless hand, scattering droplets onto the little Italian-made Speedo that was straining its seams to contain him. *Oh, God.*

"I'm working. Temporary reassignment, actually.

My counterpart in England was supposed to head up the Pacific islands tour, but I made him an offer he couldn't refuse, so, here I am."

"You . . . you *arranged* to be here?"

He gave me a sheepish palms up. "Guilty."

"You knew you were going to be here, and you never bothered to mention it to me?"

"I didn't want to spoil the surprise."

What was it with the men in my life and surprises? Geesch! I shook my head, sighing, but deep down inside, I was grateful that at least Duncan hadn't shown up in spike heels and lipstick, like my ex had in Ireland. "So what did you offer your counterpart in England that he found impossible to refuse?"

"Two weeks of my personal leave allotted to him, plus the phone number of a sexy Hollywood starlet who's renting an apartment in Rome."

My eyes widened with shock. "You're giving up two weeks of vacation to be on this cruise?"

"You're missing the point." He smiled into my face, gracing me with one of his patented steamy looks. "I get to be on this cruise . . . with you."

Aw, that was so sweet!

The sliding glass door *whooshed* open behind us. "There you are, Mr. Lazarus," called a man with an aristocratic English accent. I glanced toward the voice to find an elderly gentleman in a tweed sports jacket and vest shuffling onto the deck. "We've run into a spot of bother in the dining room. Would you be so kind as to lend us some assistance?"

"I'm on it," Duncan responded, then to me, "The

curse of the chronically employed. Duty calls." He kissed his forefinger and touched it to my lips. "Mark your calendar. We'll continue this conversation later." He gave me a sassy wink, then strutted off toward the Englishman, the floodlights illuminating his too-long hair, his Mediterranean tan, and all six feet two inches of his wet, muscled flesh.

"Duncan!" I called at his retreating back.

He turned.

"Nice bathing suit."

He flashed me an evil grin before shaking out his towel and wrapping it around his waist. "I'm in cabin seventy-five-oh-five, just in case you get lonely."

I stared after him, assaulted by embarrassing waves of emotion, lust, guilt over the lust—and most disturbing of all, envy. *His stateroom was on deck seven?* Man, Landmark was a lot more generous with its employee accommodations than the Windsor City Bank. *Deck seven?* Damn. That was even above the waterline.

I sampled all the goodies from every food island in the Coconut Palms Cafe before returning to my cabin in the bilge. Okay, it really wasn't the bilge, but the dimly lit corridor, the uncarpeted floor, the painful creaks and groans from the bulkhead, and the steady thrum of nearby engines gave it the feel of the third-class passenger deck on the *Titanic*. I opened my door and flipped on the light, illuminating a narrow, windowless cabin half the size of Nana's. If I sat down on the side of the bed, I'd practically skin my knees on the opposite wall. I sighed with nostalgia. This place had "Four Star Swiss Hotel" written all over it.

As I closed the door, I noticed a sheet of white paper lying on the floor and bent down to pick it up. Tilly's treasure map of Kauai. She must have photocopied Nana's map and slid it under my door so I'd have it for our big day tomorrow.

Stashing my shoulder bag on the vanity, I grabbed my Hawaiian Islands guidebook and sat down at the foot of my bed. I found a map of Kauai and compared it to Tilly's. No doubt about it. Griffin Ring's drawing was the island of Kauai, but would we actually find buried treasure in the place where he'd marked his huge black X?

One thing was for sure. We'd have to be on the lookout for other people searching for buried treasure, because if someone else on the kayak adventure flashed a copy of Griffin Ring's map, dollars to doughnuts, we'd be staring into the eyes of the person who killed Dorian Smoker.

"I don't want my picture taken," I announced to the photographer the next morning. I'd made it as far as the end of the gangway before I'd noticed him lurking in front of a huge painted sign that identified our first destination as the island of Kauai.

"It's not an option," he informed me, barring my way. "If you're a passenger on this ship, you have to have your picture taken. Read the small print in your cruise documents."

I narrowed my eyes at him. "I'll say this very

calmly. I overslept. I haven't had time to apply my mascara yet. *No one* takes a picture of me without my mascara. Get it?"

He aimed his camera at my face and pressed the shutter. "Got it. You'll find this posted in the picture gallery on deck five later today. You can purchase copies for fifteen dollars. That's a real bargain, lady. Kahuna Cruise Lines charges twenty."

A lightbulb went on over my head. A cruise ship was like a movie theater. The real money wasn't in the price of admission; it was in the concession stand items. The alcoholic beverages. The spa services. The photographs. "You make a killing on these photos, don't you?"

The photographer smiled broadly. "It's what keeps us afloat. Next please."

We were docked in Nawiliwili Bay, a protected cul-de-sac of a port surrounded by mountains whose lofty, razor-sharp edges were softened by waves of lush, tropical vegetation and infested by insects that would probably make an Iowa rootworm look as cuddly as a pet hamster. I was stutter-stepping down the quay behind a group of slow-moving women when I saw a man in an orchids-gone-wild Aloha shirt hold up an event sign that said KAYAK ADVENTURE, with an arrow pointing toward a corrugated steel building that looked like a converted warehouse. Since I was running late, I scooted around the women and scurried toward the warehouse, passing long-haired girls in grass skirts who were swishing their hips to a tune strummed by two guys with ukeleles. I hadn't had any success contacting Nana and Tilly this morning, so I hoped they'd been able to get tickets for the excursion and were already on the bus. I wasn't sure I could handle the whole buried treasure thing all by myself.

As I entered the building, I wondered if all two thousand passengers had signed up for shore excursions, because the place was more crowded than the annual tractor pull at the state fair. People scurrying left. People scurrying right. People standing in one spot, mouths hanging open, looking confused.

I checked my watch: 8:15. By Iowa standards, I was already late for the 8:30 departure.

"Hey, pretty, tell me you're taking the Allerton Garden tour so I can fawn over you all day."

I wheeled around at the sound of Duncan's voice and shuffled back a self-conscious step when I realized he was practically on top of me. I gave him a quick once-over, from sandals, to shorts, to polo shirt, then smiled up at his sun-bronzed face. "You look a lot taller with clothes on." I waved my ticket in the air. "Wailua River Kayak Adventure."

"Damn. That was my first choice. How'd you talk your group into kayaking? I tried to convince mine it might be exciting to step outside their comfort zone, but the only kind of water-related activities they participate in are those that involve garden hoses, sprinkler systems, and birdbaths. Hard making inroads with people whose idea of intense excitement is an audiophone tour of an Oriental garden. Thank God for the Sandwich Island Society members."

My ears perked up like antennae. "You have Sandwich Islanders in your group?" The same Sandwich Islanders that Bailey Howard accused of wanting to kill Professor Smoker?

"They're real pistols. I think some of them may even have signed up for your kayak adventure. But do yourself a favor and don't ask them to explain anything about the Sandwich Island Society."

"Why not?"

"Because they might tell you."

Hmm. How handy was that? "How will I recognize them? Are they wearing name tags?"

He fought to suppress a grin. "They're Brits. You'll know them when you see them, with or without name tags." Linking his fingers with mine, he angled my arm behind my back and pressed me against the length of his body. "Meet me for a drink in the Anchor Bar tonight, Em. Ten o'clock." He lowered his head and whispered softly against my ear, "Don't make me beg."

I paused, hoping that something soulful and profound would accidentally pop out of my mouth.

"Allerton Garden tour!" shouted a woman who was bulldozing her way through the crowd, brandishing her event sign in the air. "We leave in five minutes. All aboard! Bus number twenty-six. Allerton Garden tour!"

"That's me." Duncan kissed my cheek and released me, then aimed a stern forefinger at my nose. "Ten o'clock tonight. Anchor Bar."

"I—"

"I'll be waiting." He took off without another word, sucked into the swarming chaos like a dust bunny into a Dirt Devil.

I stood moored to the spot, battling the sensation that the ground was seesawing beneath me. Palpitations. Dizziness. Oh, God. Was this a sign that Duncan was getting to me? Was his sexual magnetism wearing down my defenses? I ventured a cautious step forward. This couldn't be animal attraction. It had to be water on the brain, or a punctured eardrum, or some other aberrant physiological anomaly.

Turning a wide corner, I exited the building and spied a row of small eight-passenger vans queued up like boxcars in the parking lot. I squinted at the signs identifying each one. NA PALI COAST ZODIAC RAFT RIDE. WAIMEA CANYON TOUR. HILO HATTIE'S SHOPPING EXTRAVAGANZA. WHALE WATCHING EXCURSION. FERN GROTTO CRUISE. KAUAI HELICOPTER TOUR. WAILUA RIVER KAYAK ADVENTURE. *Bingo*.

I hustled over to the van and flashed my ticket at the woman holding the event sign. "Kayak Adventure. That would be me."

"You and everyone else," the woman said, laughing. "Forget the van. We had to call for reinforcements." She nodded at the full-sized, fifty-five-passenger coach parked behind the last van. "Ten people is a good day for us. Today we have forty. I've given up trying to figure it out."

Forty people? *Uff da*. This wasn't good. How was I supposed to keep track of forty people?

I quick-stepped over to the bus and got in line

behind a young couple in matching *Aloha Princess* T-shirts who couldn't keep their hands, or their lips, off each other. Honeymooners, no doubt. I pretended not to notice the young man kiss his wife's neck, and sighed as my thoughts flew back to Duncan. Damn. Duncan was the guy who wanted to marry me without even introducing me to his family, for crying out loud. Was I being fair to him? Was loyalty to Etienne making me cut off my nose to spite my face? Would a permanent relationship with either man ever allow me to experience anything more meaningful than chronic frustration and heartburn?

I felt a polite tap on my shoulder from behind. "Sorry to trouble you. Is this the queue for the kayak adventure?"

I turned around to find a man dressed in Burberry plaid knickers with a matching slouch cap. He looked to be somewhere in his fifties, all pressed and proper, with a pleasant face, and a black umbrella tucked under his arm. If the accent hadn't given him away as one of Duncan's Brits, the outfit would have. "You're in the right place," I said, smiling, and extended my hand in greeting. "I'm Emily."

"Basil Broomhead." He gave my hand a hearty shake before raising his umbrella high in the air and bellowing, "This way, Percy! Do be quick!" Then to me, "He's still adjusting to the time change. This is his first trip across the pond."

"You're dressed rather grandly for a day on the river," I commented, eyeing his knickers.

"Am I? The brochure recommended casual attire."

He fixed me with a look of sudden self-doubt. "Oh, dear. Are you telling me casual meant something other than no tie?"

Basil Broomhead. Why did that name sound so familiar? And why did it seem important that I remember? "You'll be okay," I assured him. "I think kayakers have a pretty flexible dress code. Pants and a paddle, probably."

He worried his naked shirt collar as his companion jogged up beside him. "There you are, Percy," he said distractedly, making room for him in line. He bobbed his head toward me. "I'd like you to meet Emily."

Percy nodded politely. "Percy Woodruffe-Peacock. Pleasure." He had a Bugs Bunny overbite, bulldog jowls, and looked charmingly comical in Bermuda shorts, knee-high stockings, and a starched cotton shirt with a red bow tie. He obviously hadn't read the brochure.

"I should have brought my trench coat," Percy complained, in a brittle accent. "Look at those clouds. Rain clouds, I tell you. We'll most likely get drenched, contract some tropical fever, and end up having to breathe through a respirator for the rest of the cruise. Mark my words, Basil. Nothing good ever comes of an enterprise begun in the rain."

Euw. This guy was a real ray of sunshine. I should introduce him to Bernice.

Moving forward, I handed my ticket to a man standing outside the bus and hurried up the stairs, stunned by the circus atmosphere bubbling inside. Chatter. Laughter. Screams of delight. Wow, I'd never known people to be so excited about the possibility of severe sunburn and excruciating muscle pain. I peered down the center aisle to see if I could spy Nana and Tilly, but between the tall seat backs and the people crowding the aisle as they jockeyed their backpacks into overhead bins, I couldn't see a thing. But this wasn't a problem. I'd learned a few things in my months on the job.

I leaned over to speak to the driver, then slid into the unoccupied seat behind him as he announced over the speaker system, "If Marion Sippel and Tilly Hovick are aboard, would you give me a holler?"

"We're here!" I heard Nana bellow above the din. "In the back!" Nana had gotten pretty good at bellowing in the years before Grampa Sippel had sprung for a hearing aid.

I thanked the driver, then settled back into my seat, breathing a sigh of relief. Now that I knew Nana and Tilly were aboard, I allowed myself a small, self-satisfied smile. Hey, I was getting this tour escort thing down to a science!

Percy and Basil straggled up the stairs, the last passengers to board. With a nod to me, they clambered into the seat behind me, *tsking* at the lack of decorum. "I hope they plan on handing out headphones to muffle the noise," Percy groused. "What are they laughing about? It's insufferable."

The ticket-taker pounded his fist against the side of the bus, and yelled to the driver, "You're all set to go. *Aloha.*"

The engine roared to life, the door hissed shut, and

the driver announced, "I can't leave until everyone is seated, so how about it, people?"

Twenty seconds later, we were on our way.

"I borrowed silverware from the breakfast buffet," I heard Basil whisper as we rattled into traffic. "A grapefruit spoon would have been perfect. They're serrated, you know. But the only grapefruit they offered was in sections, adrift in a sea of juice. So I had to settle for a cereal spoon. At least it's a bit more pointed than a soup spoon. What did you find?"

"A SwissChamp XLT pocketknife," Percy whispered back. "I was waffling between this one and the SwissFlame with the gas lighter, but I know better than to trust you with anything combustible. First time I turned my back, you'd have your trousers on fire. Or your hair. Or—"

"Will you *never* let that go?" Basil sniped. "Your gibes are *so* tedious. I'm not even sure why I put up with you. Do you have the map?"

Map? That definitely earned them my full and undivided attention.

"You shouldn't have folded it," Basil scolded. "I can't tell now if that line is a crease or a river. What's this smudge here?"

"It's not a smudge. It's an X. As in, 'X marks the spot.' And those squiggly lines are . . . Bloody hell. What are those things?"

I heard the paper rattling like a potato chip bag. "Snakes?" said Basil. "Night crawlers? Do you suppose there's a bait and tackle shop out there?"

An exasperated growl from Percy. "Where are your

reading glasses? Oh, never mind. The Champ has a magnifying glass. Here, I'll show you."

For a full minute I heard nothing, and then—"How many of those pullout gadgets does the Champ have?" Basil asked impatiently.

"Fifty," Percy snapped. "Fifty tools that have proven to be absolutely essential for survival in any hostile environment."

Yeah. My personal favorite was the cuticle remover.

"Just a minute. I know it's here somewhere."

Okay, I'd heard enough. Map with a big X? Stolen cereal spoons? Fifty-function Swiss army knife? If these two weren't after buried treasure, I'd eat my—

I paused thoughtfully. I'd eat anything right now. I'd missed breakfast, so I was starving. But as I pondered how to gracefully interject myself into their conversation, I realized that hunger did have its advantages.

With my heart banging against my rib cage, I turned around and peeked over the top of my seat like a new neighbor looking over a property fence. "Excuse me, do either of you recall reading anything about what we're supposed to do for lunch today?"

Percy crushed the treasure map against his chest and eyed me suspiciously. Basil removed his cap and gave his mop of wavy brown hair a scratch. "We're to be provided with box lunches. Some type of American luncheon meat, I believe, though I'm holding out a faint hope for either cucumber or watercress."

I glanced at the Swiss army knife in Percy's lap.

He'd exposed so many jiggers, it looked like a mini erector set. "Nice knife. I have one too, only it's a lot smaller."

Basil plucked the knife off Percy's lap and proceeded to flip up more tiny steel-plated arms. "You wouldn't happen to know where the magnifying glass is, would you?"

"Afraid not. But I have twenty-twenty vision. Would you like me to read something for you?"

"I should say not!" Percy answered for him. He stuffed the map into his shirt pocket, then snatched the knife out of Basil's hand and snapped all the gizmos back into the housing. "I can see perfectly well for the both of us."

"Say," I gushed, feigning sudden recognition, "I knew the two of you looked familiar. Was that you I saw at Professor Smoker's lecture on Captain Cook yesterday?"

"I don't see what business that is of yours," Percy said, scowling.

"You needn't be rude to the girl," Basil chided, aghast.

"I wasn't being rude."

"Yes, you were."

"No, I wasn't."

"Wanker."

"Wiseacre."

"Mugwump."

"Swellhead."

Yup. I really knew what buttons to push to make people spill their guts. Okay, so my interrogation techniques could use a little polishing. Guess I'd have to work on that.

"We're now entering the city limits of Lihue," our bus driver announced as I turned back around in my seat, leaving Percy and Basil to bicker ad nauseum. "Lihue is Kauai's county seat—the town that sugar built, as you can tell from the twin stacks of the Lihue Sugar Company in the distance there. Four thousand residents and two traffic lights. It might take us a while to get through morning traffic, so sit back and enjoy the sights, folks. It's only a short ride to Wailua from here."

I stared straight ahead at the line of cars backed up behind one of Lihue's two traffic lights, suspecting that Basil and Percy had indeed attended Professor Smoker's lecture. Is that why Smoker had looked so alarmed? Had he spotted the two Englishman sitting in the back of the lecture room? Had he sensed they spelled trouble?

Poor Professor Smoker. I doubted he had predicted how much trouble.

CHAPTER 6

A small company of outfitters awaited us as we arrived at the parking area for the Wailua River State Park. I was first off the bus, followed by Percy and Basil, who practically mowed me down in their rush toward the kayaks stacked up near the boat ramp. A scattering of solitary palm trees and a manicured lawn flanked the river on this side, while a Jurassic Park kind of wildness ran amok on the opposite shore complete with dense foliage, tangled brambles, and spiny mountain ridges. The river was as wide as the Los Angeles freeway here, but up ahead, it looked as winding and narrow as an old country road.

I watched the two Brits drag a giant red chile pepper of a kayak toward the river and worried that if they got too much of a head start, they'd disappear behind that first bend in the river and I'd lose sight of

them completely. Not a good way to tail men you suspected of committing a heinous crime.

I shot a look back at the bus, willing Nana and Tilly
to appear amid the crowd pouring out of both exit
doors. Nuts. What was the holdup? They were usually
the first people on and off every—

I did a sudden double take as I regarded an unexpected face exiting the bus. Eh! What was *he* doing
here?

Nils's huge body filled the rear doorway as he lumbered down the stairs like a conquering warlord,
ducking his head beneath the door so he wouldn't
knock himself out. He paused outside the bus, hitching up his cargo shorts and kicking dust off his hiking
boots as he took visual inventory of the area. His eyes
flickered with surprise as they locked on mine, then
slowly crinkled with amusement, as if he couldn't
believe I had the *cojones* to navigate the same river he
was about to navigate. He nodded, maybe a little
smugly, then turned his attention to Ansgar and
Gjurd, who were having a tug-of-war with an eight-
inch-by-ten-inch sheet of paper that looked as
though it might rip down the middle at any moment.
Ansgar bellowed something unintelligible. Gjurd bellowed something back. Nils shook his head and
seized the paper, then growled something at the two
that sent them sprinting toward the kayaks at a dead
run, hair flying, gravel crunching beneath their boots.
Nils put a bead on me again and strode directly
toward me, a man on a mission.

"I see we are of like minds today. There is no better day than one spent on the water."

I craned my neck to look up at his bearded face, suspicion creeping into my voice. "I thought you and the boys were signed up to visit the place where Captain Cook made landfall on Kauai?"

"As you predicted last night, the Cook excursions have been canceled. It's most unfortunate that no one could convince his assistant to take his place, yah? Did you read her credentials in the brochure? They were most impressive. With her knowledge, I see no reason why she could not have stepped into the professor's shoes. It is most disappointing. In the meantime, this seemed an acceptable second choice." He gestured toward our surroundings. "A navigable river. Rented watercraft. Tropical vegetation. A secret waterfall. The only things lacking are a keg of beer and a more detailed topographical map. This one is poorly drawn."

He flashed the sheaf of paper he was holding before my face for a nanosecond, but that was all it took for me to see the cow-flop-shaped island with the big X in the middle. *Poorly drawn map?* It was the same map that was in my shoulder bag! He had a copy of the treasure map!

"Where did you get that?" I choked out. Oh, my God. Did this mean the Vikings were in cahoots with Percy and Basil? How else would they have gotten the map? Had the World Navigators joined forces with the Sandwich Islanders to eliminate Dorian Smoker?

Why did people have to join forces? It made every-thing so complicated.

Nils regarded the photocopied sheet. "Ansgar and Gjurd purchased it aboard ship for much money." He slanted a narrow look at the Brits as they lugged their kayak down the boat ramp. "Too much money."

Eh! Had Percy and Basil soaked the Vikings for a reproduction of the map? Talk about unhealthy busi-ness practices. Not smart to price-gouge men who probably picked their teeth with the tip of some ancestor's broadsword. Oh geesch. Was it going to get ugly out at the Secret Falls today?

"Last one to the kayaks is a Republican!" a familiar voice boomed out.

"I want the yellow one! It matches my new san-dals!"

"I have antibacterial hand sanitizer if anyone wants to clean their paddles!"

I whipped my head around to find Dick Teig, Bernice Zwerg, Margi Swanson, and everyone else from my Iowa contingent charging toward the kayaks like a flock of excited geese. What the—? What were they doing there? They were all supposed to be on other excursions, soaking up information that I could include in my newsletter.

"You'll excuse me," Nils said in a sudden rush. "The kayaks are quickly disappearing. I'll see you on the river."

"Wait!" I grabbed for his arm, but he bounded toward the waiting kayaks, jetting past my group as if they were standing still. Okay, this called for a major time-out.

Letting fly one of my signature earsplitting whistles, I watched all nine of my Iowans skid to a halt. Heads swung around in my direction. Eyes riveted on me. I threw my arms into the air at them. "*What* are you doing here? You're supposed to be whale watching, visiting the Waimea Canyon, and shopping at Hilo Hattie's."

"This sounded more exciting!" called out Alice Tjarks. "So we exchanged our tickets."

I stared at them, dumbfounded. "Where were you sitting on the bus?"

"In the back," said Dick Stolee. "We got there early enough to stake out the good seats in the rear."

"The ones next to the restroom," Dick Teig explained. "There's a real sense of security knowing you can be on the road and only one step away from the john at the same time."

Nods. Smiles. More nods.

Oh, God. I searched the faces in the group, realizing I was short a couple of people. "What happened to Nana and Tilly?"

"Tilly accidentally flushed her visor down the toilet," Margi responded, "so she and Marion are trying to retrieve it. All I can say is, I hope she doesn't plan on wearing it anytime soon."

Oh, yeah. This was going well. "Look, everyone, I don't want to spoil your fun, but none of you have ever kayaked before. This is not a wise move. You could end up in back braces and cervical collars. You could aggravate existing conditions." I nodded toward Dick Teig. "What about Dick's arthritis? Osmond's rotator cuff? Lucille's anxiety?"

"My anxiety's better since my Dick passed on," Lucille Rassmuson announced. "I don't have to worry about his cigar ash incinerating the dog anymore. My therapist says I'm a whole new person because of it."

"Dog?" said Margi. "I thought you had cats."

"You have a therapist?" asked Bernice. "How much does that set you back a week? I bet Medicare doesn't cover it, does it?"

I rolled my eyes in frustration. "Listen to me! Paddling a kayak is hard work! It requires upper body strength. Stamina. Hand-to-eye coordination. I don't know if any of you should risk—"

"If *you're* gonna do it, how hard can it be?" Bernice challenged.

Heads bobbing. Murmurs of assent.

"Who cares about the kayaking," Dick Teig enthused. "We're here . . . for this!" He waved a sheet of white paper high over his head. "Right, gang?"

Eight other hands shot into the air, each one waving a sheet of white paper.

I looked from Alice, to Osmond, to Lucille. Uh-oh. Please tell me they weren't holding what I thought they were holding.

"I got extra maps on me," Bernice said, reaching into her tote bag. "You wanna buy one? They're sellin' like hotcakes. Five bucks apiece."

I stared at the stack of paper she yanked out of her tote. Treasure maps.

Oh, God. She'd sold them to the whole freaking bus!

"It's all my fault," Tilly anguished minutes later.

An armada of red and yellow kayaks was already splish-splashing upriver toward the first significant bend, but I was still hanging out by the bus, consoling Tilly. "Try not to dwell on it," I urged. "I have a visor back in the cabin that you can borrow. It won't match any of your skirts, but let's face it. The other one's a goner."

"That's kind of you, Emily. If only I could repair the damage I've done with the treasure map so easily." She hung her head woefully. "In my excitement yesterday, I walked away from the photocopier with new copies of Marion's map, handed her one for the scavenger hunt entry, and forgot to remove the original from the machine."

"And wouldn't you know," Nana continued, "the next person into the copy center is Bernice, who finds the map in the photocopier and decides she can make a financial killin' by sellin' it off as a treasure map. She's already took in over a hundred dollars." Nana gave her teeth a loud suck. "I never woulda guessed it, but Bernice has a real gift for commercial sales."

Tilly heaved a dejected sigh. "This is so unlike me. The errors in judgment. The forgetfulness. The signs are all there, ladies. Senile plaques. Neurofibrillary tangles. Subcortical dysfunction. My brain has neuropathologic disorder written all over it. If I were living among the Polar Eskimos, they'd stick me out on the ice as bear bait."

"No one's going to stick you anywhere," I said, giving her arm a reassuring pat.

"Crossword puzzles," Nana declared. "One a day is s'posed to keep your brain from turnin' to mush. Kinda like takin' a multivitamin."

"There's nothing wrong with Tilly's brain," I defended. "Stuff like this happens to everyone. It's just that Bernice's little entrepreneurial scheme has mucked things up for us." I scrubbed my face with my palms and groaned. "Professor Smoker's killer is supposed to be the only person other than the three of us who has a copy of the treasure map, right? But Nils and company have one. The Brits who were sitting behind me have one. I suspect every passenger on the bus has one. How are we supposed to single out the real killer if *everyone* has a copy of the map?"

A pause. Lip chewing. Cogitating.

"I have it!" Tilly's eyes lit with sudden inspiration. "What if we—"

A torrent of violent splashing caused us to glance toward the river. Twenty feet from shore, Dick Teig and Dick Stolee were engaged in a major water skirmish, armed only with their paddles, their wives, and their waterproof disposable cameras.

"Get a picture of this, Helen!" KER-SPLAT! Dick Teig slammed his paddle onto the water, drenching Dick and Grace Stolee in a fountain of spray. "Bullseye!" he crowed, mugging for the camera.

"Start focusing, Grace!" ordered Dick Stolee as he

paddled hard to starboard. "Ram-ming speed!" he yelled, aiming his prow at the Teigs' kayak.

"What do you s'pose they're doin'?" Nana asked curiously.

"Reenacting the War of 1812," said Tilly.

"The whole war?" Nana shook her head. "I don't think we're gonna be here that long, are we?"

WHOOSH! Back-paddling to a sudden stop, Dick Stolee dug his paddle into the river and rainbowed a tidal wave of water into the Teig's kayak. "Take that!"

"Oh, God. I can't watch." I covered my face and turned away. "Tell me what happens."

A strangulated shriek echoed up and down the river.

"That was Helen," Nana said. "Uh-oh. Looks like she's just realizing what that water done to her treasure map. Lookit that. It's all fell apart. Guess we shoulda used heavier stock."

"A minor setback." Tilly said. "Wait until she sees what the water did to her eyebrows." She sucked in her breath. "All right, Emily. It's safe to look now. They've changed direction. They're going upriver." She paused. "Crossriver." She let out a sigh. "Downriver."

"They're paddlin' in circles," Nana declared. "You s'pose they'll ever notice?"

Oh, God. Shaking my head, I turned back to Tilly. "Okay, what were you saying about how we should go about identifying our killer?"

Tilly parted her lips to reply, then suddenly froze, her eyes widening with alarm. "I do remember entertaining an excellent idea, but . . . I . . . I don't recall what it was." She thumped her walking stick on the pavement in frustration. "The two of you should probably go on without me. By the end of the day, I might not remember your names. Goodness, I might not remember my *own* name."

"Not a problem. Just lookit your name tag," Nana advised, grabbing on to Tilly's arm and dragging her toward the river. "The real problem is, if we don't get our tushes into one a them boats, we'll never *get* to the Secret Falls. You comin', Emily?"

That's what I loved about Nana. No matter the situation, she always managed to stay focused.

The last two-man kayak sat on the boat ramp, directly behind a banana yellow one whose nose was already in the water. An army of young people in *Kauai Kayak Adventures* T-shirts crowded the ramp, throwing out rapid-fire instructions as they eased the yellow kayak farther into the water for boarding. One of them separated himself from the group and jogged up to us.

"Three of you?" He wore a Florida Marlins baseball cap and reminded me of one of the cheery youngsters who directed you to the proper car, tram, or space ship at Disney World. "You're in luck." He whistled down to his companions at the water's edge. "Hold up launching that one! I've got another passenger for you!"

After directing Nana and Tilly toward the two-man kayak, he hurried me to the end of the ramp where the yellow kayak sat bobbing in the water. A life jacket and double-ended paddle were shoved at me, and as I donned the jacket, I caught my first glimpse of the person who was snugged into the stern of the craft.

My stomach slid down to my ankles. Oh, no. "Jonathan?" I noticed a fresh wad of duct tape spiraled around his little Coke bottle glasses, as if he'd recently walked through a doorway without opening the door first. He wore a full coverage canvas hat with a duckbill visor and ear flaps and neck flaps that would shield him from everything from UV rays to frostbite. The word *Microsoft* was embroidered in gold metallic thread across the bill, a blatant admission of where his loyalty lay in the computer wars. I saw some swirly lines in black Magic Marker beneath the gold stitchery, but I was too far away to read it. I did note, however, that he repeated the Magic Marker color theme in the black socks he was wearing with his brown wingtips and white walking shorts. I guess he'd need a little help before he hit the cover of *GQ*.

"Emily! Hey, I didn't know how I was going to do this with one arm in a sling, but you've saved the day. Hop in. Geez. This is so great! Maybe my luck is changing for the better."

If his luck was changing for the better, mine was definitely taking a turn for the worse. "Jonathan! What a surprise. I thought you might be holed up in your cabin . . . trying to contain your curse." Or scrubbing Strasbourg pâté out of his trousers.

A buoyant smile brightened his face. "You won't believe it! Everything's changed since last night. I had a long talk with the captain, and he really set me straight."

"He—uh—he convinced you that you had nothing to do with the incident yesterday?"

"Better than that. He told me to get a life. And he strongly recommended island excursions as a first step. Beth used to tell me to get a life all the time, but it had more impact coming from someone in uniform. So here I am."

The captain probably wanted him off the ship to save it from sinking! Speaking of which—I eyed the kayak with sudden trepidation. "Um . . ." I held a finger up to the kid in the Marlins cap. "You know, I have a tendency to get miserably seasick and I just remembered that I left my Dramamine back on the ship, so maybe I should—"

"The Wailua's the tamest river in the world," said the kid, as he and another guy muscled me down into the molded plastic seat in the bow. "Even the tour boats that cruise up to the Fern Grotto don't make much of a wake. No one's ever gotten seasick on the Wailua." A skinny guy with a peach fuzz beard and aviator sunglasses handed me a small white box that I suspected was lunch.

"Anything good?" I asked.

He laughed out loud at my question, which I didn't think boded well for those guests who were anticipating cucumber and watercress.

"A few things before you head out," said another guy with a long ponytail and freckles. "Around this first bend here there's a fork in the river. Every time you see a fork, bear left. When you come to an island, paddle past the fallen tree and haul your kayak onto shore. Here's a map of the trail to the Secret Falls." He handed me a blue index card. "It's not real detailed, but all you have to remember is to follow the path along the river until you come to a wide stream, then follow the stream inland. Don't follow any of the smaller streams unless you're an expert hiker. Those paths are pretty treacherous. The Secret Falls is probably a half mile from where you turn inland. Any questions, ma'am?"

"Yeah, about those smaller strea—" I blinked in horror. Ma'am? He called me, *ma'am?* I stared at him, my question caught in my windpipe like a half-chewed Twinkie. To be a ma'am you had to have white hair, no waist, and a ruff of loose skin hanging from your throat and arms. *Nana* was a ma'am. I couldn't be a ma'am; I was too young to be a ma'am!

"Forget what you were saying, ma'am?"

EH! He said it again!

"Okay, you two." He slapped our heavy-duty plastic hull. "We're cutting you loose." The whole crew gave us a shove that sent us skating away from the boat ramp into deeper water. I stared at my shoulder bag, wondering if I'd brought along anything sharp enough to cut through my wrists. Teenagers calling me ma'am? Why didn't I just end it all now before I had to join the rush for support hose and orthotic inserts? I didn't want to age gracefully. I didn't want to age at all!

"I hope you won't think I'm being a know-it-all,"

Jonathan apologized from behind me, "but that paddle isn't going to work unless you stick it in the water."

When I saw that we were floating in the direct path of the Teigs' kayak and about to be rammed, I muckled onto my paddle and dug it into the water. Right. Left. Right. Left. Aging was one thing; getting a close-up of Helen without her eyebrows was a whole other kettle of fish.

With a stiff wind at our backs, I powered us through the water like the Energizer Bunny on a battery high. I hadn't kayaked for years, but the rhythm and motion were coming back to me. I guess kayaking was something you never forgot how to do, like riding a bicycle. Or sex. Although I hadn't had sex in so long, I'd probably need a diagram to remind me which body parts went where.

Left. Right. Left. Right.

"You paddle like a real pro," Jonathan called out. "I bet you've done this before."

"In college. The university was built on a lake."

"My vo-tech school was built right next to the city dump. Talk about great location. Anytime we needed a spare computer part, all we had to do was walk across the street and scavenge for it."

We were at the back of the pack, a hundred feet away from the next kayak, staying close to the snarl of water-hugging shrubs that lined the riverbank. I liked being close to shore. It seemed a lot less risky than the middle of the river, where the water was a lot deeper. My only major concern now was making sure I didn't run out of sunblock.

"There's supposed to be an authentic re-created folk village around one of these bends," Jonathan chirped behind me. "It's only a bunch of huts, but an overhead shot of them appeared in one of the opening scenes of my favorite movie of all times. *Outbreak*. Did you see that one?"

"I saw the trailer. You like medical thrillers?"Left. Right. Left. Right.

"Not particularly. But I love it when Hollywood portrays someone as beautiful as Renee Russo falling for a loser like Dustin Hoffman. It's like watching my life unfold on the big screen. We're also supposed to pass the field where Harrison Ford was chased by those hostile natives in the first Indiana Jones flick."

Hey! Just like Captain Cook!

"And the seaplane he jumps into was sitting on this very river. Doesn't that give you goose bumps?"

I couldn't help smiling. "You sound like a big movie buff, Jonathan."

"I'm sorry. Am I talking too much?"

"No, I think it's intriguing."

"Really? Beth always told me I was really boring when I started talking movies. She was the interesting one. Boy, you should have heard her discuss her method for peeling tomatoes. It was absolutely riveting."

The more I heard about Beth, the more I began to think Jonathan had gotten the better end of the deal when she'd left.

"Did you see that old John Wayne film, *Donovan's Reef?*" he continued. "The weird water-skiing scene that's supposed to take place on the open ocean was actually filmed on the Wailua. Probably back near the boat ra—"

I nearly leaped out of the kayak at the sound of a horn blasting behind us. I swung around to find a flat-bottomed barge with a pitched canopy chugging down the middle of the river in our direction, looking like a supersized roadside vegetable stand without the vegetables. FERN GROTTO TOURS was splashed in big red letters across the side, and when the horn stopped blaring, I could hear Hawaiian music echoing out over their speaker system. Tourists hung over the sides, toasting us with icy beverages and waving giddily at the scenery. The floor space was crowded with beer-bellied men in T-shirts and shorts swirling their hips and jerking their arms as if they'd all been zapped with the mother of all stun guns. One guy got so out of control, he swatted himself in the face with his hand and went down like a bull elephant. I shook my head. This was what happened when you tried to teach the hula to a bunch of white guys whose main source of exercise was pressing buttons on the remote control.

I waved as they passed, thinking how cool and refreshed they looked under the protective covering of the roof. The sun was sweltering.

"Do you remember that old Elvis Presley movie, *Blue Hawaii?*" Jonathan continued as I quartered the kayak into the barge's wake and met the foot-high waves head on. WHAP. WHAP. WHAP.

"It's the one set in a Polynesian resort surrounded by a grove of palm trees."

The waves sloshed against our hull and pitched us back and forth before rolling toward the shoreline and making a *whooshing* sound against the bank. Piece of cake—we didn't even get swamped. The kid in the Marlins cap had been right; this was one tame river.

"Do you realize we passed the resort where that movie was filmed when we turned off the highway? The Coco Palms. It's been closed since '92 because of hurricane damage, but Tattoo from that old TV show, *Fantasy Island,* used to drive his jeep through that very grove after he yelled, 'De plane, de plane!' "

"Hello, dear!" called Nana as she and Tilly glided effortlessly past us in their blue kayak. "I think the two Dicks are headin' out to sea, so if they don't show up at the Secret Falls, you'll know where to look for 'em. Too bad your cell phone's on the fritz. You coulda put the Coast Guard on speed dial."

My shoulders slumped involuntarily. Oh, God. They couldn't possibly get lost at sea, could they?"

"How's that for a coincidence," Jonathan piped up. "Did you know *Gilligan's Island* was partially filmed on the island of Kauai?"

I gave Nana a weary thumbs-up. "Thanks for the warning."

"You bet." With barely a splash they propelled themselves forward, heads high, backs straight, paddling left and right in perfect unison. My mouth fell open as they sliced through the water at a pace that defied every speed record known to man for nonmotorized watercraft. Wow. They were really fast.

"Where'd you learn to kayak?" I yelled after them. "The Senior Center?" The town had recently added an Olympic-size swimming pool to the complex, thanks to a generous donation from Nana. Windsor City now had the distinction of being home to the second largest body of water in Iowa, so anything was possible.

"The Limpopo River in Africa," Tilly shouted back. "A matter of necessity. The crocodiles were hungry. If I wasn't fast, I was lunch!"

"Did you ever see *The African Queen?*" Jonathan chimed in, as Nana and Tilly became a speck on the horizon. "That particular movie wasn't filmed in Kauai, but *Throw Momma From the Train* was. And *Body Heat.* And *Honeymoon in—*"

"So what's been your favorite part of the cruise so far?" I cut him off. I'd obviously judged Beth a little too harshly.

"That's easy: the scavenger hunt. I collected more good junk than you can ever imagine. A dozen erasers. A bunch of paper clips. And I met scads of people who were really curious about my arm. I've got all their names here in my backpack."

I heard the distinctive *zzzzt* of a zipper being opened and some grunts that reminded me of the sounds I make when my cars keys get lost in my shoulder bag. "Here we go. Buford Whitelaw, indoor environmental consultant. Melissa Beard, certified transpersonal hypnotherapist. Raymond Robinson, Alpha vending services."

I peered over my shoulder at him. "What did you do? Make a list?"

"They gave me their business cards. We only needed one for the scavenger hunt, but people were really willing to give them away, so I collected a whole stack. Cyrus Pittz, All faiths cremation service."

Uff da. Was he planning to go through the whole stack? Left. Right. Left. Right.

"Vanessa Lyon, Globalcom Technologies. Percy Woodruffe-Peacock, Sandwich Island Society. Dennis—"

"WHAT?" I turned around so fast, I heard my spine crack. "You have Percy Woodruffe-Peacock's business card? Can I see it?"

"You know him?" Jonathan asked as he handed me the card.

"I've met him." I stowed my paddle and allowed us to drift as I skimmed the card. "Name, address, and society affiliation. Not much help. You don't happen to know what the mission statement of the Sandwich Island Society is, do you?"

Jonathan shrugged. "Sounds like it has something to do with owning Subway Sandwich franchises. That'd be my guess."

Why hadn't I just asked them on the bus? That would have been the smart thing to do. Nuts. "Thanks anyway," I said, handing the card back. Taking up my paddle once more, I stroked quickly to angle away from the overhanging branches onshore, then heaved a sigh when Jonathan started chattering again.

"Hey, Emily, did you see the writing on the back of the card here? Some words scribbled in ink. You want me to read them to you?"

"Be my guest." Left. Right. Left. Right.

"At the top it says, Hit Parade, and under that are two names. Dorian Smoker and Bailey Howard." He paused. "Smoker. Isn't that the name of the guy you were talking about at dinner last night? The one who got pushed overboard?"

I stilled my paddle midmotion, my heart suddenly racing. "Yeah. It's the same name." Dorian Smoker's name appears on a "hit parade," then he conveniently ends up dead? Hit parade. Was that a deceptively innocent way of saying, "Hit List?"

I suspected I'd just learned the mission statement of the Sandwich Island Society.

"So a bunch of actors from the *Jurassic Park* movie were forced to ride out the hurricane in the ballroom of the Westin Kauai Lagoons in Poipu," Jonathan babbled, his wingtips clomping close behind me, rustling the leaves that littered the ground. "That was back in '92. I thought the first movie was much better than the sequels. Didn't you?"

I managed to tune him out as I blazed a trail in the direction of the Secret Falls, kicking leaves and twigs out of my way as I went. Our index card map was comically inadequate in the landmark department, but I wasn't worried. Finding a waterfall in the woods should be child's play for someone who'd found Victoria's Secret in the Mall of America without having to consult the directory.

I rolled to a stop, listening for sounds that might indicate a distant waterfall, but all I heard was chirping birds, creepy insect sounds, and the burble of water rushing over pebbles in the stream to our right. "Do you have any idea how far we've walked so— OOFF!"

I skidded face-first into the leaves and underlying mud, air whooshing painfully from my lungs as Jonathan fell like a ton of bricks on top of me.

"I'm sorry!" he yelped, elbowing my head and stepping on my shoulder bag as he scrambled to his feet. "I didn't know you were going to stop. Are you all right? Did you break anything?"

I opened one eye to find him crouched in front of my face, nose to nose with me, his head close enough for me to see that the mysterious black scrawl on his duckbill was in actuality the signature of someone by the name of—I squinted and tried to focus. Bowel Gas? Man, penmanship in the electronic age had really gone to hell in a handbasket.

I spat a mouthful of local flora and fauna at him. "I'm fine, just . . . give me some room." I boosted myself to my knees and swiped a gob of mud from my chin. "I suppose I should look at the bright side. A mud treatment like this would cost me big bucks aboard ship." I pondered the gunk on my hand. "You suppose it's the right kind of mud?"

"I'm sorry, Emily," he apologized again, helping me to my feet. "It was an accident. I didn't mean to—"

I held up my hand for silence. "I'll warn you next time I decide to stop. Okay? Now, can we just keep walking?"

I set a pace traipsing through the leaves and mud at double time, keeping my eyes peeled for hidden tree roots and my ears pricked for the roar of a waterfall.

"You're a nice person, Emily," Jonathan's voice echoed out behind me. "If I'd fallen on Beth like that, there would have been hell to pay. Did I tell you I thought I saw her last night? Outside the infirmary. Wouldn't that have been an awful coincidence? Beth showing up on the cruise with her new boyfriend? I'm sure glad I was wrong, but no kidding, her tattoo was exactly like Beth's."

A cluster of ferns tickled my mud-caked shins as I ducked beneath the branch of an unfamiliar broadleafed tree. "A lot of women are into permanent disfigurement these days," I conceded, "as long as it's done tastefully."

"Beth called it durable body art. She said using one's anatomy as a living canvas was very cutting edge."

I could remember when having two holes pierced into the same ear was considered cutting edge. Oh, God. I *was* a ma'am. I *was* getting old.

"Did you know that the shoulder has replaced the chest as the venue of choice for body art these days? Unless you want something more panoramic, like the Pacific fleet. That's where Beth's tattoo was. On her shoulder. A pink rosebud with a trail of leaves twining after it. It was awesome."

I slapped an insect dead on my arm and kept walking. "What were you doing in the infirmary last night? Were you sick?"

"Captain's orders. He recommended I ask the doctor for something to calm me down. But the person who really needed the tranquilizer was the blonde who looked like Beth. Man, she was chewing out that girl in the yellow vest something fierce. What a temper."

I arched my brows at that. Bailey had been wearing a yellow vest yesterday. And she'd left the infirmary last night before the second seating. "Do you remember anything else about the woman in the yellow vest? Age? Hair color?"

"She was probably your age. Midtwenties or something."

Aw, bless his myopic little eyes.

"And her hair was all pulled back into a long curly ponytail. You couldn't miss her hair. It looked like she'd backed into a cat. That's about all I can remem—No, wait. She was wearing really stylish glasses. The kind I might be able to afford after I find a new job."

Bailey. It had to be. But why would anyone be picking on her? Especially after what she'd been through yesterday. Then again, if she was number two on someone's hit list, being yelled at was the least of her problems. Which reminded me.

"Hey, Jonathan, would you do me a favor and save Percy Woodruffe-Peacock's business card? The captain might want to take a look at the writing on the back. It could be important. Okay?"

"I won't let it out of my sight," he said, sounding thrilled to be asked.

As we forged ahead through a little mushroom field, I became aware of a noise in the background that I hadn't heard before. A far-off sound that was neither bug nor bird. A deep, continuous rumble that echoed through the forest and sent shock waves up my legs.

"Do you hear that?" asked Jonathan, impressing me that he could hear anything through those ear flaps of his.

I nodded. "Sounds like a freight train, which means it's either a tornado . . . or our waterfall!"

We bounded over rocks and gullies and hurtled decaying tree trunks. When the rumbling grew so loud that it vibrated the bones in my chest, I spied an unexpected plateau through an opening in the trees, and a river of angry white water cascading downward into a circular pool that was rimmed by spurs of fractured rock.

I stepped into the opening and stared in awe, my mouth hanging open. The Secret Falls. Wow. I hadn't expected them to be so tall. So noisy. So . . . so . . .

"I say!" I heard Basil Broomhead shout over the roar of the falls. "I do believe we've found it!"

CHAPTER 7

A chorus of groans and curses thundered in disappointment. To the left of the pool, where a sweep of sparsely forested terrain sloped upward to an impossible height, heads popped up from behind rocks, trees, ferns, and stumps, like ducks in a shooting gallery. Basil knelt before a freshly dug hole, thigh to thigh with Percy, brandishing a clod of mud in the air. "See here! I've found it!" Percy thwacked his arm and looked to be admonishing him to shut up. Basil screwed his face into a petulant pout and thwacked him back.

"So what have you found?" Nils yelled at him.

"Hey, I was digging in that spot first!" shouted the honeymooner who'd been all over his bride. "Whatever that thing is, it's half mine!"

"Nice try, bud," a middle-aged woman in a straw hat balked. "Finders keepers."

Oh, no! Poor Tilly. It was so unfair that someone else had found her treasure. Talk about rotten luck. I regarded the mob of treasure hunters who'd abandoned their minor excavations to gather around Basil.

On the other hand, if Professor Smoker's killer had set his sights on acquiring whatever Griffin Ring had buried here over two hundred years ago, Tilly's not finding the treasure knocked her out of contention as a future target for foul play. That certainly made *my* life a lot less stressful.

I observed the mob dynamic playing out around Basil and smiled. Gee, how nice that he'd found the treasure. And so quickly.

I caught movement in the tail of my eye and shifted my gaze to find Nana picking her way toward me over the rocks. "I guess you heard," I said in greeting. "Someone found the treasure. Is Tilly devastated?"

"*Pffft.*" Nana waved her hand dismissively at the crowd. "It won't be nothin'."

Crows of laughter suddenly erupted from the crowd, along with hoots and snickering. As quickly as the crowd had gathered, it dispersed, leaving Basil and Percy to ponder a silvery object resting in Basil's palm.

"Can you see what that thing is?" I asked Nana. She'd undergone cataract surgery a few years back, so her eyesight was even better than mine.

"Bud Lite. Some other fellas already dug up two other cans. I'm thinkin', six-pack."

Not knowing whether this was reason to be encouraged or *dis*couraged, I looked out over the landscape, searching for familiar faces. "How come I'm not seeing any of our group out there in the fray?"

"Alice, Osmond, Margi, Bernice, and Lucille are on them rocks over there, gawkin' at the waterfall. They never seen one before. Bernice and Lucille seen them famous Rhine Falls when we was in Switzerland; they just can't remember doin' it. Don't know where the Dicks and their wives are—probably halfway to Tahiti by now. And you might wanna separate Bernice and Margi on the trip back upriver 'cause a Margi's eye."

"What's wrong with Margi's eye?"

"Nothin', other than it's big as a boiled cabbage because Bernice steered 'em into them branches what hang over the riverbank."

I winced. "Is she in much pain?" I started to go for my Excedrin.

"Nah. She's got a cold pack on it now, so that's holdin' the swellin' down."

I stilled my hand. "Wow. She's prepared for any emergency, isn't she? She actually brought a cold pack with her?"

"What she brung with her was one a them jumbo condoms a hers, so she just filled it with water and tied it off. Works real good. Only thing is, folks are startin' to stare 'cause they're wonderin' what she's doin' with a breast implant stuck on her face."

Jonathan came bulldozing through the leaves on his pale, spindly legs to stand cautiously beside me.

"Wow," he said, gaping at the waterfall. He clomped around in the other direction. "Wow," he said, gaping at the slew of divots gouged into the ground. "Funny no one mentioned land mines to us."

I remembered my manners and introduced him to Nana, who scrutinized his hat with wistful eyes. "My Sam used to have a cap with earflaps like them. Only his was beaver. A real nice one, too. Used to wear it ice fishin'. L. L. Bean. Had a lifetime guarantee against pillin', mattin', and mites." She sucked the corner of her lip into her mouth. "Can't recall what I done with it after he passed on."

Jonathan whipped off his hat to show Nana the duckbill. "See this? Mine's signed by Bill Gates. It's a little hard to decipher his handwriting, but it really says Bill Gates. This hat is my most prized possession."

"My Sam was partial to that hat a his, too." A grin suddenly lit Nana's face. "Shoot. I remember now. I buried him in it."

Oh, God. "Where did you say Tilly was digging?"

"She's not. She's so upset about the mess everyone's makin', she's just rockin' back and forth, mutterin' Swahili under her breath."

I eyed her skeptically. "You know Swahili?"

"Learnin' Channel special." She gave the bottom of my tank top a tug. "Emily, them two hotties what we saw in the lecture room yesterday are diggin' holes hell-bent for election. The blonde is drawin' some kind a chart, and the brunette is takin' measurements. Like they done stuff like this before." She bobbed her head toward a humpbacked rock in the foreground. "There they are. Eleven o'clock."

I've often wondered what the state of accurate direction-giving would be if the first clocks had been digital instead of analog. I followed her gaze. The two women were less conspicuous today than they'd been yesterday, dressed in cropped T-shirts and mid-thigh shorts, elbows pumping as they hollowed out a section of black earth. They appeared calm, focused, and methodical. Scientific, almost.

"They certainly are tidy," I observed. "Look how they're storing all the soil in that one isolated spot. Everyone else is so haphazard." I studied their movements with an eagle eye. "They sure act like pros. They even look like they've gotten their hands on some special kind of digging implements. What do you think those things are?"

"Teaspoons," said Nana. "They'd be better off with cereal spoons, but there was a run on 'em at breakfast this mornin'." She pulled an enormous spoon from the pocket of her jacket and regarded it proudly. "I got the last one."

I shook my head. "So tomorrow's breakfast crowd shovels down their Cocoa Puffs with what? Forks?"

"But, Emily, don't you think it's suspicious that them two are here lookin' for"—she sidled a look at Jonathan—"you know what? They got a map and everythin'."

I sighed. "I'd be all over them if they were the only ones digging. But look at this place! Everyone's digging. Everyone has a map!"

"That's the thing, dear." She lowered her voice to a whisper. "Bernice didn't sell them two girls a map. She didn't have to. They already had one."

My eyelids flapped up into my head like jet-powered window shades. "Excuse me?"

Jonathan made a choking sound beside me. "That's her." Spinning around so that his back was facing the digging activity, he angled his head toward me and said in a stage whisper, "The blonde with Beth's tattoo. She's here!" He stabbed a finger toward the humpbacked rock.

I looked from the blonde, to Jonathan, to the blonde again. *That's* the blonde he was talking about? She really got around. Staring daggers at Professor Smoker yesterday afternoon *and* cussing out Bailey last night. And . . . she had a map. The synapses in my brain started firing off like the cannon section in the *1812 Overture*. Okay, now I was suspicious. I was *really* suspicious.

"I'm so nervous, my knees are shaking," Jonathan confessed as he straightened his hat. "Did she catch me looking at her? Is she staring at me?"

He was wearing earflaps. *Everyone* was staring at him.

"IS THERE SOMEBODY HERE NAMED EMILY ANDREW?" a male voice belted out.

I looked out across the grounds to find a middle-aged guy in a lime green muscle shirt and flowered shorts waving a baseball cap in the air. I waved back. "I'm Emily!" But who in the world was he?

He trotted the short distance toward me, the flab

beneath his muscle shirt bouncing up and down like the contents of a half-filled water balloon. He gave me a flinty look as he slapped a cell phone into my hand. "It's for you. And I don't give a damn if it *is* an emergency. I have to pay the roaming charges, so you better make it short."

"An emergency?" I stared at the phone in dread. Oh, God. Had something happened to Mom or Dad? My brother Steve or his wife? The boys? Heart hammering in my chest, I raised the phone to my ear. "H-hello?"

"*Ciao, bella.*"

"Etienne? Oh, my God. Are you all right? What's happened? Where are you? What's wrong?"

"You're angry with me," he said rather tightly in his beautiful French/German/Italian accent. "That should explain exactly what's wrong."

I opened my mouth to reply, my thought process derailed by the three curious sets of eyes riveted directly on me.

"You needn't deny it," Etienne continued. "You left without calling. You didn't send a good-bye email. I feel fortunate that you bothered to send me your itinerary."

I smiled stiffly at my expectant audience. "Hold on, would you?" I said to Etienne. Then to the trio, "It doesn't sound good. You suppose I could have a little privacy?"

Mr. Muscle Shirt executed a serious eye roll before jabbing a finger in the direction of where he was digging. "I'll be over there when you're done."

Nana took Jonathan by the arm. "You go ahead, dear. Don't fret none about us. We'll just mosey around some."

I settled on a nearby rock, my initial dread transforming into butterflies. "I'm back," I said into the phone. "But you have me really freaked out. How did you know that guy was on the kayak adventure with me? How did you know he had a cell phone? How did you get the number?"

"I'm a police inspector, Emily. I do things like that regularly."

"Yeah, well—"

"Do you want to tell me why you're angry with me?"

I pinched my lips and stared dismally into space. "I was hoping we might have this conversation in person."

"This is the best I can do for the moment. I'm working a big case that's just come in, so—"

"You're *always* working a big case." I heaved a despairing sigh. "You're always . . . busy."

Silence.

I watched Nana pop the cap off a Magic Marker and scribble something on Jonathan's cast. Aw, that was so sweet.

I heard throat clearing on the other end of the phone. "Long-distance relationships are the hardest relationships to maintain," Etienne said with well-practiced Swiss logic.

Okay, that was encouraging. At least he was thinking about the "r" word. "You've finally come to that conclusion, have you?"

"One of my coworkers just bought a satellite dish. He saw it on an American television show. Have you ever heard of Dr. Phil?"

Men! *How* could they all be so clueless? What caused it? Testosterone? Beer? Drinking directly out of refrigerator milk cartons?

"Am I ever going to see you again?" I pressed, my heart breaking. "Because I feel as if you've put me on a shelf where all I'm doing is gathering dust."

"Emily, darling, I—"

"No, don't 'darling' me! Just let me finish. I don't need a lot of glitz and glitter. I just want what my mom and dad have. What Nana and Grampa Sippel had. A simple life with each other. A shared future. Laughter. It's not flashy; it's not always perfect. But it's quiet, and steady, and in its own way, it's magical." The line crackled with static. "Hello? Are you still there?"

"I want those things, too," he said in a voice that could have melted wax. "I love you, Emily."

"I love you, too, but—"

"Don't give up on me, *bella*. Please."

I watched Nana drag Jonathan toward the rock where the cheerleaders were digging, and thrust her Magic Marker at them.

"You mean everything to me, Emily. I want what you want, but mostly what I want is . . . you. Beside me. Naked, except for a ring on your finger."

Ring? Ring was good. Ring was very good! I watched the brunette inscribe Jonathan's cast and hand off the Magic Marker to the blonde.

"Emily, will you believe me when I tell you this situation between us is going to change soon? Not months. Not weeks. But very soon?"

"What about the big case you're working on?"

"Perhaps big cases don't have a part in my life anymore. I haven't had the pleasure of meeting your parents yet, darling, but I want what they have, too. Especially if it includes you."

"What about your family reunion? Does the 'naked' and the 'ring' part come before or after your *Nonna* Annunziata's approval?"

He laughed. "You need no one's approval, *bella*, but perhaps you'd set the date aside anyway. Sicily is beautiful at that time of year, and I know an out-of-the-way cove that no one visits, except for an occasional gull. We'd have the whole beach to ourselves, and we wouldn't even have to heat up the massage oil." His voice dipped to a husky whisper. "The sun could do it for us."

Oh, God. If I said no, would I be ruining the best chance I'd ever have for true love? What if he really was willing to change? Did I love him enough to give him one more chance? Was happiness waiting just beyond this hurdle, or was my life heading toward the "Why Did This Relationship Fail?" section of some woman's magazine?

"Emily?" he prompted.

I watched the blonde slap the Magic Marker back into Nana's hand and return to her digging, never raising her head as Nana tried to strike up a conversation. After a few moments of being ignored, Jonathan clutched Nana's arm and assisted her around the pit. It was kind of sweet the way he held her forearm, guiding her to safer ground. *The same way Grampa Sippel used to do when he'd take her ice fishing with him.* I sat mutely for a heartbeat, wondering what she'd give to have Grampa back again.

"Emily? Did we get cut off?"

"No . . . I'm here." As I watched them amble toward the waterfall, I realized that my decision had been made for me. "All right. I'll wait for you, Etienne, but—"

"Say no more. I love you, *bella!* You won't be sorry. Thank the gentleman for the use of his phone. *Sei piu bella d'un angelo. Voglio essere con te per eternita.*" And then he disconnected.

"Etienne? Etienne! What does that mean?" Damn. I got goose bumps when he spoke Italian to me, but I hated not knowing what he was saying. If I could remember any of the words, I could ask Duncan to translate; he was fluent in five languages. But how tacky would it be to ask the competition to translate the sweet nothings of the front runner?

Nuts. What was I going to do about Duncan?

I boosted myself to my feet, a little unsettled about what might be in store for me, but feeling good about having gotten a few things off my chest. The muscle shirt guy was in the back forty, heaving chunks of moss over his head, so I headed off in that direction with his phone, making a detour along the way.

"Have you reached China yet?" I asked the cheerleaders as I hovered beside their ever-deepening hole.

The blonde paused, sank back onto her haunches, and gazed up.

"What?"

"China. Didn't you ever see that Bugs Bunny cartoon where he dug a hole and ended up in China?"

She looked me up and down, her eyes pebble hard in her ultratanned face. "Is that what you do in your spare time?" she asked condescendingly. "Watch cartoons?"

I flashed her a benevolent smile. I wasn't the one who was going to look like a thousand-year-old raisin by the time I reached forty, so I could afford to be pleasant.

"My brother watches cartoons," the brunette volunteered, still digging. "He's actually done an analysis that draws a striking parallel between Elmer Fudd's relentless pursuit of Bugs and the path our current administration is taking in its foreign policy."

Where else but in America could you watch Looney Tunes for a semester and earn credit toward a college degree? "Where's your brother studying?" I inquired.

"Miss Clukey's Nursery School. He's five."

My youngest nephew had attended nursery school. We'd been pretty impressed when he learned to count to ten. "I'm Emily, by the way," I said in introduction. "And you are?"

"Shelly Valentine," said the brunette, bobbing her head.

"Busy," said the blonde, returning to her excavating duties.

"Dammit, Jen," Shelly complained. "Will you watch what you're doing? You're contaminating my quadrant."

Dissension in the ranks. Oh, goody, I loved it when that happened. I looked blithely from one to the other, ever the cordial observer. "If I'm not mistaken didn't I see the two of you at Professor Smoker's lecture yesterday?"

"So?" Jen grumbled, never looking up.

"So, you must be really broken up about what happened to him after the lecture."

"We're crushed," she said sarcastically.

"It was a horrible blow." Shelly brushed a strand of hair off her face with her wrist, leaving a smudge on her cheek. "I don't understand how anyone could hurt Dori. He was so lovable."

"Dori?" I asked.

Shelly looked faintly embarrassed. "That was our pet name for him. Everyone in his inner circle called him Dori."

"So how did one go about getting admitted to Professor Smoker's inner circle?"

"By sleeping with him," Jen said matter-of-factly. She looked up, spearing me with her eyes. "Do you have a problem with that?"

Yup. Tilly had sure hit the nail on the head with that one. "Hey, it's your life."

Jen let out a derisive snort. "Your generation is so sexually repressed. In case you hadn't noticed, we've moved out of the Dark Ages. University professors don't live in ivory towers anymore. The really hot ones sleep around, and in case you weren't aware, no one was hotter than Dori."

"Did he sleep around a lot?" I ventured.

" 'A lot' is an empty term," Jen lectured smugly. "It's a measurement of exactly nothing. It's unspecific. It's not quantifiable. It's—"

"Did he sleep with all his female students?" Maybe that was specific enough for her.

"Not at the same time!" Shelly piped up. "He was hot, he wasn't kinky."

"I have a question of my own," Jen fired back at me. "Who the hell are you?"

I gave her a palms up. "Just someone who's out looking for buried treasure, like you. I saw that map and I couldn't resist. How many times in your life do you run into an honest-to-goodness treasure map?"

"Not often," Shelly said affably. "We don't even know what we're looking for, but I guess we'll know it when we see it."

"That's what I figure, too," I agreed. "Where'd you get your map?"

"From—Ow!" Shelly dropped her spoon and cradled her hand against her chest. "Watch what you're doing, will you?" She glowered at Jen. "That hurt! Look, you broke the skin."

Jen expelled an exasperated sigh. "So hit the infirmary when you get back and ask for some Neosporin."

"She can even show you where it is," I informed Shelly, then redirected my attention to Jen. "Talk around the watercooler is that you went ballistic on

Bailey when she was leaving the infirmary last night."

Her eyes lengthened to unfriendly slits. "Who told you that?"

I shrugged. "It's a confined space. Word gets around."

"Listen, Sherlock, whatever I said to Bailey is my business, so why don't you go dig a hole someplace and do us all a favor by jumping into it."

To borrow a phrase from Nana, "I don't think we're going to be here that long." I smiled and gave her an impish wink, but as I turned away, I was struck with an impulsive thought that caused me to turn back. "Was Professor Smoker sleeping with Bailey, too?"

Jen studied me evenly. "Bailey never made the cut. Dori had this . . . rule. The women he slept with?" Her lips curved into an icy smile. "They had to be viviparous."

"Warm-blooded," Tilly explained a few minutes later, her voice uncharacteristically dull. "Or more technically, bringing forth living young instead of eggs. Nearly all mammals are viviparous."

So Jen was implying that Bailey wasn't warm-blooded? Euw. That wasn't very nice.

We were sitting on a craggy rock near the flowage from the falls, Tilly in a near depression as she observed the chaotic methodology of the treasure hunters. "I hope they realize they can't leave those holes exposed like that. They have to fill them in. This is a state park.

All park entrants are required to leave things exactly the way they found them."

"Are you going to do any digging yourself? That's why you're here. That's why Nana's packing stolen flatware. Come on, Tilly. It's your treasure."

"There'll be nothing left to dig when these scavengers finish their assault. Look at them. How could any treasure survive this kind of destruction?"

I could think of only one way to console her. "Have you eaten lunch yet?" Carbohydrates worked wonders for depression.

She waved off my offer. "I've lost my appetite." Her eyes flitted toward the flattened white box I dug out of my shoulder bag. "They must have provided us with more than one lunch option. My box doesn't look like that."

I raised the crushed container to eye level. "That's because Jonathan didn't step on yours."

Halfway through my mashed peanut butter and jelly sandwich, I glanced at the three Norwegians to find Ansgar and Gjurd high-fiving Nils, then hunkering back down to observe something in their hole. Uh-oh. Looked as if they might actually have found something.

Their wide backs formed a protective shield as Nils fussed with his backpack. He removed a towel and handed it to Ansgar, who glanced cautiously over his shoulder, obviously on the lookout for prying eyes.

"I say!" I heard Basil call out. "I've found it! I've really found it this time."

Percy smacked him on the head as groans and hisses filled the air. I watched people fling clumps of earth toward them, followed by moss, leaves, and what looked like a rusty engine part. "We don't believe you!" a woman yelled.

"You ever heard of the boy who cried wolf?" the guy in the muscle shirt yelled.

Basil and Percy tented their arms over their heads and knelt protectively over their pothole while the Norwegians shrugged into their backpacks, tamped all the soil back into their hole, and headed out. Considering that their ancient ancestors hadn't gotten beyond the pillage and burn stage, these guys were proving to be real neatniks. The evolutionary process at work.

"Another false alarm," Nana complained as she ambled our way with Jonathan in tow. She stopped in front of us and handed me her Magic Marker. "You wanna sign Jonathan's cast? He's still got some space open."

"Have a speedy recovery," I wrote, signing my name. I checked out what other people had written. "This cast is full of germs. Avoid contact with your eyes and mouth after touching it. Margi."

"I broke my arm once, too, and I bet it was a lot worse then yours. Bernice."

"There's something about you that reminds me of my Sam," penned Nana.

"Get lost!" read another message in huge block letters. The sentiment had no name attached, but instinct told me the author was probably dear old Jen.

"EEEKKKKK!!!" A scream rang through the trees. "IT'S BIGFOOT!"

Pandemonium broke out as a hideously fat beast swathed in leaves bounded down the hill.

"EEHHHH!" shrieked the newlywed in the *Aloha Princess* T-shirt as she pelted through the trees away from it.

"Somebody shoot it!" her husband yelled as he pelted after her.

Nana whipped out her camera and squeezed off a quick shot, pondering afterward, "You don't s'pose he meant with a gun, do you?"

"Holy crap!" cried Jonathan. "That thing could be a carnivore!" At which point he took off down the trail like a streak of chain lightning.

"Bigfoot is a phenomenon indigenous to the Pacific Northwest," Tilly expounded as the beast thrashed through a stand of saplings. "I'm rather perplexed why it's making an appearance in the South Pacific."

"Maybe it's lost," said Nana.

Tilly pointed to it with her walking stick. "Naturally, the legend of Bigfoot has expanded over the decades. In Canada it's known as Sasquatch. The Lakota Indians call it Chiye-tanka. The Sioux refer to it as Big Man."

The ground shook as our fellow kayakers charged past us like stampeding wildebeest. Basil. Percy. The guy in the muscle shirt. Over rocks, around trees. Through ferns, moss, and mud. Screaming. Shrieking. Yelling.

"But I'm not sure if the Hawaiians have a comparative humanoid ape in their mythology."

The beast flailed its arms, bounced off a tree, then staggered dizzily. "It sure is fat," observed Nana. "Probably hard to find nutritious food in Dumpsters these days."

Tilly waggled her walking stick at it. "The cranium is extraordinarily large. It must boast a massive brain to have a head that big, which means its intelligence level could be well above that of a typical anthropoid ape. The leaves have me puzzled, though. Bigfoot is reputed to be a furry creature—a great, solitary, gangly beast who's been walking the earth for six thousand years. Why is this creature's epidermal layer covered with mulch instead of fur? I hope it doesn't have jungle rot."

"Them other ones might be solitary," Nana announced, nodding toward the hill. "But this one's not. He's got relatives."

Three more fat, leaf-covered creatures came tumbling down the slope behind him.

"Looks like they all been eatin' outta the same Dumpster," Nana observed.

"A nuclear family," marveled Tilly. "Astounding. I wonder if they're grouped into matriarchal or patriarchal units." She heaved herself to her feet. "Perhaps I'll ask."

"ARE YOU CRAZY?" I seized her arm. "You can't go near that thing! Look at it! It's vicious. It might be rabid. If you get anywhere near it, it might—"

It stumbled into a pothole and fell flat on its face with a painful *WOOF*.

"Ouch." Nana winced. "That had to hurt."

"I'll be fine," Tilly assured me, removing my hand from her arm. "I faced down the Abominable Snowman near the summit of Mount Everest. This creature is small potatoes in comparison."

"Yeah, but he brought along the whole family!" I paused stupidly as her words caught up to my brain. "You've seen the Abominable Snowman?"

"Actually, it turned out to be an unnaturally tall Sherpa guide who'd lost his way in a storm, but if you ever visit Nepal, you'll discover that I've become something of an urban legend."

The creature dragged itself clumsily to its feet and in a fit of wildness and rage, pounded its way straight for us.

"Um, I think we better move," I said, grabbing Nana, but Tilly strode brusquely to intercept him.

"You there," she yelled, utterly fearless as the thing stopped, growled curiously, then catapulted toward her as if she were the Big Mac he'd ordered for lunch. Faster. Closer. Faster. Closer. *Oh, my God! He wasn't going to stop!*

THWACK! She clubbed him in the midsection with one swing of her walking stick. *BOOM!* He went down like a six-ton sack of flour.

"She's somethin', isn't she?" said Nana.

Circling the moaning carcass, Tilly nudged leaves from its face with the tip of her cane, then peered down at the thing with such blatant disappointment, I had to call out, "Bad news?"

"The worst." She glanced back in our direction. "It's only Dick Teig."

I guess the good news was, at least he wasn't on his way to Tahiti.

"How much time before the bus leaves?" Jonathan asked worriedly.

Riiiight. Leeeeft. Riiiight. Leeeft. The wind that had pushed us upriver was now in our faces, so we were bucking a powerful head wind as I paddled back downriver. I checked my watch. "Forty-five minutes."

"We're going to miss it, aren't we?"

"I can't be sure," I said breathlessly. I figured we had another mile to go, but my shoulders and arms were burning so much from the exertion, I didn't know if I could make it all the way back. Riiiight. Leeeeft. Riiiight. Leeeft. "Maybe Nana will ask the driver to wait."

I had no one but myself to blame for our late start back. After deleafing the Teigs and Stolees, who'd taken the wrong trail to the Secret Falls and ended up traipsing through hikers' hell, I'd sent them down the correct trail under the watchful eyes of Nana and Tilly, then stayed behind to tamp all the upturned soil back into its proper place. The Vikings had set such a good example, I felt obligated to follow suit. I hooked up with Jonathan back at the kayak, but by the time I arrived everyone else had already taken off, leaving us to navigate back on our own.

Riiiight. Leeeeft. Riiiight. Leeeft.

As I navigated a wide turn around a bend, a gust of wind slammed into us like a class-three hurricane, lifting our bow out of the water and driving us back as if we'd hit a giant deflector shield. My hair flatlined. My eyebrows nearly blew off my face. My cheeks stung. I bowed my head against the force of the gale, realizing with horror that the river was now acting as a wind tunnel.

"My hat!" cried Jonathan. "My Bill Gates hat!"

Riiiiiiiiiiiiiiight. Leeeeeeeeeeeeft.

"Over there! To the right! Hurry, Emily! Right, right, right. You've gotta save my hat!"

TOOOOOOT! TOOOOOOT! The horn from the Fern Grotto tour boat blasted behind us. I whipped a look over my shoulder to find it suddenly within spitting distance, its flat little bottom and canopy bearing down fast.

Forty yards.

Thirty yards.

Holy shit.

Rightleftrightleftrightrightrightleftright.

TOOOOOOOT! blared the horn. *OH, GOD!*

Twenty yards.

Ten yards.

Rightleftrightleftrightrightrightleftright.

"Turn around!" Jonathan screamed, grabbing his paddle and plunging it into the water like a rudder to stop me. "That hat is one of a kind! The only one ever offered on eBay. A collector's item! You've gotta turn arou—"

CRRRRRRRRRRRRRRRRRUNCH!!!

CHAPTER 8

"Peas will help bring down the swelling."

"Peas?" I peered at the female doctor in the emergency room cubicle. "Dried or frozen?"

"Frozen. Preferably in a bag. Without butter sauce. Just keep refreezing them."

"Baby or snow?"

"Whichever is cheaper. Don't make the mistake of eating them afterward." She stuck her pen in the pocket of her lab coat and offered me a warm smile. "You're done here, Miss Andrew. Ice that lump for a few days, and you'll be fine. But I'd advise against any more kayaking trips on the Wailua. Next time, you might not be so lucky to escape with only minor bruises. Be thankful you were wearing your life jacket."

"Do you know anything about the condition of the man who came in with me? Jonathan Pond?" I tested the matzo ball of a knot over my eye, hoping the swelling might have gone down already, but no such luck. I looked down at myself, assessing the damage. My clothes were damp, my shoulder bag was water-logged, and my new short, sassy, ridiculously expensive, frizz-free hairdo was in ruins.

In other words, I was a mess.

On a brighter note, at least I'd been wearing water-proof mascara.

"I don't know anything about Mr. Pond, but I can check for you."

She returned in ten minutes with an update. "He's scheduled for more X-rays and a CT scan, so we're going to keep him overnight. His doctor wants to make sure there's nothing going on other than the broken arm."

"Can I see him?" Although I didn't know if that was such a good idea since all I really wanted to do was . . . WRING HIS FREAKING NECK!

"He's having a psych evaluation at the moment, so probably not." She lowered her voice. "He apparently keeps babbling something about a hat. You wouldn't know anything about that, would you?"

A cab picked me up at the hospital in Kapa'a and transported me to Kojima's market, where I forked out a month's rent for a bag of generic frozen peas minus butter sauce. Living in an island paradise had to be the most idyllic thing on earth, until you had to eat. I figured the leading cause of death in most island communities wasn't heart attack, but sticker shock.

We headed south on Route 56, through Waipouli,

Wailua, Kapaia, and Lihue, arriving at the cruise ship terminal in Nawiliwili just as the sun was setting. My peas were in a major thaw, so my primary goal on ship was to make a mad dash for my mini refrigerator, though my so-called "freezer" compartment probably wasn't big enough to store my 'Giant Economy Size Family Pack' of baby peas. Nuts. I should have bought broccoli florets; they probably would have taken longer to thaw.

"Miss Andrew," the security guy at the ship's entrance said as I handed him my room key/identity card. He checked the information in his computer, then made a little whistling sound. "I'm going to have to keep this, so you'll need to visit the Guest Relations Desk on deck four to be issued a new one."

"A new key? What's wrong with that one?"

"Your name is flagged on the computer. That's all I can tell you."

"Why is my name flagged?"

"They'll tell you at Guest Relations, ma'am."

I was so irritated by this further disruption of my schedule that I didn't even bother getting upset about the "ma'am" thing. I charged up to deck four by way of the central staircase and took my place at the back of a ridiculously long line where people were purchasing tickets, exchanging tickets, and switching table assignments. By the time I got to the desk, twenty minutes had elapsed and I had enough water in my plastic grocery bag to support marine life. "Do you have another key for me?" I asked the agent wearily. "Emily Andrew?"

He punched something into his computer, consulted the screen, then unlocked a drawer, riffled through the contents, and handed me an envelope. "A new stateroom assignment for you, Miss Andrew. Sorry for the inconvenience."

"What happened to my old stateroom?"

"You've been upgraded."

I bobbled my grocery bag, sloshing water everywhere. The agent grinned. "Ice cream?"

"Baby peas. Why have I been upgraded?"

"I'm not at liberty to say, but your steward has already moved your belongings, so you can go right up to your new cabin."

I glanced at the number on the envelope. Cabin number fifteen-fifty-eight. "What deck is this on?"

"Deck ten." He gestured with his thumb. "Straight up."

"And you can't tell me why I'm being moved?"

He gave me a two-handed palms up and shook his head. "Sorry. Enjoy your peas."

I hopped the elevator to deck ten and found cabin fifteen-fifty-eight close to the elevator bank on the ship's starboard side—which said to me, outside cabin! I inserted my key and opened the door, then stood paralyzed in the doorway, sure someone had made a terrible mistake.

The room expanded to penthouse proportions. Directly opposite me stood floor-to-ceiling glass panels that looked out on a long private balcony. A baby grand piano occupied the center of the room on a circle of inlaid tile. Pillars rose to my right and left, guarding the foyer, while other pillars marked the entry to the bedroom and the dining area. An elegant sectional sofa wrapped around the outer wall, perfectly positioned for its occupants to watch the flatscreen TV that occupied the interior wall. Potted plants abounded. Plush pillows. A circular coffee table with a quartet of armchairs surrounding it.

I crept farther into the room, my eyes flitting from corner to corner. Recessed lighting. Glass dining table. Minibar. Wet bar with full-sized refrigerator. Hot damn! I raced across the floor, dropped my bag into the sink, and stuffed my baby peas into the freezer.

I ranged a look across the room to the bedroom and sprinted in that direction. *Oh, my God.* King-size bed with closet space galore and glass doors opening onto the balcony. I slid the closet door open to find my clothes hung up and all my shoes neatly arranged on the floor. I ran into the bathroom, dazzled by the whirlpool tub, the separate shower, and double sink. It even had a bidet, though I had yet to figure out how to use those things.

I strolled back out to the living room, wondering who was to blame for assigning me the wrong stateroom, because somebody had definitely goofed up. In my experience giving a guest an upgrade usually meant transferring them to a room with a coffeemaker, or a toilet that flushed. It never meant giving them the room with the baby grand.

I picked up the phone, hesitant to make the call,

but knowing it was the only thing to do. The way my luck usually worked, I'd just get settled in when the real occupants of the room would show up at the door. And guess who'd be out on her ear?

"This is Emily Andrew in cabin fifteen-fifty-eight," I announced to the man who answered my call. "There's been a mistake. I'm not in the right room. This looks like the penthouse suite, and my cruise package basically entitled me to an interior cabin in the bilge."

I heard a flurry of clicks on a computer keyboard. "There's no mistake, Miss Andrew. Cabin fifteen-fifty-eight, which is our Royal Family Suite with balcony, is your new assigned cabin."

"But I didn't *pay* for a Royal Family Suite with balcony."

"The extra charges have been paid by someone else."

Someone else? "Does the 'someone else' have a name?"

More keyboard activity. "Your benefactor wishes to remain anonymous. Is there anything else?"

I had an anonymous benefactor? *Uff da.* Was this a scene straight out of *Great Expectations,* or what? "So this is actually my cabin? No one is going to kick me out? I have your word on it?"

"My name is Jason. If you have any problems, feel free to contact me and I'll take care of it personally. Although, you do realize that occupancy in our Royal Family Suite with balcony does entitle you to concierge service?"

I sat down after I disconnected, stunned. Was concierge service like having your own valet or butler? Someone to press your clothes and polish your shoes and draw your bath for you? Hmm. I wondered how they'd feel about styling my hair and blow-drying my shoulder bag.

I was gazing around the room, trying to guess how much this cabin had set someone back, when it hit me. Duh! This wasn't about the money. It was about all the intangibles I'd talked about earlier. Intimacy. Nurturing. Commitment. It was Etienne's way of making amends for his long absence!

I leaned back in my chair, accustoming myself to the opulence of my surroundings. Wow. He didn't do anything halfway.

Awash with excitement, I slid the phone over, read the printed instructions on how to make an overseas call, and punched in Etienne's number. I didn't care if the going rate *was* an astronomical $7.50 a minute. A surprise like this was simply too spectacular to ignor—

"This is Miceli."

"You are *the* sweetest man! This is the most incredible, the most romantic—"

"Please leave a short message," his voice continued. "I'll get back to you." *Beeeeeeeeeeeep!*

I opened my mouth, disappointment spilling out in fractured phrases. "You're not . . . Shoot! Umm . . . I wanted . . . Never mind. Umm . . . Will you—"

CLICK.

Damn! Well, he'd know it was me. He'd call me

back. But in the meantime, I couldn't keep my good fortune to myself. I punched up another number.

"You won't believe where I am," I gushed when Nana picked up.

"Emily? Are you all right, dear? We been real worried about you."

"I'm fine. Never been better! I'm in a cabin with a whirlpool bath, a baby grand piano, and get this, concierge service. And . . . I'm in love!"

"No kiddin'?" A pause. "Who with?"

"With Etienne, of course! He's talking about a ring, Nana. And commitment. And he surprised me with this unbelievable room upgrade. I could burst!"

"How nice for you, dear. Is that fella Jonathan there with you? We was frettin' about him, too."

"Jonathan. Oh, my God. Wait 'til you hear about Jonathan." I gave her the blow-by-blow—from boat mishap, to rescue, to ambulance ride to the hospital. "They're keeping him overnight for observation, but I expect they'll release him tomorrow. So, did the bus driver wait for us at all before he decided to take off?"

" 'Bout fifteen minutes, then he said he had to get us back to the ship 'cause he was on a schedule. But a couple a them outfitters stayed behind with a van to drive the three a you back once you showed up. I guess they have to make allowances for people bein' late when the wind kicks up like it done today."

"Three of us? Who else was missing besides me and Jonathan?"

"One a them Norwegians. The wiry one what wears his hair like Farrah Fawcett used to. It was the strangest thing. All three a them was at the boat ramp when we got back, but when it come time to leave, the little one went missin'. Nils said we should go on without the little fella 'cause he sometimes liked to explore on his own, so that's what we done. The Coconut Market Place is just up the road from there, so I'm thinkin' he went shoppin' for souvenirs."

Souvenirs, or a pawnshop to get rid of whatever he and his buddies had dug up at the Secret Falls today? I suspected he'd make his way back to the ship with a lot more money than when he'd left.

Frustrated, I slumped down in my chair and rubbed the knot on my forehead. None of this was turning out the way I'd hoped. I just wish I knew what the Vikings had found, why one of them had disappeared, and if those two incidents were connected to Professor Smoker's death. "Switching gears completely, what are you and Tilly signed up for tomorrow? Are you going to try to do your zodiac raft trip?"

"Nope. We're all doin' the same thing we done today, only we're actually gonna dig. No more gawkin' at the scenery. Tomorrow, we're gettin' down and dirty." She lowered her voice in a secret agent kind of tone. "We even picked up some dessert spoons for what Tilly calls 'more refined diggin'.' "

Oh, God. I shook my head tiredly. "You stole more silverware at dinner tonight, didn't you?"

"You bet. But we're gonna give it back!"

Okay, so what if the Vikings *had* already found the treasure? Nana and the gang would still have a good time looking. They'd certainly had a great time today. And no one had gotten hurt.

Well, no one except . . . me. "Sounds good, Nana. Go for it."

"You wanna join us, dear?"

"I'm doing Kauai by air tomorrow, but maybe I'll catch an aerial view of you paddling up the Wailua from the helicopter." Which reminded me in a round-about way of a question that had been burning a hole in my brain since yesterday. "Say, Nana, this might be a stupid question, but who discovered America?"

"Bjarni Herjulfsson," she said without missing a beat. "Why do you ask, dear? I thought everyone knew that."

Having missed dinner, and deciding that half a peanut butter and jelly sandwich wouldn't sustain me until morning, I took a quick shower, blow-dried my hair and my shoulder bag, and reluctantly left the luxury of my Royal Family Suite for the Coconut Palms Cafe, which was now only one deck above me.

The cafe wasn't a popular place at night. Most passengers preferred ordering from the menu in the main dining room rather than schlepping a plate around an archipelago of food islands. But for those who preferred casual cuisine to elegant, the cafe was the place to be, the bonus being, you had the whole restaurant, and every morsel of food in every over-flowing serving tray, all to yourself.

I filled a plate with a sampling of fruit salad, tropi-cal salad, pasta salad, spinach salad, and seafood salad, then pondered where, amid the sea of empty tables, I wanted to sit. This was more overwhelming than walking down the cereal aisle at Fareway Food!

I finally set my tray down at a table conveniently located near the dessert station. But as I pulled the chair out, I realized I didn't have the whole cafe to myself.

At the far end of the room, in a shadowy corner far removed from the soft spill of overhead lighting, I saw a solitary person hunched over a plate of food, her back facing me. And though I couldn't see her face, I had no trouble recognizing who it was.

"Last time I saw you, you were planning to head home." I set my tray down on her table. "What happened?"

Bailey Howard slid her designer specs higher on her nose as she looked up at me. "All flights out of Kauai are booked solid. Aloha Airlines apologized profusely, but they're down a plane because of instrument problems, so I'm out a seat until we arrive in Maui." Her gaze drifted to the lump over my eye. "What did you do? Get coldcocked by a coconut?"

"Boating accident. Mind if I join you?"

"Be my guest. After the day I had, I could use some company."

"That doesn't sound good. What happened? Did it go badly with the police?"

She shook her head. "They were really nice. Took my statement, then told me I was free to go. Easier said than done. So I ended up spending the entire day in my cabin, climbing the walls."

I set my flatware out, shook out my napkin, and dug in while Bailey scanned the cafe with wary eyes.

"I probably shouldn't be here right now, but one more minute in that cabin and I would have ended up in a rubber room. That cubicle isn't a stateroom; it's a prison. If I had claustrophobia, I'd never be able to survive."

If she had claustrophobia, she probably would have been advised to cash in her 401K so she could afford the cabin with the piano, flatscreen TV, Jacuzzi, and floor-to-ceiling glass wall with attached balcony. "I—uh, I got a chance to talk to one of Professor Smoker's students today," I said as I chomped down on a pineapple chunk. "A woman by the name of Jen. I think you probably know her. Blond hair? Killer tan? She accosted you and Professor Smoker after his lecture yesterday?"

"Jennifer French." She exhaled a quick breath. "The bitch."

A waiter in a red vest and pressed trousers took my drink order and hurried off to fill it. "I got the impression from a brief conversation that she thinks the same thing about you."

Bailey leaned back in her chair, taking a moment to polish her glasses on her napkin. "You know what I wish? I wish the earth would open up and swallow Jennifer French whole."

"I heard she was yelling at you outside the infirmary last night."

"*You* heard? The whole ship probably heard!"

"What's her problem?"

"I gave her an F on a final exam last semester, and she won't let me forget it."

"You flunked her? You were teaching a course?"

"Yeah. For the past two years." She paused for the waiter to serve my iced tea before speaking again. "I was Professor Smoker's teaching assistant. Jen cheated on her final exam, so I flunked her. Well, *we* flunked her. She pleaded her case before the honor board, but they arrived at the same conclusion. She'd gotten hold of copies of past exams, so she knew in general what the final essay question would be, and that's cheating."

"A lot of colleges make previous final exams available to students. Where's the crime in that?"

"Professor Smoker *never* made his exams public. That's the difference. We have a strict code of honor at the university, and Jen violated it, so she got exactly what she deserved. An F."

Uh-oh. "Did that F prevent her from graduating?"

"Of course it did. But she's not going to lay that at my doorstep. It was her own fault. She tried to convince Professor Smoker to overrule the board's decision, but their ruling is always final. Not that that meant anything to her. Why do you think she's on this cruise? She wanted to get Professor Smoker alone in paradise so she could work on him to manipulate the board into changing its decision. Unfortunately, she made such a scene after the lecture yesterday that he told her not to approach him again until she grew up. She left in a huge huff, which is pretty typical behavior for her."

"And that's the last time they saw each other?"

"As far as I know."

But I wasn't so sure. "If you and Professor Smoker parted company while he checked out the golf simulators, they could have seen each other again." I looked her square in the eye. "It could have been Jennifer who confronted him at the rail. You said yourself you weren't sure if the person was a man or a woman."

"But . . ." Bailey's eyes widened in shock. "Are you implying that Jennifer might have killed Professor Smoker? Look, she may be a certifiable nutcase, but I don't think she's capable of murder."

"You'd be surprised who's capable of murder." I chased a shrimp around my plate with a fork, trying to look nonchalant. "I guess you knew Jennifer was sleeping with the professor."

Bailey's mouth tightened in what I gauged was either anger or pain. "They all wanted a piece of him. It was a constant feeding frenzy. They were always throwing themselves at his feet, and he couldn't say no."

Seemed intellectuals had trouble with the simple thiings in life, like one syllable words.

"But I can't *believe* she'd kill him over a freaking grade!" She propped her elbows on the table and braced her forehead in her palms. "What was the big deal? She could have signed up for another semester. Gone to summer school. Taken a course online. It wasn't the end of the world."

"Maybe it was to her. Did she miss out on the job of a lifetime because she didn't graduate on time?"

"How should I know? Her major was archaeology. I don't keep up with all the disciplines. But I suppose—" She expelled a long puff of air and pinched her eyes shut. "I think I read something about a private firm holding interviews on campus to recruit seniors for a major dig someplace in Africa. Maybe that's what set her off. But this is so deranged! The World Navigators and the Sandwich Islanders hated Professor Smoker. They're the ones who threatened his life. They're the ones he was supposed to be worrying about. Not Jennifer French."

Sandwich Islanders. Damn. "Um . . . speaking of Sandwich Islanders, you're probably not in the mood for any more bad news, but I saw Professor Smoker's name scribbled on the back of one of their business cards today."

"Why is that bad news?"

"Because the scribbling appeared to be a hit list, and Professor Smoker's name was at the top."

"Hit list? Are you serious?" She pressed her fingertips to her mouth. "You see? I told you they hated him. I told you—"

"The really bad news is, your name was next."

"My—?" Panic starred her eyes like Independence Day sparklers. She clutched my arm. "Where's the card? Let me see it. If the police need evidence, this'll—"

I groaned. "I don't have the card."

"Who does?"

"No one does. It's sitting in a backpack at the bottom of the Wailua River." I tapped the lump above my eye. "The boating accident I mentioned? I got wounded. The backpack drowned."

"So . . . so what am I supposed to do?" She slapped her hands on the table and tapped her fingers in agitation. "I'm on the Islanders' hit list. Jennifer hates me. Everyone knows I witnessed Professor Smoker's murder. And the Navigators are threatening to file suit against the cruise line if I don't take over the lectures for all the Cook excursions. They *really* want me off on my own, and one can only ask why. So tell me: how am I supposed to fend off all my detractors until we reach Maui?"

I wondered if that was a rhetorical question, or if she really wanted an answer.

"Well?" she prodded.

Okay. She really wanted an answer. "This probably isn't the answer you want to hear, but I think your only option is to stay in your cabin and order room service."

"I can't *stay* in that cabin another day!" she wailed. "I'll lose my mind. There's only one movie channel and it keeps replaying *Weekend at Bernie's*—a film about a man who spends a normal weekend partying and water-skiing. The only thing is, HE'S DEAD! How can you water-ski if you're dead? The worst movie in the history of filmmaking . . . and they keep torturing me with it!"

"Have you checked the listings for tomorrow?" I hedged.

"No. Why?"

"There's a sequel."

She slumped forward onto the table and crossed her arms over her head. Poor thing. *Weekend at Bernie's II* did seem like cruel and unusual punishment. "If you want to escape from your cabin tomorrow, you could come on the helicopter tour with me."

She uncrossed her arms and lifted her head. "Are you crazy? Helicopters are death traps. They crash all the time over here. No way are you going to get me into one. You have any other suggestions?"

I shrugged. "You could sign up for the Wailua River Kayak Adventure. My group of Iowans are planning to do that tomorrow. You've already met my grandmother and Tilly, and there's nine more that'll be going. You'd be pretty safe if you stick with the group."

"Kayaking sounds a lot more inviting than another day climbing my cabin walls." She bobbed her head back and forth with indecision. "Okay, I'll do it. But will you come with me while I buy my ticket?" She darted a look around the room. "I'd feel better if I wasn't alone."

After accompanying Bailey to Guest Relations and escorting her back to her room, I headed for the General Store on deck five to check out rental costumes for the big Halloween party.

Racks of costumes filled half the store's floor space, satisfying every fantasy imaginable. Southern belles. Belly dancers. Pirates. Clowns. Cowboys. Vampires. Gladiators. Mother Goose characters. Knights. Ladies-in-waiting. Marvel Comic characters. Disney characters. Looney Tune characters. Civil War generals. Roaring Twenties flappers. Hollywood movie stars. And a healthy assortment of fruits and vegetables. There were shelves of wigs, theatrical makeup, beards, mustaches, full-face masks, half masks, and a wall of accessories that included medieval and modern weaponry, gaudy jewelry, eyewear, fake teeth, and enough feather boas to start an aviary. I made a quick choice, grabbed it off the rack, charged it to my room, then made my way through a series of adjoining rooms until I arrived at the room I was looking for.

The Picture Gallery was a maze of glass display cases showcasing all the photos our eager photographer had snapped so far. I heard oohs, aahs, and peals of laughter as passengers milled in front of the cases, poking fingers at faces they recognized. I was hoping that if some individual photos of the group turned out well, I could use them in my proposed newsletter.

I circled the perimeter, reading signs labeled DAY ONE—AT SEA and DAY TWO—WELCOME TO KAUAI. Squeezing between two groups of onlookers, I worked my way to the front of the DAY ONE case and began skimming pictures.

I found a rather striking photo of Nils, Ansgar, and Gjurd as they boarded the ship—boy, Ansgar's hair was really photogenic—and a typical one of the two Dicks as they made horns of their fingers behind their wives' heads. I cringed at the photo of myself in my big orange life vest during the lifeboat drill. Why did I always have to have my mouth open and my eyes closed? Though I supposed some people might accuse me of going through life that way.

I scanned random shots of guests gambling in the casino, one of Bernice scowling into the camera as she explored the spa, one of Margi opening a moist towelette packet with her teeth, and several photos of Professor Dorian Smoker as he delivered the last lecture he would ever give on Captain James Cook.

I studied the man in the navy cardigan and baggy Dockers, wondering what mysteries he'd taken to the grave with him. He'd seen his killer's face. If only he'd left some kind of clue behind that would help us identify who it was. Were we overlooking something?

I scrutinized the half dozen other lecture room photos, spying Nana and Tilly, but discovering that yours truly was completely hidden behind a man whose head was even larger than Dick Teig's, if that was possible. I picked out Nils near the front, bookended by Ansgar and Gjurd, and nodded with satisfaction when I located Percy and Basil in seats near the back. So they had attended the lecture. Why wasn't I surprised?

There were scads of people I didn't recognize at all, and a few who looked vaguely familiar. Was that the muscle shirt guy sitting beside Gjurd? Sure looked like his stomach. And there was Bailey in the front row, looking studious and intelligent as she hung on Dorian Smoker's every word, her head angled so that her hair looked like an explosion in progress. I focused more intently on the photo, trying to identify the man sitting directly behind her. The hair and glasses made me think it could be

Jonathan, but it was hard to ID someone with only half a head. I noticed a blurry image of Jennifer French standing near the back wall, but couldn't find Shelly anywhere. Of course, the photographer's lens hadn't captured everyone who'd been in the room. Me, for example.

I returned back to the boarding photos, and after poring over what seemed like a couple million, I found a terrific picture of Osmond and Alice and a really cute shot of—

I did a quick double take, arrested by the image of a man whose shoulders filled the entire photo and whose eyes looked hot enough to singe glass. Wow, Duncan really dressed up the ole *Aloha Princess* backdrop. I wondered how his excursion had—

Duncan? Oh, my God! I checked my watch. I was supposed to meet him in ten minutes!

I charged into the Anchor Bar a few minutes later and paused at the entrance, allowing my eyes to adjust to the room's lack of light. I squinted at the petite sofas and pedestal tables that crowded the floor and whistled at the focal point of the room—a circular acrylic bar that was illuminated with the blues and aquamarines of a tropical sea. As I stepped into the room, I could make out a handful of couples occupying couches at opposite ends of the room, but nowhere within the intimate confines of the Anchor Bar could I see Duncan's mane of blond hair, which could only mean one thing.

I was early.

Struggling to catch my breath, I sat down on one of the sofas and smiled at a miniskirted barmaid as she headed in my direction.

"Are you Emily?"

I guess I'd been foolish to think she might actually ask me what I wanted to drink. "I'm Emily, but I'm a little afraid to ask why you're asking."

She handed me an envelope. "A really good-looking guy stopped in a while ago and said to give this to a brunette named Emily who'd be coming in around ten. Guess that would be you. Can I get you a drink? Mr. Universe already paid for it."

I stared at the envelope, feeling a little unsettled. "I'll let you know after I get through reading." As she headed back toward the bar, I ripped open the envelope and began reading Duncan's handwritten note.

I apologize for standing you up, Em, but as they say, the best laid plans of mice and men . . . Two of my people tracked me down with a security issue. They don't trust their room safe to hold some valuables they have, so as you read this, I'll probably be wrangling with the ship's staff about placing whatever it is that Percy and Basil have in the ship's vault. Please don't wait for me; this could take forever. Documents to sign, etc. But do you suppose you and I could try this again tomorrow night? Same time? Same place? Unless you'd rather have me meet you in your new cabin. I hear the view is pretty spectacular from the balcony on deck ten.

Duncan

I read the note a second time, riveted by the part about Percy and Basil. Had they actually discovered something out by the Secret Falls besides Bud Lite cans? Nuts! Why hadn't I paid closer attention? But if the two Englishmen had found Griffin Ring's treasure, what had the Vikings found? And who was in possession of the original map? The Vikings, the Brits, or the cheerleaders?

I sagged against the sofa back, reading the note again and again. By the time I finished reading it a fifth time, I realized something else.

If Duncan knew I'd changed cabins, did that also mean he was responsible for the upgrade? But Duncan didn't have that kind of money, did he? *Uff da.* Was it possible that Duncan, not Etienne, was my benefactor?

I blinked stupidly.

Damn. I'd never even thought of that.

CHAPTER 9

"So what's the good news?" a man in khaki shorts and an expensive Tommy Bahama flowered shirt asked as he stepped off the scales.

"Three hundred sixteen pounds," a female assistant behind the counter announced. "Honey, we're going to have to send you up in a bird all by yourself."

He laughed good-naturedly. "I ate a big breakfast. I'm usually a svelte hundred and seventy."

That morbidly obese passengers qualified to fly in their own private helicopter was a real shocker. But what shocked me even more was that Tommy Bahama actually made shirts in super-plus jumbo triple X sizes.

I was seated in the waiting area of the Kauai Helicopter Tours office, a vintage World-War-II-style building at the Lihue Airport, watching people weigh in for our flight. I'd never given it much thought

before, but apparently one of the secrets of helicopter safety is the even distribution of weight in the
passenger cabin. Hence, the scales and the weighing-
in routine. I regarded the guy in the Tommy Bahama
shirt as he lowered all five foot three inches of himself into the chair beside me and cringed when I felt
the floor deflect beneath us. *Creeeeeak. Urrrrr.
Sssssssss. Creeeeeak.* Oh, God. Was that the floor or
his chair?

"This your first time up?" the guy asked me, as
another vanload of people arrived.

I nodded. "You, too?"

"Yeah. They tell me these things have a lousy safety
record, but I'm a real risk taker, so I figured, what the
hell. I have no fear. No phobias, no nothing. In my
book, fear is a complete waste of time. I can do it all.
Needles. Snakes. The dentist. I mean, look at me. My
doctor tells me I'm a walking time bomb, but he's not
scaring me, either. Not one bit."

I watched a crowd of newcomers file through the
door and sat up a little straighter when I saw a face I
recognized.

"When your time's up, it's up," the guy droned on.
"We're not gonna live forever. You can try all that
health food crap, but it's not gonna prolong your life
by one minute, so you might as well throw your
money at a helicopter ride instead." He gave my bare
knee a friendly pat with his huge, sweaty palm. "So,
are you married? Good-looking girl like you, I'm
thinking we might have a future together."

"Would you excuse me a moment? I'm meeting

someone." I plucked his hand off my knee and scooted across the floor, sidling up to Shelly Valentine as if she were a long-lost friend. "I need you to save me," I said in a desperate whisper. "Will you pretend we're together so Jabba the Hutt will hit on someone else?" I bobbed my head in his direction.

Shelly looked beyond me, shivered a little, then gave me a huge hug. "I'm so happy to see you!" she said in a loud voice, then in an undertone close to my ear, "I'm glad to help. I figure I owe you one after the way Jen treated you yesterday."

We moved forward in the line, heading toward the scales.

"She's not with you today?"

"She decided to stay on the ship for an all-day spa treatment. Maybe they'll be able to extract cellulite, toxins, and that big mean streak of hers. Frankly, I don't see how Dori put up with her. She's so moody. Just because you're *in* pain doesn't mean you have to *be* one. No wonder she doesn't have any friends."

"I thought you were her friend."

"Me? Hah! Not in this lifetime."

"Then what were you doing on the kayak adventure together yesterday?"

She tossed her long, glossy dark hair behind her shoulder. "I didn't have anything better to do. She wanted help excavating something that was supposed to be buried near that waterfall, so I agreed. Jen and I are both archaeology majors; we've both had the same methods courses. Since I have another year of school to go, I figured I could use the practice."

"Isn't this a strange time of year to be on a cruise if you're in school?"

"I took the semester off. The course work got so intense, I needed to take a breather."

If she thought college was bad, wait until she hit real life.

"Step onto the scales there, honey," the woman behind the counter instructed Shelly. After we weighed in and filled out the necessary paperwork, we wandered into an adjoining room and sat down to await further instructions.

"Remember when you asked Jen and me yesterday where we got our map?" Shelly asked. "I don't know why Jen was being so secretive, but she wouldn't tell me where she got it, either. Isn't that weird? I don't know what the big deal was. It looked to me as if everyone had one."

I couldn't help entertaining a suspicion that unlike everyone else, Jennifer may have acquired her map from Dorian Smoker himself—right before she pushed him overboard. "You mind if I ask where you and Jennifer went after you left Professor Smoker's lecture?"

Shelly's mouth angled in disgust. "I don't know where Jen went, but I went back to my cabin and had a good cry. I thought I was going to have Dori all to myself for ten days. I share him enough throughout the year. Then *bam!* Jennifer shows up. I was *so* disappointed."

She heaved a pathetic sigh. "I know women of my generation are supposed to be too liberated to get jealous, but . . . I guess I'm guilty of being way too sensitive. Don't tell Jen that I cried about it, okay? She'd only make some snide comment and laugh at me. I hate to admit it, but she's a lot more socially evolved than I am. She didn't even fall apart after she flunked that ethnographic methods course last semester, but she was really steamed. I mean, she had a job lined up and everything."

She had a job lined up? YES! I knew it! "So what kind of jobs are archaeology majors applying for these days?"

"The L. S. B. Leakey Foundation? Olduvai Gorge in Tanzania? They're beginning excavation on a new site on Bed One. That's the level where the strata dates back over a million years. She was supposed to be in charge of cataloging all the Pleistocene artifacts, but since she didn't graduate, they gave the position to someone else. She really blew that one."

A man's voice blared out over a loudspeaker, causing us both to jump. "When I call your name, please proceed across the street to the gate I assign you." He read off a litany of names, eventually announcing, "Emily Andrew, Shelly Valentine, and Carl Leatherman, gate nine."

We joined the exodus out the door and straggled across the street in uneven groupings, hiking toward our gates in the ankle-high grass that flanked a tall chain-link fence. Inside the barrier, a fleet of helicopters sat like chess pieces on slabs of pavement with yellow markings, the entire compound ringed by a field of scrubby bushes that swept toward a range of dark volcanic mountains. Shelly and I passed through the fence at gate nine and walked to the edge of the tarmac, eyeing the craft that was to be our home for the next hour. "Isn't it supposed to be . . . bigger?" she asked, aping the subject line of the SPAM that flooded my in-box these days.

I gave it a once over. "Without the tail and rotor blades, it's about the size of my VW bug, so it can probably hold at least fifteen college students. Six if they all want seats."

"When your time's up, it's up, right?" insisted a male voice behind us. "I heard these things have lousy safety records, but I don't care. I'm not afraid of anything. Walking under ladders. Confined spaces. Lightning. I can do it all."

I shot a horrified look at Shelly. She shot one back. I looked over my shoulder, my stomach sinking to my ankles at the sight of the guy in the Tommy Bahama shirt. NOOO! This was beyond cruel! This was criminal! Unconscionable. Unbelievable! Un . . . unconstional!

"Excuse me," I said to the woman whose ear he was chewing off. She wore an ID badge around her neck and was carrying an official looking clipboard. "I think there's been a terrible mistake. Doesn't he get his own helicopter?"

"Ladies, ladies, ladies," Carl continued, draping a flabby arm around each of our shoulders. "This is your lucky day. You get every mouthwatering inch of me all to yourselves."

In the next instant Shelly seized his wrist, spun

beneath his arm, and in a quick, fluid motion, flipped him onto his back as if she were a short-order cook and he was Humpty Dumpty on his way to becoming a cheese omelette. The earth shook. Debris floated upward. "Don't touch me," she yelled into his stunned face, stabbing her forefinger at his nose. "Don't ever touch me! You got that?"

She brushed off her hands and stormed to the other end of the tarmac, swinging her arms to loosen her muscles and muttering to herself. I stared after her, speechless. Wow. The only other people I'd ever seen execute moves like that were the Terminator and Nana.

Reminder to myself: Don't get on Shelly Valentine's bad side.

I walked over to her. "That was pretty impressive," I said as she methodically cracked one knuckle after the other. "How'd you do it?"

She shrugged. "I signed up for a self-defense course at the university during my freshman year, and I keep taking refresher courses. Best thing I ever did. Not bad for an amateur, huh?"

Not bad for a professional, either.

"You!" the female official blasted, leveling her pen at the flattened carcass of Carl Leatherman. "Any more manhandling of the passengers, and you're outta here. You!" she called to Shelly. "The World Wrestling Alliance moves belong in the gym. Understand? Okay, Valentine and Andrew in the front seat. Leatherman in the back. No eating or smoking allowed. Enjoy your flight."

Subdued and grass-stained, Carl struggled onto his fat little feet, looking decidedly pouty. Ignoring us, he squeezed though the door of the copter and wedged himself into the back passenger compartment. Shelly and I strapped ourselves into the front seats. Our pilot climbed aboard next, a confident looking forty-year-old who, after introducing himself as Bogart, went to work with mute efficiency. He handed us protective headphones, checked his instruments, flipped some switches, powered up the rotor blades, and then, after a slow vertical liftoff, swooped into the air like a giant dragonfly off a lily pad.

We banked high to the left, my body vibrating from teeth to toenails, the whir of the rotor blades louder than New York jackhammers. My feet tingled with the sudden height, but I had to admit, the scenery unfolding before us was even more awesome than the sight of "60% OFF" stickers during Emerhoff's semiannual shoe sale.

I dug my Canon Elph out of my shoulder bag and began snapping pictures. A deserted crescent of white sand beach, washed by blue-green water and nestled within a leafy swath of emerald green jungle. A lighthouse perched on the lip of a rugged headland. A narrow-mouthed bay with a long finger of rocks forming a breakwater around a local marina. Sailboats. Powerboats. And there was our cruise ship! I wondered if I could pick out my cabin from here. I gave Shelly a little poke to point it out, but she still looked pretty miffed about the Carl incident and in no mood to take pictures.

As we flew over what looked like a huge resort hotel, I heard static over my headphones, followed by a few strains of some classical overture, and the voice of James Earl Jones on a prerecorded tape. "Directly below you lies the Menehune Fishpond, a nine-hundred-foot mullet-raising pond reputed to have been built in one night by a race of small, hairy people who inhabited the island prior to the Polynesians."

I shot a picture of the pond, then glanced over my shoulder to see if Carl wanted me to move my head so he could get a picture, too. But Carl wasn't looking at the Menehune Fishpond. Carl looked too frightened for sightseeing. He was clinging white-knuckled to a safety strap, his eyes pinched so tightly, he'd need a crowbar to pry them open again. Even his lips were quivering—or maybe he was mouthing a silent prayer. Huh. It seemed that after a lifetime of facing down needles, snakes, and dentists, he'd finally found something that scared the crap out of him.

More music played as we soared over razor-backed mountains with scrubby flanks and geometrically challenged fields in a patchwork quilt of pea green, celery green, moss green, and pistachio.

"The mile-long lane of trees you see in the distance is a stand of rough-bark swamp mahogany imported from Australia and planted by a local cattle rancher over one hundred and fifty years ago. It's known as the Tree Tunnel and it shades the country road leading into Poipu."

We swayed right and left and swooped off again

toward the west, approaching terrain that was as fierce as it was uninhabitable. Towers of stone rose like the spires of a gothic cathedral, lacy with erosion, craggy with age. Water gushed through rock and cascaded over steep precipices, spilling into pools that looked peacock blue in the sun.

"To your right is the waterfall Steven Spielberg used in the opening shot of the movie *Jurassic Park*," announced James Earl in his melodic baritone.

Angry gray ridges. Huge, inaccessible caves. Grassy plateaus. I snapped a picture of the waterfall for Jonathan and smiled to myself. My good deed for the day.

After a rousing interlude by Rachmaninoff, James Earl continued his travelogue. "Directly ahead of you is Waimea Canyon. Mark Twain once dubbed it the 'Grand Canyon of the Pacific.' Ten miles long, one and a half miles wide, thirty-six hundred feet deep, it borders the Alakai Swamp and is chiseled from red bedrock that eons of rain and sun have bleached to the color of an old clay pot."

Even in direct sunlight, the colors of the canyon were muted into soft earth tones. Pale peach. Light pink. Soft coral. Warm beige. Deep valleys. Rocky pinnacles. Impossible waterfalls. Rivers meandering toward the sea. With Rachmaninoff blasting in our ears, we hovered over one waterfall, dipped into a valley, banked high over a sharp crest, and charged like a Valkyrie toward the open sea. I checked behind me to see how Carl was faring.

On the upside, he didn't look so scared anymore.

On the downside, he had the same "car sick" look my brother Steve used to get before he'd upchuck his lunch in the front seat of Dad's pickup. Gray skin. Moist brow. White lips. Uh-oh.

"Are you all right?" I yelled at him.

He clung silently to the safety strap, sweating, eyes still clamped shut. I was obviously failing in my attempt to penetrate the racket created by rotor blades, James Earl Jones, and Rachmaninoff.

"ARE YOU ALL RIGHT?" I persisted. When he still gave no indication of hearing me, I turned back toward the front console. Ignoring the lure of the scenery for a moment, I glanced left and right for—

Aha! I grabbed a motion sickness bag from a pocket beneath the instrument panel and pivoted around to drop it onto Carl's lap. There might be a supply in the backseat, but if he kept his eyes shut, they'd be as useful to him as the Weight Watcher's point system. In fact—

I grabbed the rest of the bags and pitched them behind me, figuring he'd thank me when we landed. That Tommy Bahama shirt was probably dry-clean only.

"On the horizon is the famed Na Pali coast," James Earl announced in my ear. "An impenetrable expanse of valleys and four-thousand-foot cliffs, sitting cheek to jowl with the pounding surf." We swept out over the whitecapped ocean and looked northeast toward the successive waves of knife-edged rock that scalloped the towering cliffs. A petticoat of sea foam skirted the base of the cliffs, all swirly and frothy white. "The 1976 remake of *King Kong* was partially filmed in one of these valleys along the coastline," James continued. "Valleys with names like Koahole, Awaawapuhi, and Honopu."

We swooped toward the mainland like a pesky gnat, buzzing into the mouth of a primeval valley that looked like the land time forgot. Giant monoliths of stone, shaped like arrowheads and slick with centuries of moss, rose like skyscrapers before us. Lush greenery carpeted the valley floor. Boulder-strewn streams sliced mean paths through the terrain, seaming the land like permanent scars.

I took a panoramic shot of the arrowheads as we circled around the valley, but as we headed back out to sea, I heard a thump, felt a lurch, then tumbled against Shelly as the chopper pitched wildly to port.

"Mayday," Bogart fired into the mouthpiece on his headset. Shelly screamed as she slammed into the door. I struggled to push off her, but we were too far off-balance. I felt like a bug pinned to a display card; I couldn't pull myself upright.

"Mayday, mayday," Bogart repeated. Fighting the g force, I muscled myself high enough to peer into the backseat. My heart fluttered at the sight.

Carl lay in a huge, lifeless heap, all three hundred and sixteen pounds of him slumped against the window on the left side of the chopper, like a shifted load on a logging truck. He'd finally opened his eyes, but they were obviously blind to the sudden blur of scenery that whizzed past our windshield as we started plunging toward earth.

No! This was a mistake! Carl was the time bomb. His time was up, not mine! I exercised. I went to church. I ate my vegetables. THIS COULDN'T BE HAPPENING TO ME!

As Bogart fought to stabilize us, I clutched Shelly's arm and closed my eyes, suddenly realizing why this was happening.

My hair. It had to be my hair. My shorter, sassier, ridiculously expensive, frizz-free locks. No wonder this was happening—God didn't recognize me!

"I was sure it was motion sickness," I confessed as I lobbed a stone over the edge of the bluff. It hit the rock-encrusted beach fifty feet below us and ricocheted toward the pounding surf.

Employing some pretty masterful maneuvers, Bogart had managed to set us down on the grassy headland at the valley's entrance, a fairly level plateau overlooking a cliff face of sheer rock. The helicopter had sustained only minor damage, but it wasn't going anywhere with Carl still in it. And neither were we.

"Cardiac arrest," Shelly countered as she lobbed her own stone over the side. "Or a brain aneurysm. I knew that guy spelled trouble from the get-go. The mouthy ones are always trouble." She spun around, shielding her eyes as she checked the sky. "That rescue copter sure is taking its time. I have a manicure scheduled for three o'clock. Look at this." She wiggled her fingers in the air. "I broke two nails on that wild-goose chase yesterday. I was terrified I was going to break another one today."

Shelly was happy she hadn't broken a nail. I was happy I hadn't broken my neck. This illustrated one of the great strengths of today's college coed. She could quickly suppress the trauma of a near-death experience to face the challenge of an even greater crisis: the unrepaired hangnail. Yes, today's collegians really had everything in perspective.

I tossed a look back toward the helicopter to find Bogart leaning against the body of the craft, carrying on an animated conversation by cell phone. I shook my head. "Bailey warned me about helicopters. Wait 'til she hears about this. She'll be *sooo* happy she opted for watercraft rather than aircraft today."

Shelly lifted her brows. "Are you friends with Bailey?"

"Passing acquaintances."

"You seem to know a lot about her, for being a passing acquaintance."

"I know enough to realize that, contrary to what Jennifer implied, Bailey is definitely warm-blooded. Or should I say, viviparous."

Shelly grinned. "Jen likes to throw out those ten-cent words when she's around civilians. Makes her feel intellectually superior." She dug the toe of her sandal into the turf. "I suppose you've guessed by now that Jen isn't a Bailey Howard devotee."

"Because of the honors board thing. Yeah, Bailey brought me up to speed about that."

"Well, Jen might not be one of my favorite people, but I can't blame her for feeling the way she does."

It was my turn to be surprised. "You don't think she should have been called on the carpet for cheating?"

"I'm not talking about the cheating allegations. If she did cheat, she deserved the punishment she got. I'm talking about the other issue."

Right. The other issue. "What other issue?"

She spent all of a nanosecond wrestling with the principles of ethics and confidentiality before filling me in. "This is Jen's take on the matter, not mine, okay? But according to Jen, Dori had something that Bailey wanted. Unfortunately, Bailey didn't have the patience to wait to come by it honestly, so she facilitated a way to acquire it more quickly. In the end, Bailey wins the ultimate prize, and Dori—Poor Dori gets a one-way ticket to the great beyond."

I gave myself a mental V-8 Juice smack on the forehead. Oh, my God! Was she talking about the journal? Had Bailey wanted Griffin Ring's journal? "But . . . but . . . Bailey needed Professor Smoker to sign off on her dissertation. Why would she jeopardize all those years of study by killing him before she had her degree in hand? I mean, for all she knew, the journal could have been worthless. And then what's she left with? Absolutely nothing!"

Shelly frowned. "Journal? I'm not talking about a journal."

"Then what *are* you talking about?"

"She wanted his job!" Shelly looked shocked that I hadn't figured it out for myself. "She wanted to be at *his* desk, in *his* office, at *that* university. It was her main goal in life, or weren't you around her long enough to pick up on it?"

Why was this growing more confusing? I shook my head. "How can an unofficial Ph.D. who's completely green behind the ears expect to end up in the chair vacated by the world's leading expert on Captain James Cook? Come on. Talk about unrealistic expectations. That doesn't happen."

"Oh, doesn't it?" She flashed a smug smile. "Budget cuts. The administration would have to hire an assistant professor to replace Dori, because with all the belt-tightening that's going on, they wouldn't have the funds to hire a full professor. And Bailey has made quite the name for herself on the Captain Cook front, so she'd probably be a shoo-in, especially with her degree so near completion. The campus paper called her the 'best and the brightest' graduate student in the history department. The adjective they failed to include was 'most ambitious.' "

As the faint whir of rotor blades echoed in the distance, Shelly looked up and gestured toward a dark speck in the sky. "Our rescue copter. 'Bout time."

As the chopper approached and circled overhead, I had a numbing thought.

If what Shelly implied was true, I might have sent my little group off today in the company of a cold-blooded killer.

CHAPTER 10

"Say 'ah,' " the emergency room doctor instructed, tongue depressor in hand. He looked pure Hawaiian and could have been the poster child for Coppertone tans, BioSilk hair care products, and Rembrandt tooth-whitening systems. Back home the doctors were walking advertisements for Rogaine, Dentu-Grip, and Dr. Scholl's Gel Insoles. They weren't so easy on the eyes, but their lack of movie star looks was a whole lot less intimidating.

"There's nothing wrong with my throat," I objected impatiently, my legs dangling over the edge of the examining table. "Look, my cruise ship leaves port in less than an hour, and if I'm not on it, I'll have to find my own way to Maui. They make that very clear in our travel documents. It's our responsibility to return to the ship on time, and if we're not aboard when the gangplank goes up, it's *adios muchachos.*"

"*Aloha malihini*," Dr. Akita corrected. "When in Rome." He waggled his tongue depressor again, unmoved by my appeal. I finally gave in and opened wide.

"Ahhhh."

He clicked on his Penlite. "You're right. There's nothing wrong with your throat." He pitched the wooden depressor and returned his Penlite to the pocket of his lab coat.

"My being here is a waste of your valuable time," I pressed on.

"Your helicopter crashed. It's protocol."

"It didn't crash, it was more like a hard landing. My traveling companion didn't even break a nail."

"Have you seen the edema over your eye?"

"Old injury. I did that yesterday."

He went through the mandatory routine of checking my heart and lungs and testing my reflexes, and when he was done, he scribbled something onto a clipboarded form, then turned back to me. "I'll sign your release and you'll be free to leave. I'll also have the front desk call you a cab. Lihue's impossible to get through at this time of day, so your taxi driver may have to gun it to get you back before your boat leaves."

He shook my hand and smiled. "By the way, I hope you're not prone to seasickness. The weather advisories are warning of a fairly significant squall forming southwest of here. If your next port of call is Maui, I'm afraid you may be heading right into it."

"A storm?" I sagged with relief. "Thank God!

That'll give me more time to get back to Nawiliwili. The ship won't leave port if there's a storm brewing, will it?"

"Port is the worst place a ship can be during a storm. A vessel the size of your cruise ship is always much safer riding out a storm at sea."

"You're kidding, right?" The tidal wave scene from the *Poseidon Adventure* flashed before my eyes. The *Poseidon* hadn't been safe at sea; the *Poseidon* had gone belly-up five seconds into the movie and all the important cast members drowned!

Dr. Akita regarded me indulgently. "The most dangerous thing a ship can run into during a storm isn't wind, waves, or rain. It's land."

Land? "But what about that old saying? 'Any port in a storm.' "

Dr. Akita grinned wryly. "I believe that applies mostly to birds."

Ten minutes later, I sat on a bench outside the emergency entrance, waiting for my taxi to arrive and trying not to freak out about having only forty minutes left before the *Aloha Princess* sailed into the sunset without me. With most people, disasters happened in threes. With me, they seemed to happen in twelves. Was it simply old-fashioned bad luck or one of those annoying quirks of the new math?

I lent a passing glance toward the sky, wondering if Carl had been transported back to Lihue yet. Our rescue chopper had dropped off the medical examiner and some other officials at the crash site, then flown Shelly and me back to the airport, where we were transferred to Wilcox Memorial Hospital. Shelly ended up getting released from the ER so fast that she popped into my cubicle to tell me she could probably still get her nails repaired, so she'd see me around.

I'd learned a few surprising facts about Shelly today. She could deck a horse in three seconds flat. She could shake off adversity like a dog shakes off water. She could ditch a friend in favor of a cheap manicure. I'd known other people like Shelly Valentine, and they all ended up the same way.

They really went places.

Come on, come on, I willed the taxi. I slid to the opposite end of my bench to see around the ambulance that was partially blocking my view, then anxiously watched cars entering the long drive that fronted the hospital. I peeked at my watch, tingly warmth creeping up my throat as each second ticked by. Where was the freaking taxi?

The emergency room door slid open and two paramedics sauntered out, one lighting up a cigarette, the other waving a styrofoam cup in his hand. "It's a state park," the guy with the cigarette said. "The trails need to be marked better, and if they're not, we're going to be out there hauling more dead bodies to the morgue."

"They don't want to disturb the island's natural beauty by posting signs."

"Hey, I'm grateful for the work, but my overtime will kill them."

I spied a car with a roof light turning into the drive and popped up to get a better look.

"Kevin!" A woman in blue scrubs hurried out of the building to join the two paramedics. "What's this I hear about you taking a hike today? I've been telling you to do that for years."

The guy with the cigarette gave the woman a quick hug before tossing his stub to the ground and crushing it under his foot. "Must be a full moon. There are way too many weird things happening today. Did you hear about the copter crash on Na Pali? One fatality there. We're heading out to the airport right now for pickup and transport."

My ears perked up. They were talking about Carl. Oh, God.

"What about the one you just brought in?"

The car with the roof light drew close enough for me to read the writing on the plastic. KAUAI CAB. Yes! My taxi!

"DB on the trail in the state park."

"Accident?" asked the nurse.

I frantically flagged the cab down. I checked my watch. Thirty-five minutes and counting.

"Not likely," Kevin responded. "Head bashed in. No ID. What does that sound like to you?"

"The Tourism Board will be doing some fast talking about this one," the paramedic with the styrofoam cup chimed in. "Nothing stems the flow of tourist dollars like a violent death on a hiking trail."

I shivered at their conversation, suddenly glad to be leaving the "garden island."

"You my fare to Nawiliwili?" the cabbie asked, through his open window.

I nodded. "I have less than thirty minutes to catch the boat. Can you get me there in time?"

He grinned with the cool confidence of a man who lives for speed. "Piece of cake."

As I climbed into the backseat and slammed the door, the nurse's voice drifted toward me. "Did the CSU close the trail?"

"For a while, but it's probably open again by now."

"Which park was it? Polihale?"

"Wailua. The Secret Falls trail."

The Secret Falls trail? A body had been found by the Secret Falls? But . . . but that's where Nana and the gang had been today. Oh, my God! What if the body belonged to someone I knew? What if—

My cabbie peeled away from the curb like a Grand Prix driver on a straightaway; tires screeching, rubber burning. Eh! I toppled onto my side in a tangle of arms and elbows, realizing that the gravitational pull of a nosediving helicopter was small potatoes compared to the g force produced by Hawaiian cab drivers. I forced my head up to read the identification card attached to the dash.

PIERO DONATI.

Donati? I dug my fingers into the back seat, holding on for dear life as we screamed around a corner on two wheels. *Thank you, Jesus!* There was no way I was going to miss the boat with this guy driving.

He wasn't Hawaiian.

He was Italian!

* * *

We roared into the cruise ship terminal with a full six minutes to spare. I tipped the driver handsomely, dashed through the terminal, flashed my ID at the computer security guy, then ran up the central staircase to deck seven. "Nana?" I yelled as I pounded on her cabin door. "Are you in there?"

Five seconds passed.

Ten.

More pounding. "NANA!"

The door opened a crack. Nana poked her eye into the gap and peered out at me like the mythological Cyclops. "You got anyone with you?"

"No, I'm by myself. Are you all right? I just heard about the—"

"You can come in, then." She opened the door another few inches, hauled me into the room, then slammed the door shut. "I woulda answered sooner, dear, but I had to clear me a path." She lowered her voice to a whisper. "We got company."

I looked beyond her and pressed a grateful hand to my chest when I saw who the company was. "Eh! Thank God you're all here! I was so worried!" I paused. "You *are* all here, aren't you?" I squeezed past Nana, maneuvering into the cabin so I could count all their fingers and toes. The Stolees. The Teigs. Lucille. Margi. Bernice. Alice. Tilly. They were bunched shoulder to shoulder on the sofa, on the beds, on the floor. I looked left and right. "Where's Osmond?"

I heard the resounding *whooooosh* of a toilet being flushed.

Okay, everyone present and accounted for.

"He's retaining water," Bernice nodded toward the bathroom, "so he's taking pills to get rid of it. He's become a human fire hydrant."

"Smokey the Bear should hire him to put out forest fires," Alice chimed in.

The bathroom door opened and Osmond appeared, adjusting his hearing aids as he stepped out. He regarded all the faces looking up at him and smiled perceptively. "Powerful suction, hunh? You want me to flush it again?"

"Oh, boy, you guys, I was really sweating it," I confessed as I dropped my shoulder bag to the floor and sank down cross-legged beside it. "Someone discovered a body on the trail to the Secret Falls today, and I was terrified it might be one of you."

"You always think the worst," said Bernice. "You're such an alarmist."

Life teaches us many lessons. One of the important ones it has taught me is never to take offense at anything Bernice Zwerg says.

"Was it a hiking accident?" Tilly asked.

"I overheard a grisly conversation describing the body, so it doesn't sound like an accident. Did any of you see anything? Were you anywhere near the trail when it happened?"

"I'm afraid we're not going to be much help to you, dear," Nana lamented. "We were on a trail, but it wasn't exactly the one to the Secret Falls." Ten sets of eyes telescoped roundly on Bernice.

"What?" she complained. "You didn't have to follow

me. You could have gone the other way. What are you? A bunch of lemmings?"

"We didn't want you to get lost," Grace Stolee rationalized.

"Well, don't go pointing fingers at me," Bernice sniped. "Margi started it."

"I did not!" defended Margi.

"Did so!" said Bernice.

"No, suh."

"Yes, suh."

I looked from one woman to the other, wondering if it was possible for a Norwegian to win a Mexican standoff.

"All right!" Margi gave in. "Maybe I was partially responsible, but . . . I couldn't help it. Once I get started paddling in one direction, it's hard for me to change course."

No doubt about it, Margi had all the makings of a great political leader.

"But you headed down the wrong fork of the river," Dick Teig scoffed. "How come you didn't go the same way we went yesterday?"

"I thought it *was* the same way we went yesterday. It looked the same. Trees. Water. More trees. More water. How can you distinguish one way from another if everything looks alike?"

"Yeah," Dick Stolee agreed. "They could use better landmarks in this place. Signposts. Billboards. A few silos."

I rolled my eyes. "So did you come across anything

on the right fork of the river that you didn't find on the left?"

Grins. Quiet sniggers. "We did find one thing of interest," Tilly said, dipping her head toward the opposite end of the room.

I followed her gaze to find a wooden box the size of a church hymnal sitting on the lighted vanity.

"It's constructed of teak," she continued. "One of the hardest and most durable woods known to man. Polished exterior. No nails. No hinges. No locks. It's the hardwood equivalent of a brick."

I nodded. "You found a wooden brick?"

Tilly smiled. "We found Griffin Ring's treasure."

"YOU WHAT?" I leaped to my feet and stumbled over a host of outstretched legs to reach the vanity. I peered down at the box, awestruck. "This is Griffin Ring's treasure?"

"Tilly thinks so," said Osmond, "but personally, I think it's a doorstop."

It was apple-peel smooth, dark and unblemished, the parallel striations in the wood grain its only decoration. "Can I touch it?" I asked, my hand hovering over the top.

"Go ahead," said Tilly. "Everyone else has."

I lifted the box into my hands and shook it slightly, my eyes widening when something rattled inside. "Oh, my God. There's something in here."

"Automatic eyebrow pencil," said Helen.

"Tylenol gelcaps," guessed Lucille.

"Electronic digital oral thermometer," said Margi.

"Energizer rechargeable batteries," theorized Alice.

Bernice shook her head, smirking. "You people are so out of touch. That thing is two hundred and forty years old. If there's Tylenol in there, no way is it going to be in gelcap form."

I lifted the box above my head, turning it this way and that. "How are you supposed to get into it?"

"It's some kind of puzzle box," Tilly said. "It probably has two pressure points that enable the lid to slide off, but we haven't found them yet. These kinds of boxes have been quite popular throughout the centuries. People have a great fondness for enigmatic household accessories."

I shook it again, trying to imagine what was thunking around inside. Could it be the Ring family heirloom Tilly had talked about? A brooch? An antique weapon? A priceless figurine? "How will you get it open if you can't find the pressure points?"

Tilly nodded toward Nana. "Your grandmother suggested an X-ray."

"And I've offered to take it to the clinic when we get back home and have one of the technicians do it on the QT," Margi said conspiratorially.

I shrugged. "Why wait until then? You could have it x-rayed downstairs in the infirmary."

I saw dubious looks being exchanged. Eyebrows being arched. Nana cleared her throat. "We decided we're not tellin' no one aboard ship about it, dear. It's Tilly's treasure, and we don't want anyone causin' her no fuss. We all took an oath a silence. Even Bernice."

"But we conducted an independent poll and the result was, no one believes her," Osmond said, which prompted every eye in the cabin to rivet on the wiry-haired gossip.

"*What?*" Bernice griped at everyone. "Don't look at me like that! I wouldn't rat out Tilly."

"Would so," said Margi.

"Would not," said Bernice.

"Yes, suh."

"No, suh."

Bernice would probably rat out the pope, but on a more practical level, hadn't we just had this conversation? "So, where did you find the box?" I tossed out.

"We was readin' the squiggles on the map wrong from the beginnin'," Nana explained, as she and everyone else whipped out their own personal copy. "This squiggle here is the fork in the river, not an imitation wave. And all these other little squiggles are a little waterfall, not the big one at the Secret Falls. And the X shows where you gotta stop, not where the treasure is buried. You can't go no farther there 'cause the river narrows down too much and gets too shallow."

"After we reached the impasse and went onshore to eat our box lunches, we found the little waterfall in a lovely glade," Tilly continued. "But we have one of the Dicks to thank for finding the treasure."

Dick Teig shrugged. "It was nothin'."

"Go ahead," Helen urged proudly. "Tell Emily what you did."

He lifted his shoulders again. "I sat down."

Applause. High fives. Laughter.

"On what?" I asked, noting that the teak box wasn't splintered into a bazillion pieces.

"A heap of rocks by the waterfall. It looked pretty stable until I sat myself down, then the whole pile dislodged beneath me."

Hunh. I guess even rock piles had a maximum weight limit. "Is that where you found the box?" I asked. "Under the rocks?"

"Show her, Dick," Grace Stolee instructed her husband.

Dick unwedged himself from his seat on the sofa and handed me his camcorder. "Just press the button there, and it'll play back."

I set the box back down on the vanity, punched the button on the camcorder, and watched the action unfold on the display screen.

Dick Teig, flat on his butt near a little waterfall, a surprised look his face. Laughter in the background.

Dick shaking his fist at the displaced rocks behind him. Growly noises from his throat.

Dick tilting his head as if he's just noticed something of interest in the cavity where the rocks collapsed.

Dick rolling over onto his hands and knees for a better look. More hoots and hollers, with people talking over each other.

The back of Dick's head.

A blank screen.

I waited for the picture to return. And waited. And waited. "There's nothing on the screen," I fussed. "It's gone blank."

"I know what you're looking at," Dick Stolee spoke

up. "It's not blank. That's just a close-up of Dick's head."

I squinted at the image. Oh! I should have been able to figure that out. Duh.

The picture wobbled, followed by a more steady shot. Okay. Here we go. Hands grappling at the rock. Yanking. Wrenching. Grunting. Muted gasps of surprise.

A close-up of the top of an old chest that looked to be the size of a shoe box. "Oh, my. That thing looks like a real antique. What's it made of? Looks like some kind of metal."

"Lead," said Tilly. "The perfect vault for a wooden box. It won't rust. It won't weather. And the lid was sealed so tightly, it didn't allow any moisture into the chamber that might have caused the teak to decay."

I scanned the floor of the cabin. "Did you bring the chest back with you, too?"

"It was much too heavy to transport in our kayaks," said Tilly. "And we weren't at all sure about handling the lead, so we left it there."

I returned my attention to the display screen to view fists beating on the lid. Dueling voices. An angry *Uff da* as someone broke a nail. A Swiss army knife angling into the picture. The lid of the chest being slowly levered off. Oohs. Aahs. An initial shot of the teak box lying within the lead chest. A slow three-sixty of the stunned reactions on everyone's face.

"Balls!" yelled Dick Teig. "Check out the time!"

Gasps. Shouts. Wails.

The floor seemed to tilt as the group struggled to

their collective feet. Bumping. Shoving. Hysterically out of control. "How did that happen?" cried Helen. "It's a quarter past six! We'll never make dinner on time!"

Not only had my group lost all sense of direction, they seemed to have lost all sense of time. Wow. Folks back home were never going to believe this.

They rushed toward the door, jamming up in the tiny entryway like jellybeans escaping a narrow-necked bottle. "My camcorder!" Dick Stolee called back to me, extending his arm through the crowd.

As I attempted to depress the button to stop the replay, I stood motionless for a heartbeat, my eyes glued to the display screen as Bailey Howard's image stared back at me in the final frame. Oh, geesch! How could I have forgotten about Bailey? I was happy to see she was still alive.

The most disturbing and baffling question now was . . . who was dead?

CHAPTER 11

With the elevator being hogged by the dinner crowd, I took the stairs back up to my cabin, my mind churning with unanswered questions.

If Tilly and the gang had found Griffin Ring's treasure, what had Percy and Basil found that needed to be stored in the ship's safe? What had Nils and the boys dug up that Ansgar had taken off with? Did I dare believe anything that Jennifer or Shelly had told me? And what about Bailey? Was she the dedicated grad student she appeared to be, or an ambitious killer with a flair for hip eyewear? The real problem for me was, whose version of the truth was I supposed to believe when everyone seemed to have an ax to grind?

I hit deck ten sucking in air like a Hoover WindTunnel. Inserting my room key into its slot, I realized this was the result when your only cardiovascular activity of the day was a protracted scream in the cockpit of a crashing helicopter. And a protracted scream might not even be classified as cardiovascular. It might be pulmonary.

I pushed open my door, puzzled by an unexpected smell. I sniffed the air suspiciously. *What in the—?* I punched the light switch on the wall, then stood paralyzed as I gazed around the interior of my Royal Family Suite.

Roses. On every surface. In every space. An ocean of color in coral and pink, cream and red, lemon and blush. I looked from arrangement to arrangement, feeling as if I'd either stepped into the Secret Garden, or the Serene Reflections viewing room at Heavenly Host Funeral Home. Sweetheart roses. Long-stemmed roses. Tea roses. Miniature roses. Damask roses. In sprays and bouquets, vases and baskets. On the floor. On the counters. On multitiered pedestals that stretched from one end of the suite to the other. If there were any roses left on the islands of Hawaii, I'd be very surprised.

I inched my way into the room, shifting flower stands here and there to create a path, overwhelmed by the fragrance, the color, the sheer number of arrangements. If these were fruit baskets instead of flowers, we'd be saying good-bye to world hunger. Halfway into the room, I noticed a particularly elegant arrangement set on a high pedestal by the baby grand—a tall glass vase filled with a sweeping bouquet of deep pink roses, baby's breath, and lush greenery . . . with a white envelope taped to the vase.

Handwritten on the front of the envelope was a solitary word that I suspected was *Emily*.

I tiptoed awkwardly through the forest of flowers and ripped the envelope off the vase. I didn't recognize the handwriting on the front, but felt a trill of anticipation as I lifted the flap and removed the card. My hand shook as I read the neatly printed words:

> Will you marry me?

My stomach executed a little somersault. My feet tingled. OH, MY GOD! This was so . . . so unexpected. So romantic! So wonderful!

My gaze dropped to the signature.

There was none.

No signature? I flipped the card over. Still no signature.

Okay, so who had popped the question? Etienne or Duncan?

My stomach roller-coastered to my ankles.

Oh, no. This was terrible.

"I'll have the broiled tenderloin steak," Margı Swanson told Darko half an hour later, "but I want it without the guacamole sauce, the smothered onions, the hearts of palm, or the choron sauce. And I'd like extra bacon bits on my potato, no chives in the sour cream, and butter on the side. And for dessert, I'll have the Grand Marnier cake." She closed her menu, but snapped it open again a moment later. "Or do you think I should order the Rock Cornish game hen? What's a game hen anyway? Is that like a dwarf chicken?"

I'd tackled bovine reproduction in Switzerland and poultry reproduction in Ireland, so I'd let Darko handle this one.

He bowed his head to Margi and smiled. "How would you like your steak?"

Good comeback. I suspected Darko had been asked this question before.

As he finished taking her order, I looked around the empty table, wondering where the rest of our dinner companions were. I'd been twenty-five minutes late for dinner, but I'd still beaten Jonathan, Nils, Gjurd, and Ansgar. Margi had been so happy to see me, she didn't even ask if I'd washed my hands before coming to the table.

Darko appeared at my side, pencil and paper in hand. "Madame?"

"I'll have the chocolate mousse, the parfait Rothschild, the almond kiwi cake, the chocolate eclair, the cherry pie, and the Grand Marnier cake."

He didn't bat an eyelash. "And for your entrée?"

"That is my entrée."

He clicked his heels as if he were wearing a pair of ruby slippers and dashed off to the kitchen.

Margi wagged a finger at me. "If you ignore the food pyramid, you're going to end up looking like the Dicks."

I narrowed my eyes at her. "I'm in the midst of a romantic crisis. The only thing that's going to make me feel better right now is comfort food . . . or hallu-cinogens."

"I had a romantic crisis once," Margi confessed in a wistful tone. "You might find it hard to believe, but back when I was your age, I had two men vying for my hand." She slapped her hand over her heart. "Clyde Converse and Virgil Stump. Clyde pumped gas at the old Sunoco station, and let me tell you, his technique was something to behold. No one pumped gas like Clyde. The way he handled that hose—whip-ping it off the boot, sticking the nozzle in your gas tank door, depressing the trigger . . . It gave me goose bumps." She flattened her hand on my forearm. "And you wouldn't believe what he could do with wind-shield cleaner and a squeegee."

I frowned as I felt a subtle shift in the ship's motion, as if we'd just hit a dip in the road.

"Virgil bagged groceries at the IGA. The fastest bagger ever recorded; Dick Stolee timed him once. And he never so much as cracked an egg. He was the most versatile man, Emily. He could carry on a regular conversation at the same time he was separating your canned goods from your bakery products. That man could walk and chew gum at the same time. Both Virgil and Clyde were such gentlemen, and they never seemed to mind one bit that I was a little overweight. They understood about inner beauty. Clyde buttered a dozen ears of corn for me at the annual Corn Festival, and you know what a messy job that is. Virgil bought me half a pig when the IGA overordered, and he had the bacon cut thick, just like I like it."

She shook her head dreamily. "They were so thoughtful. It was a real dilemma for me. They were both such nice young men. How's a gal supposed to chose between two fellas when they're both wonderful human beings?"

I sat with bated breath. Was Margi about to solve my romantic dilemma with a simple parable from her youth? I stared at her, waiting for an answer.

She dug out her hand sanitizer and began cleansing her hands. "I touched that menu, didn't I? Lord only knows who handled it before me."

I waited for her to finish.

She stashed the sanitizer back into her pocketbook, leaned back in her chair, and smiled casually.

"So who did you chose?" I practically screamed into her face.

"Oh! Neither one, actually. Clyde came down with a bad respiratory infection after he serviced a swine truck and died real unexpectedly." She gave her head a grief-stricken shake. "Prolonged exposure to ammonia fumes. Sad thing is, he might have been okay if the driver had needed half a tank instead of a fill-up."

"And Virgil?" I asked hesitantly.

"Well, the year Windsor City first started its Winter Carnival, the IGA sponsored an ice sculpture contest, only instead of ice, the contestants were supposed to use canned goods. Alice Tjarks won hands down with her version of the KORN radio tower, built exclusively from sixteen-ounce cans of French-cut green beans and one can of chopped pimento. The pimento was supposed to represent the red light at the top of the tower, but a lot of folks thought chile peppers might have been a better choice. Anyway, Virgil got taken out when he was dismantling Lars Bakke's replica of the family grain elevator. Buried under two thousand cans of creamed corn. They tell me he died instantly."

I studied her for a long moment, lost for words. "Oh, my God, Margi. That's so sad. How did you get through it without completely falling apart?"

"Cake and powdered doughnuts. In times of emotional crisis, carbohydrates are a great blessing. And some good came of the whole thing."

I regarded her hopefully. "You met someone else?"

"The Sunoco station went self-serve. And the IGA replaced all their sixteen-ounce cans of creamed corn with ten-and-three-quarter-ounce ones. That in itself probably saved a lot of lives."

That, and the fact that the Winter Carnival had gone the way of Grampa Sippel's old Edsel.

"I hope your romantic crisis turns out better than mine, Emily. But if it doesn't, you come see me. I don't have hallucinogens, but I've got the next best thing." She dipped her head toward mine and said in a guilty whisper, "Little Debbie Hostess Cakes."

"Hi, ladies. I'm sorry I'm late."

We glanced up to find Jonathan circling the table to his chair. "I didn't leave myself enough time to dress. Tomorrow I'll have to start earlier. Have you ordered yet?"

He stood stiffly beside his chair, his head perched

on a cervical collar like a three-minute egg on an egg cup. Both his arms were immobilized in casts and slings, and his oversized Hawaiian shirt hung miserably askew.

I clapped my hands over my mouth, gasping. "Jonathan! Oh, my God! What happened to you? Your arm! You broke your other arm?"

"The ulna." He dropped his gaze toward his left arm. "I'd never heard of an ulna before yesterday. But it's not so bad." He elevated both arms slightly. "I kind of like the symmetry."

Margi flicked her finger toward his waist. "You missed a buttonhole."

"If I stopped to fix it, I never would have gotten here."

"What about your neck?" I asked, wincing at the foam rubber doughnut circling it.

"They think I might have suffered a little whiplash when we got rammed yesterday, but it's not a big deal. On a scale of one to ten, the pain is only a nine, and I hardly know I'm wearing the collar. It's pretty comfortable, actually." With a self-sufficient gesture, he braced his calf against the rear leg of his chair and coaxed it away from the table, his attention focused directly on me. "And speaking of yesterday, I want you to know how grateful I am for what you did for me. If you hadn't muckled onto me when you did, I might—"

The chair tottered sideways and crashed to the floor with a resounding boom. Jonathan cringed at the sound and flashed an apologetic half smile. "I guess I need a little practice moving dining furniture with my leg."

I rushed around the table to set the chair upright, then helped him get seated properly.

"What I was saying about yesterday," he continued, as I returned to my chair, "I would have drowned if you hadn't clamped your hand under my chin and hauled me to safety. I really owe you, Emily."

"It was only four feet to shore," I said in embarrassment. "And you were wearing your lifejacket."

"Don't be fooled by her modesty," Margi admonished. "She specializes in water rescues."

"About your hat," I hedged. "I'm really sorry about—"

"Forget the hat. That stupid hat nearly got both of us killed. I'm better off without it. In fact, when I get back home, I'm going to trash all my Microsoft stuff and buy a Mac . . . once I find a new job, of course. Take *that,* Mr. Bill Gates."

Wow. He actually sounded like a normal person. Was that possible? I slatted my eyes, scrutinizing him. There was something else different about him, too. Aside from the new confidence and determination in his voice, I detected a subtle physical change. Something different in his appear—"You're wearing new glasses!"

Gone were the Coke bottle lenses in the klunky black frames patched together with hunks of duct tape. Tonight he was wearing frameless eyewear in a space age design of platinum and polymer that showcased sleekness and sexy angles. These weren't ordinary correctional lenses. These were the kind of glasses Hollywood trendsetters with twenty-twenty vision bought just to look cool.

He grinned extravagantly and blinked for effect. "Sergio Tacchini. From Lenscrafters designer line. Nice, huh?"

"They're not nice. They're spectacular!" Leave it to the Italians to do for eyewear what Victoria's Secret had done for cleavage. I stared at him, amazed. "And your hair's different! It's ... it's ..."

"Razor cut and streaked with amber highlights. They tell me highlights are the latest thing in men's hair care." His smile dazzled me with its sudden brightness. "I even had a facial."

And maybe had his teeth whitened? I hoped his newfound confidence hadn't gotten the better of him. Facials and teeth-whitening systems were expensive, even for people with full-time jobs. But there was no doubt about it. Jonathan Pond looked and acted like an entirely different person. He should have gotten rammed by a tour barge years ago.

"That's some impressive team of psychiatrists you saw while you were in the hospital," I acknowledged.

Jonathan blinked his eyes in a simulated nod. "They gave me some dynamite advice."

Margi perked up, her curiosity getting the better of her. "Excuse me, but I'm part of the medical community. Would it be too rude of me to ask what kind of advice they gave you? I might be able to pass it on to some psychotic in Windsor City someday."

"Oh, sure. They told me I didn't have to return

my volcanic rock to the actual field where I found it to have the curse lifted. I could return it to any island, so long as it was Hawaiian soil. So I dumped it in the shrubs outside the cruise terminal. What a rush—I could actually feel the curse being lifted! At first I thought it was my jockey shorts riding up, but then I remembered I was wearing boxers. It was surreal. I felt like such a new man when it was over that I decided to have a makeover. What a great day!" He smiled boyishly. "And I know it's only going to get better."

The room seemed to dip again as Darko appeared with a menu for Jonathan. "Wooo." Jonathan sank back into his chair. "Did you feel that?"

"Bad weather ahead," explained Darko. "But we have big stabilizers. Very big. *Pffft*. You will feel nothing."

He snatched more menus off the sideboard and presented them to Nils and Gjurd, who suddenly appeared out of nowhere. Nils nodded politely as he lumbered to his seat. Gjurd sat down without making eye contact. I glanced over my shoulder, then back at the two men.

"No Ansgar this evening?"

Nils peered at me over the top of his menu, his expression guarded. "He will be here. Shortly." But there was enough doubt in his voice to merit a question mark.

"The three of you sure left the Secret Falls in a hurry yesterday," I said conversationally. "You missed all the excitement."

Gjurd looked at Nils. Nils looked at Gjurd. They both looked at me. "What kind of excitement?" Nils asked, distractedly.

"We found Bigfoot," said Margi. "But it wasn't the real one. I think the real one's in Washington or Oregon."

I smiled at the two Vikings. "So what did you guys find? Beer cans? Arrowheads? A few misplaced weapons of mass destruction?"

Nils's bearded face became a blank. "We found nothing." He rapid-fired some Norwegian at Gjurd, who rapid-fired some back. "Gjurd says we found nothing, also."

Oh, right. They were high-fiving each other to celebrate the fact that they'd come up empty. I don't think so.

Darko checked his watch as he hovered over them. "Your other companion," he said to Nils. "He will be joining us this evening? Yes? No?"

Nils cast a long look down the main aisle of the dining room. "Yah, he's aboard the ship. His name was in the computer for reboarding earlier, but we don't know where he is. He's not been back to our cabin."

Gjurd uttered a few incomprehensible sentences, causing Nils to nod agreement. "Gjurd says perhaps Ansgar found a woman and is taking up residence in her cabin instead of ours." The two men elbowed each other conspiratorially. "Ansgar is very pretty so this is entirely possible, yah? It could mean that tonight, he will be ordering room service."

The floor of the dining room suddenly pitched right, eliciting screams, gasps, and a clattering crash of china from the kitchen. Menus jetted off the sideboard and went airborne. Saltshakers and pepper shakers tumbled over. Jonathan turned white. Margi turned green. In the next instant we lurched symmetrically to the left, eliciting more screams, gasps, and a tinkling of shattered glass.

Clinging to the table, I remembered Darko's claim that the ship had big stabilizers. As I watched the water pitcher on a neighboring table skate off the edge and crash to the floor, I found myself making a rash prediction.

They weren't going to be big enough.

CHAPTER 12

The bad thing about having a stateroom full of flowers is that when the ship is bucking forty-foot waves, the flowers end up in a watery heap on the floor.

The great thing about being in the Royal Family Suite is that with a single call, you can summon the concierge, who'll have the whole mess cleaned up while you sip frozen strawberry margaritas in the intimate confines of the Anchor bar.

It was 9:45 P.M. and I had the room all to myself, save for the bartender and a chunky, middle-aged bald guy with a trendy goatee who was obviously as immune to seasickness as I was. He occupied a table at the far end of the bar, chugging one cocktail after another and staring out into the violent blackness beyond the bow, his blaze orange and screaming yellow shirt making me happy that Hawaiian prints had never caught on in the forty-eight contiguous states.

I sat near the entrance, waiting for Duncan to arrive and wondering how I'd react if he admitted to being the secret benefactor who'd upgraded my stateroom, filled it with flowers, and asked me to marry him. I stared into my frothy pink margarita, unsure how many I'd have to knock back before the answer became clear.

Etienne or Duncan? Etienne or Duncan? Old World or modern? Elegant or rugged? Caged or uncaged? Predictable and dependable or wild and untamed?

Nuts.

I took a swig of my margarita. How could I decide? It . . . it was like trying to choose between double chocolate cake or fudge brownies. Impossible! I wasn't even sure how to broach the subject. Should I be direct or subtle? Lay all my cards on the table when he arrived or beat around the bush?

I licked a band of crystallized sugar off my glass, shifting my gaze to the doorway as the ship's photographer rocketed into the room like a seasoned veteran of countless storms at sea. Oh, God. He wasn't going to take pictures, was he?

"How about a smile?" he asked, stopping in front of my table.

I regarded him drolly. "Business a little slow tonight?"

He pressed the shutter, blinding me with his flash. "Yeah, unless I want pictures of guests with their heads down the john. I know my clientele. Those shots don't sell worth beans." He wandered toward the bar, snapped a picture of the only other *Aloha Princess* guest who didn't have his head down a toilet, then propped himself up on a stool at the bar, looking as if he were calling it quits for the night.

I wish he'd call it quits for the rest of the cruise.

As I licked another stripe of sugar off the rim of my glass, the overweight guy with the goatee heaved himself out of his chair and zigzagged across the floor, nodding to me as he staggered past my couch. I smiled in return and toasted him with my margarita. Any landlubber who could avoid slamming into a wall in these conditions deserved to be toasted. As he propelled himself toward the exit, the door swung open and Duncan appeared, lunging for a decorative chrome rail as the floor seesawed dramatically. The bald guy saluted him and charged out of the bar while Duncan anchored himself to the rail, looking like a shipwreck in the offing.

Uh-oh. I was getting a bad feeling about this.

When the floor leveled out a few degrees, Duncan made a mad dash across the floor and slid onto the sofa beside me. "Thanks for . . . meeting me," he choked out, his voice low and raspy.

I eyed him speculatively. "Are you all right? You look a little . . . how should I say this . . . seasick."

He shook his head. "I don't get seasick."

Of course he didn't. That was why his complexion was the color of old pavement.

"I apologize for last night, Em. Balmy English." He leaned back on the sofa, looking glad to be off his feet. "I'm not sure what they put into that vault, but from the way they were acting, I wouldn't be surprised if it turned out to be a transcript of the eighteen deleted minutes from the Nixon tapes. They didn't finish signing documents 'til after midnight. Those two really know how to stifle a guy's love life."

Recalling the hit list on the back of Percy's business card, I wondered if Duncan's love life was the only thing the two Brits had stifled recently. "Duncan, remember when you suggested yesterday that I should do myself a favor and not ask the Brits about their society affiliation? Well, I didn't, but now I wish I had. So, what's the big deal with the Sandwich Island Society?"

He massaged a spot on his forehead as if he were willing away a migraine. "They're zealots. One-issue fanatics. No sense of humor. If you don't share their beliefs, they'd just as soon—"

"Kill you?" I said in a preemptive gasp.

He lowered an eyebrow at me. "They'd just as soon back you into a corner and talk at you until you decide to change your point of view."

"My point of view about what?"

"About Captain James Cook. They blame him for everything from the rise in oil prices to the disappearance of Elvis. They despise him for destroying the culture of the Sandwich Islands and for contaminating every South Sea island he set foot on. They claim he introduced disease and political strife and created social unrest where none existed. They're happy to tell you that because of Captain James

Cook, the Sandwich Islands lost their true identity. According to Percy and Basil, *they* would have done a much better job of preserving the culture."

"Get you something from the bar?" the bartender asked as he approached our table. "Beer nuts? Popcorn?"

Duncan waved him off, looking as if he could easier stick pins in his eyes than entertain any thought of snack food. He backhanded a line of sweat from his upper lip and shifted position on the couch.

"Are you sure you feel okay?" I asked skeptically.

"Maybe I'm a little queasy," he confessed. "Too much Tabasco in my Bloody Mary."

Right. He was a little queasy like some women were a little pregnant. "Duncan, maybe you shouldn't be here tonight. I wouldn't mind taking another rain—"

"So you met Percy and Basil," he cut me off, twining my fingers with his. "What did you think of them? Entertaining, huh?"

I frowned at his question. "Why does the name Broomhead sound familiar to me? I know I've heard it before, but I can't remember in what context. Did he invent something, or sue someone, or get his name in the *Guinness Book of World Records* for some oddball reason?"

Duncan shrugged. "I think Basil is related to some famous Englishman, but don't ask me who. I try not to listen when they start dragging out the family crests. It gets to be so overblown." He drew my hand to his mouth and kissed each of my fingertips, causing darts of electricity to needle my arm. "I'll tell you what, the next time I see him, I'll inquire."

"Would now be too soon?" I checked the time. "It's not too late. He might still be up."

A pause. "Are you serious? Now?"

"If it's not too much trouble."

He fixed me with a puzzled look. "Just so you know, neither Basil nor Percy was at dinner this evening. I suspect that means they may both be incapacitated, in which case, I'm not going to make the mistake of disturbing them."

Incapacitated . . . or gone? Now there was an intriguing concept. Had they gotten out of Dodge before anyone could shake them down about Professor Smoker's death? Could they have missed dinner not because of illness but because they were no longer aboard the ship? Euw, boy. "Were you on the same excursion as Percy and Basil today?"

He shook his head. "I haven't seen them since last night. I took a big group to Smith's Tropical Paradise today. I don't know what they did."

Gears started grinding in my head. Could they have gone back to the Secret Falls in search of another windfall? Had they found something again today? Or had something or some*one* found them first?

The dead body on the trail loomed large in my thoughts as we plunged into a trough and bucked out again. I grabbed my margarita and steadied it as the floor slid up and down. Back and forth. Left and right. Twitching my mouth at the annoyance, I stared hard at Duncan. "Okay, here's the thing. What would you say if I told you that Basil Broomhead and Percy Woodruffe-Peacock have created a hit parade of—"

"I'msorryEmily," he choked, clapping his hands over his mouth. As we belly flopped into another trough, Duncan raced across the floor and ripped through the doorway like an Iowa twister, leaving me to stare dumbly after him.

No! He couldn't leave! We hadn't even touched on the important stuff yet. What about my upgrade? My flowers? *My proposal?* I NEEDED TO KNOW! Was it him or Etienne?

Damn. Pouting at my missed opportunity, I raised my glass into the air to signal the bartender for a refill. I should have known better than to insert murder into the conversation.

I'd been way too subtle.

The computer room was tucked away on deck four, opposite the business/copy center and conference rooms. I staggered left and right as I negotiated the corridor, my steps governed by the pitch and yaw of the bucking ship and *not,* I told myself, by the two margaritas I'd polished off in the last half hour. Reaching the computer room entrance, I grabbed the doorframe to steady myself and peeked inside.

It was a small interior room whose banks of overhead lights looked down on four rows of buffet-size tables equipped with the latest flatscreen monitors, split keyboards, and tower CPUs. I suspected that the place was usually busy twenty-four/seven but tonight, it was as dead as the rest of the ship.

Unlatching myself from the door frame, I shuffled off-balance to the nearest workstation and sat down, feeling a little daunted by all the spiffy hardware. Computers weren't my medium. I could turn them on and off, all right. It was the stuff in between the "on and off" that sometimes gave me hives. I did much better with a catalogue and a phone. But this Basil Broomhead thing was driving me nuts, so I was going to get to the bottom of it in the only way I knew how.

I'd Google him.

I swiped my room key through the proper slot, encouraged when I gained instant online access and thrilled when the screen I called up actually appeared. I typed the words "basil broomhead" into the search field, and seven-tenths of a second later saw that my inquiry had produced two hundred and six hits. All right! Now we were getting somewhere.

I scrolled slowly down the page, discovering a Broomhead dance page, a University of Sheffield calendar that included someone named Broomhead, an article from *Horse & Hound* that quoted Basil Appleyard, several genealogical sites for people named Broomhead, a Broomhead Gallery and Museum, various awards and prizes offered by men named Basil, a listing for a block of new flats that had been built in Broomhead Park, but no Basil Broomhead. I clicked on the next page and sighed. Ten down. Only a hundred and ninety-six to go.

Twenty minutes later, having scrutinized all two hundred and six listings and finding diddly-squat, I decided to broaden my search. I typed the word "broomhead" into the search field and two and two-tenth seconds later was looking at a grand total of—

I winced at the number on the screen. Please tell me that wasn't right. Twenty-two thousand eight hundred hits? I'd be there until I was eligible for social security!

I heard a door slam shut in the corridor but ignored it as I tried to figure out how best to attack my problem. I needed help from a computer whiz. Someone with expertise in advanced searching techniques. Someone who could hack and find as easily as I could cut and paste.

There was only one solution.

I needed Nana.

I cocked my head as a muted, rhythmic humming filled the corridor. Photocopier. Geesch, I guess Etienne wasn't the only workaholic. Hard to believe someone would be up at this time of night slaving away in the business center. This was a cruise! Those of us who didn't have our heads stuck down a toilet were supposed to be having fun!

I clicked the "Start" icon to turn off the computer, but paused when another idea hit me. Hmm. Maybe a back door approach would prove more successful. Returning to the Google screen, I typed in the words "Sandwich Island Society," accruing a total of fifty-five hits in five-tenths of a second.

I scrolled down, finding websites that listed officers, purpose, and conference sites, but nowhere on the websites nor on connecting links did I find any information that expanded what Duncan had already told me. Nuts. While I was at it, I typed "World Navigators Club" into the search field and was given the opportunity to explore twelve thousand eighty-seven possible connections.

Right. Like that was going to happen.

I scanned the information on the first page, pausing when I ran across the name *Nils Nilsson*, and a web address with a snippet of text that read, *former president of the World Navigators, arrested on suspicion of assault with intent to . . .*

Eyes glued to the screen, I clicked on the address and zipped through an Associated Press article dated five years ago. *Oh, my God.* According to the article, Nils had been taken into custody for assaulting Dr. Hiram Quilty, a respected Boston College history professor, with a baseball bat. *Euw.* But even though there were witnesses to the assault, the professor refused to press charges, explaining that he never really got a good look at his attacker and was hesitant to trust eyewitness accounts of men who'd been drowning their sorrows over another Red Sox loss in a pub on Boylston Street. Nils was subsequently released and no formal charges were ever filed. The police suspected that Nils's friends might have used strong-arm tactics to influence the professor's decision, but they could never prove the allegation.

I stared wide-eyed at the screen. Nils Nilsson had clobbered a history professor with a baseball bat? His friends might have threatened the man further? Who were the friends? Ansgar and Gjurd? A tingle crawled up my spine. Was it just me, or did I see a pattern linking Nils Nilsson to the foreshortened life expectancy of university history professors? And I bet I knew what kind of history.

I brought up the home page for Boston College and clicked on the faculty/staff directory. *Aha!* Just as I'd suspected. Dr. Hiram Quilty was a professor of world history, the Early Explorers Period, from 1400–1799. And dollars to doughnuts, he pushed the theory that Christopher Columbus had discovered America, and that James Cook had been *the* penultimate explorer ever to sail the seven seas.

I powered down the computer, my heart thumping in my throat. I was paired up for dinner with a man who was not only suspected of assault with intent to kill, but whose favorite hardwood was a baseball bat.

I zigzagged to the door and into the corridor, where the sounds of the photocopier continued to hum. As I passed the glass window that fronted the copy center, I saw a familiar head of blond hair hunched over the copy machine and felt a little embarrassed when Jennifer French gazed up to find me looking at her. I flashed her a smile and gave her a little finger wave.

Not surprisingly, she didn't wave back.

As I headed for the elevator, I wondered what was so important that she'd be copying it close to midnight on a stormy night at sea.

Nana answered her door on my second knock, opening it a crack to peek out. "Emily! Come in. Come in, dear." She threw the door wide. "Isn't this

storm somethin'? I never seen nothin' like it. And
lookit you. You're not even curled up in a ball wishin'
you was dead."

That's what I loved about Nana. No matter the
day, the hour, or the situation, she was always happy
to see me. "I'm sorry for the surprise visit," I apologized as I crossed the threshold, "but I have a favor to
ask. How would you feel about doing a late-night
computer search? I started the process, but your
advanced search skills are more refined than mine.
I'm looking for information on a name: Basil
Broomhead. I got twenty-two thousand eight hundred hits on the last name, so I need you to whittle it
down to something more manageable. I'm not sure if
Basil Broomhead has any connection to Professor
Smoker, but I kinda think he might, so your search
could really help."

"AAAGHHCKK! AA-AAGHHCKK!"

I stared at the bathroom door, cringing at the
sounds. "Oh, no. Tilly?"

Nana nodded. "She says she done okay in some
typhoon in the South China Sea some years back
when she was escapin' a boatload a pirates, but this
here storm has done her in. You okay, Til?" she asked,
tapping on the door.

The toilet flushed with a wall-vibrating *WHOO-
OOSH*.

Nana nodded with satisfaction. "Yup. She's okay."

"Tilly encountered pirates in the South China
Sea?" I marveled as I seated myself on the sofa. "Real
pirates? I didn't realize pirates were still around."

"Oh, sure. But more typically, they're wearin' business suits and workin' on Wall Street." She sat down on the sofa beside me. "This storm's leveled everyone. You shoulda seen 'em at supper. They was staggerin' back to their cabins even before the entrées showed up. Old folks, young folks. Even Bailey's sick. I seen her earlier in the evenin' when I went to her cabin to give back the tube a sunblock she lent me today, and she looked worse'n Tilly, if that's possible. Kinda like she could be dead by mornin'. They could *all* be dead by mornin'."

"AAAGHHCKK! AAAAAAAGHHCKK!"

Nana shook her head. "This whole thing has got me to thinkin', Emily."

"About what? Not signing up for any more cruises?"

"About the wave machine I was thinkin' to buy for the new Senior Center pool. Maybe I should go with the waterslide instead."

I nodded. "A waterslide would be nice. So you're not sick?" I asked switching gears. "Not even a twinge?"

"Nope. But between you and me, dear, all this buried treasure business has got me pretty antsy. I could really use somethin' to take the edge off."

Even though I'd only been on the job a year, I was seasoned enough to know that it was a bad sign when the holiday grew so exciting, the guests started having nervous breakdowns. "Do you want me to take you down to the infirmary?" I asked in concern. "I bet the doctor could prescribe a low-dose tranquilizer that might calm you down."

"A pill?" She scrunched her face up like an apple doll. "I don't want no pill. I was thinkin' more like a good stiff Shirley Temple. With extra cherries."

I rolled my eyes.

"Them extra cherries give it a real kick."

"AAAGHHCKK! AAAAAAAGHHCKK!"

I winced at the bathroom wall. "Poor Tilly. Is there anything I can do?"

"Well, if you want me to check out that fella's name on the internet, you could stay here until I get back. I don't wanna go off and leave Til by herself."

"Deal." I gave her a high five. "Basil Broomhead. See what you can dig up."

She bustled around the cabin, changing into her sneakers and grabbing hold of her pocketbook. "What have I forgotten?" she asked rhetorically as she stood in the middle of the room.

I reached into my shoulder bag, pulled out my wallet, and handed Nana a twenty-dollar bill. "Buy yourself a couple of Shirley Temples while you're at it."

"You don't need to do that, dear. I'm filthy rich."

I smiled affectionately. "Don't stunt my generosity. Drinks on me. Okay?"

She flashed me a smile as she removed the bill from my hand. "I don't know if the bars handle cash, but I'll try. You're a good girl, Emily. I'm glad your nice young police inspector has woke up enough to realize that. And to do somethin' about it."

"But he *hasn't* done anything about it!" I tossed my head back and dug my fingers into my scalp. "He . . .

he's left me in limbo!" Which was not a preferred destination for any Catholic these days, since its existence had been struck from the books.

Nana speared me with a quizzical look. "Wasn't it him what got you upgraded to that nice Royal Family Suite with balcony?"

"I'm not sure now! It could be him. It could be Duncan. And no one has said anything about the roses."

"What roses?"

"Don't ask. It's too frustrating to even talk about. Etienne hasn't returned my phone call. Duncan's seasick. I don't know what to do! How can I choose between them? I'm so confused."

"Maraschino cherries," Nana said with quiet authority.

"Excuse me?"

With a little spring in her step, she came to sit beside me. "Back when I was a girl, my pa hired a couple a young men to help out on the farm during the summer. Real nice fellas. Good-lookin'. Hardworkin'. Polite. And not to toot my own horn or nothin', but they was both a little sweet on me."

I inhaled a patient breath. "Is this a parable?"

She fluttered her hand to quiet me. "Anyway, my ma used to make the best homemade ice cream, so for dessert at our noon meal, she'd serve us all ice-cream sundaes with nuts, chocolate sauce, and one maraschino cherry to top it off. Them cherries was a real delicacy back in them days. And we all liked 'em so much, we'd save 'em to eat last. Yup, them cherries made it reeeeal easy to know which one a them fellas deserved a second look."

I bowed my head with trepidation. "Please don't tell me that one of them choked on a pit and died . . . which narrowed the field to one."

"Maraschino cherries don't got pits."

Right. I knew that. "Okay, so how did you know which guy deserved the second look?"

"It was real simple, dear. The one what sat to my right used to steal the cherry from my bowl and pop it in his mouth before I could get to it. The one what sat to my left used to make up for it by givin' me his."

Aw, that was so sweet. "So what happened to the guy who sat on your left?"

"I married 'im."

The floor dipped beneath us, causing my stomach to float up to my throat. "Whoaaa. That was a good one."

"AAAGHHCKK!" echoed from the bathroom.

Nana patted my knee. "I'm outta here. I got work to do." She gave the room a final once-over. "I keep thinkin' I'm forgettin' somethin'."

"Come back if you figure out what." I walked her to the door, my mind still focused on a detail of her story that still bothered me. "Nana, if the guy on your right used to steal the cherry from the bottom of your ice-cream dish every day, how come you didn't just eat the cherry first?"

She stared at me oddly, her eyes glazing over. "You're right, dear. Hunh. I never thought a that."

I returned to the interior of the cabin, watching

the rain that pummeled the porthole for a while, mesmerized by the brute force of the storm. I hoped the glass didn't pop out. That never happened. Did it?

Feeling my mouth go a little dry, I opened the minirefrigerator in search of water and came face-to-face with Griffin Ring's teak box, perched on a shelf between a tube of Fixodent and a bottle of prune juice. I blinked in surprise. Gee. What an odd place to hide a treasure. But when I eyeballed the safe above the refrigerator, I realized the box was too large to stow there, so the refrigerator was actually a brilliant place to hide it. Hmm. Had the girls found the correct pressure points to open it yet?

Sliding the box off the shelf, I walked to the sofa and sat down, cradling it in my hands. I shook it gently, listening to the mystery object rattle inside and wishing that I'd been born on the planet Krypton so I'd have X-ray vision. I slid my palm across the top and fingered the sharp-angled corners, but it remained as much a brick as it had earlier. I rattled it again. What in the world was in there?

Tap tap tap.

I sidled a look in the direction of the door. "Did you remember what you forgot?" I called out. Placing the box on the sofa cushion, I heaved myself to my feet.

"AAAGHHCKK!" Tilly cried as I passed the bathroom. *WHOOOOSH* went the toilet. Yup. Sounded as if she was still doing okay.

I pulled open the cabin door, grinning as I realized

what Nana had probably forgotten. "Let me guess. You forgot your key—"

Pshhhhhhhhhht!

Pain seared my face and eyes, burning like liquid fire. "EHHH!" I screamed, clawing at my eyes. I ground my fists into my eye sockets, blinded. Then I felt the door slam me backward, driving my head into the wall like a well hit racquetball.

My life flashed before my eyes in that instant. The footlights of the Broadway stage. My marriage to Jack. Etienne's kiss in the Hotel Chateau Gutsch. The ghost in Ireland. My hair catching fire in Italy. Duncan's kiss in his little Speedo. And as I slid to the floor, I realized that if I had to live my life over again, there was only one thing I'd do differently.

I would have asked, "Who's there?" before answering the damn door.

CHAPTER 13

"Tilly was here when it happened, but she was mannin' the bathroom, so she didn't see nothin'."

Nana's voice floated toward me, distant and muffled, as if engulfed by fog.

"My granddaughter was collapsed on the floor when I come back. And the way she fell, she was blockin' the bathroom door, so I had to roll her over so's I could get Tilly out. You s'pose she got thrown against the wall and hit her head when the ship went off kilter? It couldn't a happened no more than fifteen minutes ago, but it scared me when I seen her passed out like that."

As I drifted slowly back to consciousness, instinct told me that I was flat on my back, on a surface that was softer than a floor. It also told me that I was better off unconscious, because the moment full awareness hit, so did the blistering pain. Air seethed through my teeth as I sucked down oxygen. "My eyes!" I fisted my hands against my eyelids, trying to scrub the sting away.

"Don't rub," a man instructed, tugging on my arm. "If you're experiencing eye irritation, rubbing will only make it worse."

"I can't help it!" I flapped my elbow to shoo him away and continued grinding my fists into my eyes, discovering only too late that constant rubbing made the pain worse. "Someone sprayed something into my face. It burns!" I heard heavy footsteps cross the floor, a rush of water in the bathroom sink, and the man's voice again, back at my side.

"Try this." He teased a wet cloth under my fingers. "Hold it against your eyes instead of rubbing."

The cloth momentarily eased the acid sting on my face and cooled the burn on my eyelids. I let out a relieved breath. "Bless you. That feels so much better."

"Can you tell me how you ended up on the floor?" the man asked. "I'm Dave Israelstam, by the way. Ship's doctor."

The incident replayed on the backs of my eyelids like a 3-D flick at an IMAX theater. "Someone knocked on the door. I answered it. I heard a hissing sound, and the next thing I know, my eyes are swimming in jalapeño pepper juice and the door slams me into the wall. That's the last thing I remember, other than wishing I hadn't opened the door."

"So you suffered a blow to your head. That gives me something to work with." He cupped my head in his hands, probing the back of my skull with his fingertips. "Oh, yeah. Big knot back there. You'll want to ice that."

"I already have peas," I said helpfully. The edge of the bed sank low as he sat down beside me.

"Can you tell me your name?"

"Didn't Nana tell you?"

"She did. But I'd like to hear it from you."

I would have executed a major eye roll if my eyes had been able to do anything but water. "Emily Andrew."

"Do you know what month it is?"

"I hope it's October, because tomorrow night is Halloween and I've rented a really spectacular costume."

"Isn't that costume shop somethin'?" Nana piped up. "Who are you goin' as, dear? Tilly thought I'd make a good Marilyn Monroe, but I can't see it. I think to be really convincin', I'd need to be a lot taller."

"Where *is* Tilly?" I asked.

"Over here." Her voice was a sandpaper scratch wrapped in misery. "Wishing I'd never escaped those gators on the Limpopo. Being eaten alive would have been a so much kinder way to die."

"Can you tell me how old you are, Emily?" Dr. Israelstam continued.

I sighed dejectedly. "Old enough for people to start calling me ma'am. Do you think you could ask me something a little less personal? Like my social security number? I know it by heart. I could recite it for you."

"Are you experiencing nausea? Headache? Confusion?"

"No nausea. No headache. And the only thing I'm confused about is why anyone would do something like this."

"You s'pose it was a Halloween prank?" Nana questioned.

Dr. Israelstam cleared his throat. "It's a possibility. Pepper spray compounds are sold virtually everywhere these days. And if you live in a state where they're illegal, you can order them online. I'll give security a heads-up. They have zero tolerance for antics like this. It's not the kind of experience we want to provide for our cruise guests."

I flipped the cloth over on my face, my heart slowing as I pondered a sudden, terrifying thought. "I'm . . . I'm not blind, am I?" I'd won accolades for playing Helen Keller back in high school, but felt totally ill equipped to handle the real thing.

"Pepper sprays burn like the devil, but they don't usually result in corneal damage. I'd like to check your pupils, though. Can you open your eyes for me?"

Could I? I slid the cloth off my face and tried to unglue my eyes, but they stung too badly to open even a sliver. "I can't do it. They really smart." I made a blindfold of the cloth again and pressed it to my eye sockets. The bed bounced slightly as Dr. Israelstam stood back up.

"Okay, Emily. Here's the plan. I'm going to take you down to the infirmary. We'll wash your eyes out, then I'll run a few neurological tests."

"Neurological tests? But . . . I don't need any tests. I'm fine!"

"Anything here you need to take with you?"

"Her shoulder bag," Nana piped up. "Right there at the foot a the bed."

"Really, Dr. Israelstam," I said, stalling. "I'd tap dance for you if I could see the floor. There's nothing wrong with my brain. You need proof? Listen to this. I can recite the alphabet backwards."

"Up you go." He circled his hand around my elbow, coaxing me to a sitting position.

"Z—Y—X—W—V—U—"

"Chances are, your injury is probably benign—" He eased me to my feet, steadying me with a firm hand.

"I can recite all the former presidents of the United States in order. Washington, Adams, Jefferson, Madison—"

"—but any head trauma that produces unconsciousness can be potentially serious."

"—Monroe, Adams, Jack—" I stopped midname. "How serious?"

"You could be looking at stroke. Brain hemorrhage. Coma. Death."

Death? Yeah, death was pretty serious.

"It's your call, Emily, but if I were in your shoes, I'd want to play it safe."

I exhaled a frustrated sigh, fumbling to keep the compress over my eyes. "But you don't understand. I've been upgraded to the Royal Family Suite with balcony. Do you know what that means?"

"I'll have someone from my staff call your cabin and inform your other family members where you'll be."

"No, no. It means concierge service! You can't ask me to relocate. Please. This is the best room I've ever had in my life. Do you understand? My life!"

"You'll like our rooms, too," Dr. Israelstam assured me as he guided me across the floor. "How do you feel about cozy?"

In an effort to ward off stroke, brain hemorrhage, coma, and death, the infirmary staff took my vital signs, tested my reflexes, and flashed annoying lights in my eyes at frequent intervals. Like . . . every time I was about to doze off.

"Do you know what your name is?"

I cracked a bleary, sleep-deprived eye at the nurse. "What time is it?"

"It's 2:00 A.M."

"Why do you keep asking me what my name is?" I dashed tears from my eyes and tented my hands over my mouth as I yawned. "Look, I don't normally do name tags, but if you'll let me sleep, I'll make an exception. You can slap it right on my forehead. I don't care. Just stop waking me up."

"It's on your chart: neurological checks every fifteen minutes. No sleep for you tonight, Miss Andrew. We don't want you to lapse into a coma. Can you squeeze my hands?"

I'd rather have squeezed her throat, but I couldn't say that out loud, especially when she was making such a dogged effort to keep me from turning into a hundred-and-twelve-pound brussels sprout.

"So far, so good," the nurse said after she'd completed her checks. "You can go to sleep now."

"I can? But you just said—"

"For a half hour. You're doing so well, I can start thirty-minute checks."

Oh, goody. That would give me just enough time to doze off before she woke me up again. Settling back into my pillow, I pulled the sheet up to my chin and stared up at the ceiling, thankful that at least I could open my eyes again. They still smarted a little, but the horrible burning sensation was gone.

Had Nana been right? Was this a random Halloween prank? Or had someone found out her cabin number and knocked on her door with the intent of causing injury?

But . . . who would want to hurt Nana? For what reason? Who was even *well* enough tonight to be roaming the decks? I knew firsthand that all the usual watering holes aboard ship were deserted. The only people I'd seen who were still ambulatory were the photographer, the fat guy in the bar, the bartender, and—

An image of a photocopy machine flickered in my mind.

And Jen.

I frowned up at the ceiling, wondering if that was somehow significant. She'd seen me in the corridor outside the business center. Could she have followed me up to deck seven thinking I was going to my own cabin? Could she have wanted to teach me a lesson for sticking my nose where she thought it didn't belong? Did she live in a state where it was legal to carry pepper spray?

I tossed the theory around in my head, realizing that if I was right, I could conclude that I'd been the intended target, not Nana. That made me breathe a little easier. But the pepper spray factor still bothered me. I could understand mailmen carrying it to deter vicious dogs, but why would Jen need it on a Hawaiian cruise? Did she mean to fend off potential muggers in the spa? Get rid of admirers at the pool?

I forced my eyes open, trying to stay awake. Cruises had a reputation for being incredibly safe. Why had she armed herself? To protect herself against what? If you asked me, Jennifer French could probably take on a company of Marines and come out the victor—a thought that caused me to shift my thinking around to a new angle.

What if she was carrying pepper spray not as a defensive weapon, but as an offensive one? What if she'd brought it to use on Professor Smoker if he refused to meet her demands about trying to reverse the honor board decision? What if she *had* used it on him . . . to incapacitate him right before she flipped him overboard?

My eyes froze as I relived the moment when Shelly Valentine had flipped Carl Leatherman onto his back. Shelly had taken self-defense courses at college. Had Jennifer done the same thing? Did she possess the same physical capabilities as Shelly? Might they even have been in the same class?

I noted the time on the wall clock, worried my lip in indecision, then picked up the bedside phone and punched in a number. "If you were asleep, I apologize for waking you," I said when Nana answered.

"Tilly's hurlin' in the bathroom again, dear, so I'm wide-awake. Are you doin' any better?"

"You bet. Nana, when you went down to the computer room, did you hear someone running the photocopier in the business center?"

"Nope. Was I s'posed to?"

"Did you notice if anyone was working in there when you passed by?"

"The place was empty. I know 'cause I looked through the window."

So Jennifer had left by then. Did that mean she'd finished up her work and gone back to her cabin, or that she'd followed me?

"By the way, dear, I never got to tell you earlier, but I done your computer search and I didn't come up with nothin'. It took me a while, too. About ten minutes."

"You searched twenty-two thousand eight hundred references to Broomhead in ten minutes?"

"What can I say? Response time was a little slow tonight. Anything else you want me to search for tomorrow? I already got a request from Tilly. She wants me to pull up some information on eighteenth-century puzzle boxes so's maybe we can figure out how to open—"

Puzzle box? My heart thudded to a stop. "Oh, my God! The puzzle box! It didn't fall onto the floor and break, did it?"

"It can't break, dear." She lowered her voice to a whisper. "It's in the refrigerator."

"No, it's not. I found it when I was looking for bottled water, and . . . and I took it out. I left it on the sofa when I answered the door." I hesitated nervously. "It's still there . . . isn't it?"

"Hold on." I heard feet shuffling away, then back. She picked the receiver up again. "It mighta been there when you answered the door, dear, but it's not there now."

"It's gone?" I said in a small, guilt-ridden voice.

"The only thing on the sofa is the cushions, and a few cracker crumbs, on account a I'm force-feedin' saltines to Tilly when she's not in the bathroom."

Damn! Damn, damn, damn! Why hadn't I made the connection sooner? Jennifer French hadn't been after Nana *or* me.

She'd been after the treasure.

Twelve hours after being admitted to the infirmary, I was released with a clean bill of health and bags under my eyes that rivaled twenty-five-pound sacks of flour. The rain had stopped, but the seas were still heavy enough to confine guests to their cabins, which was a blessing in disguise, because when I arrived at the Picture Gallery on deck five, I didn't have to fight the crowd. Unlike the other night, I had the whole place to myself.

I wasn't sure what I was hoping to find, but as I located the section entitled DAY THREE—KAUAI, I had a gut feeling that if I looked closely enough, something would leap out at me. The ship's photographer had been so relentless in his pursuit of the perfect Kodak moment that I expected to find some surprises amid the hundreds of photos posted in the display cases. Yet, as I eyeballed the array of glossy prints, I hoped my goal wasn't too ambitious. Geesch. Talk about looking for a needle in a haystack. But I considered it my duty, since I was the one who'd dragged the puzzle box out of its hiding place. I felt it was up to me to track it down and get it back.

I searched scads of happy faces leaving the ship for the morning excursions, and a few faces that didn't look so happy. Bailey was posed against the "Welcome to Kauai" panel all by herself, her mouth zipper straight, her eyes anxious. No surprise there. I found all of my group in sequential photos, wearing their standard seed corn hats, wind suits, and leis. *Leis?* No one gave *me* a lei. Shoot. Maybe they'd run out by the time I disembarked.

I found Duncan and reminded myself to call him when I got back to my cabin to see how he was feeling. Scanning some more, I discovered Gjurd in a solo shot without Nils or Ansgar, and Shelly looking good enough to be on the cover of *Sports Illustrated*. She wasn't wearing a lei either, which confirmed my suspicion that the supply had run out by the time I'd left for my helicopter tour.

I spotted Percy and Basil looking goofily English in

a picture high above my head and wondered where they'd gone yesterday. They were both wearing leis, so they must have left fairly early—though according to Duncan, not with his tour group. Had they gone off on their own to participate in some nefarious Sandwich Island Society activity?

I whipped through photo after photo, finding no surprises—until I reached the middle of the second display case, where I found a glossy shot of Jennifer French standing in front of the Kauai panel, her tattoo exposed, her hair a riot of straw, her expression cool and smug. I arched an eyebrow at the photo. Hadn't Shelly told me that Jen had planned an all-day spa treatment on the ship yesterday? Obviously, she hadn't spent the entire day in the spa. So where had she gone when she'd disembarked? What had she done? Could her leaving the ship explain how she'd learned that Nana and the gang had unearthed Griffin Ring's treasure?

Shoot. How come I was ending up with more questions than answers? Logically, Bailey could have told Jen about the treasure, but that seemed highly improbable since the two women hated each other so much. So if Bailey hadn't spilled the beans, who had? Bernice?

I sucked on the inside of my cheek. Bernice would normally get my vote, but the gang had threatened her within an inch of her life if she blabbed. Even Bernice wasn't willful enough to misplace all that trust, was she?

I continued with my visual inventory, running into

a slew of recreational photos. An enormous splash frozen in time as someone belly flopped into the pool. Poolside guests sipping frosty beverages. A guy making like Spider-Man as he scaled the climbing wall on the top deck. A quartet of ladies in bowling shirts playing miniature golf. A prostrate body with what looked like cooked spinach slopped all over it.

I eyed it more closely. Hey, that must be the Ionithermie treatment Nana had talked about. I curled my lips in distaste. Euw. If she saw this picture, I bet she wouldn't get anywhere near that treatment room. Spinach gave her gas.

I skimmed over a face painted peacock blue with cucumber slices over its eyes. Two women reading magazines under hair dryer hoods. A stylist wielding a blow-dryer as if it were an unholstered gun. A manicurist sitting at a table opposite—

I zeroed in for a closer look. Huh. It looked as if Shelly had gotten back in time to have her nails done yesterday, because there she was in the nail salon—I shifted my gaze from Shelly to the woman beside her—sitting right next to . . . Jennifer French? Okay, so Jennifer had spent at least part of her day yesterday in the spa. But should I be deducing something from this, other than that archaeologists-in-training probably had to sink a bundle into restorative nail care? Was it possible that Jennifer had learned about the treasure from Shelly? But how could Shelly have found out what had happened on the Wailua River kayak adventure, when she'd spent the day with me? Unless . . .

Unless Shelly and Bailey had run into each other on the ship before Shelly's nail appointment. Shelly and Bailey were on speaking terms, weren't they? That could explain it. Bailey had told Shelly, who repeated the story to Jennifer. And the rest, as they say, was history.

I dusted my hands off with satisfaction. Damn, I was good. Now all I had to do was catch Jennifer red-handed with the puzzle box and force her to admit she was the one who killed Professor Smoker.

Unfortunately, this was the part that always gave me a *teensie* bit of trouble.

Feeling confident about my theory, though, I returned to the DAY ONE—AT SEA and DAY TWO—WEL-COME TO KAUAI displays and briefly reexamined the photos I'd seen two nights ago. No new detail grabbed me by the throat. The same guests boarded the ship. The same people posed for predinner pho-tos. The same faces showed up for their prepaid excursions. I recognized the cell phone guy in the muscle shirt without effort. The honeymoon couple with the matching T-shirts. Percy Woodruffe-Peacock in his kayaking shorts and bow tie, and Basil Broomhead in his plaid knickers and slouch cap, just like that famous golfer used to wear. What was his name? I snapped my fingers to trigger my memory. Something like—

Wait a minute. I lasered a look at Basil's knickers again. Oh, my God! That was it! Golf! That's why Basil Broomhead's name was familiar to me! I'd seen it written down on the sign-up sheet for the golf simulators, directly above the name Dorian Smoker! Eh! Had the two men accidentally run into each other that first day near the simulators? Had Basil seized the opportunity to eliminate the first name from the Sandwich Island Society's hit list?

Oh, my God! Had I just blown my Jennifer French theory to hell? Was it Basil, not Jennifer, who'd killed Professor Smoker? And if Basil had done the killing, had he also stolen the treasure? But why would he want Tilly's treasure if he already had one? WHY WAS THIS SO FREAKING COMPLICATED?

Frustrated and confused, I circled around the display case, stopping dead in my tracks when I ran into Nils Nilsson on the other side, standing before a column of photos. Oh goody, just my luck. I was alone in a room with Nils Nilsson, of felonious-assault-with-baseball-bat fame. I wondered if he'd notice if I shuffled quietly backward and started running.

"Do you know how one goes about purchasing these photographs?" he asked without removing his gaze from the display case.

Since I was the only other person in the room, I guessed he was directing that question at me. "Uhh— You see those numbers in the bottom right-hand corner of each photograph? I think if you give that number to someone in the general store, they'll have copies made for you."

He nodded his thanks before slipping back into statue mode. I slatted my eyes at him. There was definitely something weird going on here. "Did you find one you like?" I asked, inching closer to see what he was looking at.

He bobbed his head toward the case. "The boarding photo. You think it's a good likeness, yah?"

"I noticed that picture the other night. Yeah, it's a great shot. You guys are really photogenic."

"It's especially good of Ansgar's hair. I think his family will like it."

"Yup. He has one great head of hair. Soooo . . ." I said, angling to snare more information, "did he ever show up last night?"

"Yah." He turned his head, looking down at me with dull eyes. "But not aboard ship. He showed up on the hiking trail to the Secret Falls with his head caved in. Ansgar is dead."

Oh, my God. The dead body the paramedics had been discussing at the hospital had been Ansgar? A lump the size of Delaware caught in my throat. "Nils, I'm so sorry."

He nodded. "There was much competition between Ansgar and me. There has always been great rivalry between Nilssons and Norstedts. But I would not have chosen to beat him in this way."

I hoped his use of the word "beat" was a linguistic faux pas and not a subliminal reference to anything more deadly.

"His identification was missing," Nils continued, "so it took the authorities many hours to notify his family. Gjurd and I will leave the ship once we reach Kona, so we can fly back to Kauai and accompany his body home."

"You're going to finish the cruise? You're not going to fly back to Kauai right away?"

"The authorities tell me they cannot release Ansgar's body for many days yet. Not until their investigation is complete. Gjurd and I feel that Ansgar would want us to finish the cruise, despite the misfortune that has befallen him."

"But . . . are you sure it's Ansgar? If his identification was missing, how—"

Nils slapped the tattoo on his upper right arm. "His name was here. Like mine. *Ansgar Norstedt. World Navigators Club.* This was how the authorities traced him."

"But . . . you said last night that his name was listed in the computer as having reboarded the ship."

He gave his beard a thoughtful scratch. "I was wrong."

A frisson of unease snaked up my spine. Okay, so if Ansgar hadn't reboarded the ship, who had?

CHAPTER 14

By three o'clock, the heavy sea had lost its fizzle, going flat as old ginger ale. By four o'clock, guests began crawling out of their cabins, looking anxious to make up for lost time. By five, I'd checked in with each member of my Iowa contingent, and by six, all eleven of them were gathered in my Royal Family Suite, listening to the sordid details of what they'd missed in the last twenty-two hours.

"I contacted the head of security this morning about the puzzle box's disappearance," Tilly informed us, "but it was a rather disappointing conversation. He wanted to know if there was anything of value inside the box, and when I said I didn't know if the contents were valuable or not, he sighed condescendingly and instructed me to reexamine my cabin. He suggested I may have forgotten where I stowed the box and might actually have hidden it on myself, as so often happens with cruise guests, and I quote, 'of a certain age.'"

Boos from the room at large. Hissing from the Dicks. "So'd you set that fella straight?" Osmond called out.

Tilly smiled archly. "I certainly did. I thanked him for his time, told him to have a nice day, and hung up the phone."

A thunder of applause. Hoots. Hollers.

Yup. Midwesterners could deliver tongue-lashings that were second to none.

Tilly motioned for quiet. "Since it's obvious we'll receive no help from ship's security, we're left with only one recourse. We'll have to band together and find it ourselves."

"Woo! Woo! Woo!" yelled the Dicks, pumping their fists in the air. Head bobbing from the women. Margi leapt to her feet and did the jump-around, knocking Osmond off his chair with an errant hip. Bernice raised her hand.

"How come Emily gets the penthouse suite when the rest of us are booked into kennels? Does the bank know about this?"

"Emily thinks her sweetheart paid for the upgrade," Nana defended. "Isn't that romantic?"

Bernice crossed her arms defiantly. "Sure he did. If you ask me, something smells funny."

"No one *did* ask you," Osmond countered as he struggled back into his chair. "So there."

"Don't pick on Bernice," Lucille Rassmuson scolded. "I smell something, too. Florally. Smells like"— she sniffed the air—"a funeral parlor."

I crooked my mouth into a smile. "I had a few flowers in here earlier, but they, uh, they didn't survive the storm."

"Hey, why am I wet?" Osmond asked as he regarded a dark stain on his pant leg.

Moans all around. "Maybe you should cut back on those diuretics," Dick Stolee teased.

"It's the carpet," I apologized. "It got a teensie bit wet . . . because of the flowers."

A half dozen hands went down to test the floor. "Teensie bit wet?" complained Bernice. "It's soaked!"

"Watch this," Dick Stolee instructed as he popped out of his chair. He bounded across the floor at a dead run, assuming a surfer's stance as he skidded the last ten yards, geysering water in every direction. I looked heavenward and shook my head. Oh, God.

Grace Stolee let out a guttural sound that I suspected her husband had heard many times before. "Would someone *kindly* tell the human squeegee that if he tears his ACL or breaks his hip, I'll be taking the bike ride down Mount Haleakala without him?"

"Si'down, knucklehead," Dick Teig barked out. "You're pissing your wife off."

Tilly grabbed the nonstick fry pan we'd confiscated from the kitchen and gave it a whack with a meat-tenderizing mallet, creating a sound like an out-of-tune Chinese gong. *BOINNNNK!* "Order, people. I'll have order!"

Osmond gave his hearing aids another tap. "Would you give that thing another whack, Til? Seems to help the ringing in my ears."

BOINNNNK! "All right, I'm turning the meeting over to Emily. She's devised a plan, and I think it's a good one. She'll give you the logistics."

"Show of hands." Osmond stood up. "All those in favor of turning the meeting over to Emily?" Ten hands shot into the air. "Opposed?"

Bernice raised her hand. "Doesn't anyone else want to know who Emily's sleeping with to get set up in a room like this?"

"The ayes have it," Osmond announced. "Take it away, Emily."

Tilly thrust the meat tenderizer at me, looking as if she wanted to get rid of it before she was tempted to use it on Bernice. I set it down on the table in front of me and stood up. "Thank you all for coming on such short notice. The thing is, we don't have much time to execute my plan. I'm afraid that once the gangplank goes down in Maui, our thief is going to hightail it off the ship with the puzzle box. So if we don't catch him or her sometime within the next three hours, we may not catch him at all."

"So what's your plan?" Dick Teig called out.

"I have a stack of photos here, and if my instincts are right, one of the people I'm about to show you is responsible for Macing me, stealing the puzzle box, and killing Professor Smoker."

"You think the three incidents are related?" inquired Alice.

"I can't prove it yet, but that's my theory."

Low groans. Head shaking. Raised eyebrows.

"What?" I protested.

"We've heard your theories before," Dick Teig complained.

"Yeah," Lucille Rassmuson agreed. "You're always wrong."

"Well, I'm not wrong this time. I'm positive I'm on the right track."

"That'd be a first," grumbled Bernice.

Okay, so I was fairly confident I was on the right track. Or . . . at least pretty sure.

All right, so it was a shot in the dark. Crime solving was not my chosen career path.

"Ignore all the sourpusses," Margi told me. "We have a few people in the group who are a little cranky because they don't like their Halloween costumes, and they're taking it out on those of us who had the foresight to rent early." She smirked at Bernice and Lucille, who turned in unison to smirk back. "Go ahead, Emily," she encouraged. "Tell us what you've got."

"Okay, I'll explain a little about the person in each photo, then I'll pass the print around the room so you can get a closer look. When I'm done, I'll assign a photo to each of you, and that's the person you'll be responsible for following until we reach Maui."

Helen Teig raised her hand. "You want us to spy on people for the next three hours? But that'll interfere with dinner. When are we supposed to eat?"

Imminent starvation was apparently a huge fear

for women weighing two thousand pounds and over. "There's only one show in town tonight: a huge Halloween buffet in the main dining room, starting at seven. All you can eat, open seating. I assume our suspects will have to eat, so do your best to keep an eye on them while you're making your way through the buffet line. If you're clever, you might even be able to wrangle a seat at the same table with them."

"How are we gonna recognize 'em if they're wearin' masks?" Nana asked.

"I've written names and cabin numbers on the back of their photos. Once you're in costume, casually stake out their rooms to check out what they're wearing, then don't let them out of your sight."

"What are we supposed to be looking for?" Dick Teig piped up. "You think someone's gonna be dumb enough to be carrying that box around with them?"

"I don't know," I admitted. "But if any of them do anything to give themselves away, we need to be there to catch them. Okay, suspect number one." I held up the first photo. "Jennifer French. Some of you might remember her as the foul-tempered blonde from the Secret Falls. She had a grudge against Professor Smoker and was in a good position to steal the box last night. If she heads for the disembarkation deck when we reach Maui, do whatever you have to do, but don't let her off the ship."

I handed the photo to Tilly and held up the next one. "Nils Nilsson. Member of the World Navigators Club, with a criminal history that includes assault against a university history professor. He apparently isn't fond of anyone who promotes explorers of non-Scandinavian descent. I think this guy could be a very bad dude."

Helen Teig shot out of her chair and snatched the photo from my hand. "Say, this is the fella that gave me a whole bag of Skittles clear out of the blue on the first day of the cruise. Why'd he do that? How'd he know I like Skittles? You think he might have been stalking me?" She held the picture up to the light, an appreciative smile teasing her lips. "He's a big one, isn't he?" A little twinkle lit her eyes. "You don't need to hand this one around, Emily. I'll take him."

"Down in front!" Bernice sniped. "The rest of us can't see!"

"This is Nils's sidekick," I said, holding up a predinner photo of my next suspect. "His name is Gjurd. I don't know anything about him other than if he hangs around with Nils, he's probably in cahoots with him. He might be his strong-arm man or something."

"What about the young fella with the pretty hair?" Margi questioned.

I held my breath for a moment before exhaling. "Ansgar. Right. Um, Ansgar was involved in that bad mishap on the Secret Falls hiking trail yesterday, and . . . and I'm afraid he didn't survive his injuries."

Margi's face turned Clorox white. "That nice young fella is dead? The one who ate dinner with us? Oh, my goodness. And to think I'd been mustering my courage to ask him a very personal question. In

English, of course. I don't speak Norwegian, except for a few cusswords."

"What were you fishing for?" crowed Bernice. "His phone number?"

"The name of his shampoo. You don't get body like that using ordinary over-the-counter hair products." She sighed dismally before looking up at me. "Two people dead in four days, Emily? That's not a normal death rate for holiday travel, is it?"

"Four's about normal," Nana said helpfully. "That's what we averaged in Italy."

"I told you that trail needed more signs," Dick Teig proclaimed. "That fella probably got lost on the same trail we did and broke his neck falling down that damned embankment."

"His neck wasn't the problem," I hedged. "It was his skull. Someone apparently altered the shape of it with a lethal blow then made off with all his identification."

Gasps. Whispers. Tooth sucking.

"So he was murdered," Tilly declared, her voice vibrating with uncharacteristic anxiety. "Perhaps by the same person who killed the professor?"

I nodded. "That's my guess."

"Which means our miscreant has struck not once, but twice?" She shook her head. "I don't like those statistics. Go on with your talk, Emily." She bowed her head in my direction, and whispered behind her hand, "And you might want to hurry."

"Basil Broomhead." I held his photo up like a cue card. "He may have been the last person to see

Professor Smoker alive." I flashed the next picture. "Percy Woodruffe-Peacock. The flip side of Percy's business card is annotated with two names: Professor Dorian Smoker and Bailey Howard. I think these annotations comprise an actual hit list. Suspect number six: Shelly Valentine."

The two Dicks elbowed each other as I displayed a DAY ONE photo of Shelly in her hot pink halter top and cheek-hugging short shorts. "Shelly may have nothing to do with any of this, but she was sleeping with Professor Smoker, so in my book that earns her billing with everyone else."

Dick Stolee rocketed his hand into the air, his tongue hanging down to his belt buckle. "I'll take that one, Emily."

Grace thwacked him on the arm. "In your dreams."

"My last photo is Bailey Howard, and you know what she looks like because you were with her all day yesterday. But I'm adding her to our picture gallery because rumor has it that her academic career could actually be furthered by Professor Smoker's death."

Margi executed a little finger wave to draw my attention. "I don't mean to sound dumb, Emily, but how would Bailey have found time to kill Ansgar if she was with us all day yesterday?"

"An excellent question. And the answer is—" I let out a ragged breath. "I don't have a clue. We have a lot of puzzle pieces that don't fit yet."

"Bailey knew we found the treasure," Bernice blurted out. "I betcha she's the one who stole it."

"She was seasick along with everyone else last

night, so that's a stretch," I allowed. "But she might have mentioned it to one of the other suspects. Or better yet"—I fisted my hands on the table and directed a long, pointed look at Bernice—"someone *else* in our group might have had loose lips and told a whole *slew* of people."

Ten heads snapped around to stare at Bernice, who shifted nervously in her chair before sticking her chin out in self-defense. "Why are you looking at me? I took your stupid oath of silence! Do I look like the kind of person who'd blow off an oath?"

"We didn't make you swear on a Bible," Lucille accused. "Maybe you took advantage of the loophole."

Osmond jumped to his feet. "Show of hands. How many think Bernice blabbed?"

Ten hands darted into the air.

"Majority rules. You blabbed."

"If I blabbed, may God send the upper deck crashing down onto my head this very second!"

Screams. Shouts. Everyone doubled over, flinging their arms over their heads to protect against concussion, cranial trauma, and all other forms of divine retribution.

I ducked down and cringed at the ceiling, relieved when the overhead panels didn't rain down on the baby grand. Five seconds passed. Ten.

Osmond poked his head out from beneath his arms to give the ceiling a distrustful look. "Damn. She might be telling the truth."

I marked the hour on my watch. "Come on, you

guys. We don't have much time left. Let's go over this again so I know we're on the same page. When I cut you loose, what are you going to do?"

"Get into our costumes," said Alice.

"Loiter casually in the corridors so's we know what our suspects are wearin' to the Halloween bash," added Nana.

"Eat," bellowed Helen.

I nodded approval. "And what's the most important thing you're going to do tonight?"

"Eat," repeated Helen.

I gave her a withering look.

"I'm going to hand out condoms," said Margi. "It's not a widely known fact, but posing in a costume can sometimes alter a person's psyche. The subject begins to assume the qualities of the person he or she is playing and can even start exhibiting the same behavior, which often causes increased hormonal activity that can trigger episodes of uncontrollable sexual arousal. It's a real problem."

Nana raised her hand politely. "I'm sorry. How's that a problem?"

Oh, God. "Okay, just to refresh your memories. Bailey is the only person among our suspects who's scheduled to disembark in Maui, so if you see anyone *other* than her leaving, jump on them. Got it? That's your primary mission this evening. I'll be in a conspicuous place in the dining room, so please check in with me every so often to let me know how you're doing. Any questions?"

When no hands went up, I nodded with satisfaction. "All righty, let's get those photographs divided up."

A minor skirmish erupted between the Dicks over who'd be assigned to Shelly Valentine, so I resolved the problem with King-Solomon-like wisdom by handing her over to Bernice.

"Thanks a bunch, Emily," Dick Teig griped as I escorted him to the door. "I'll be burning up with sexual passion, and who will I get to ogle?" He slapped the front of his assigned photo. "Some English wacko in short pants and a bow tie. I'll remember that when it comes time for your evaluation."

After I'd shown the last person out, I scooted back to the desk in the living room and read the items that remained on my list. I'd already crossed out BUY PHOTOS FROM PHOTO GALLERY and HAVE CONCIERGE PROVIDE SUSPECTS' CABIN NUMBERS. I drew a line through ASSIGN PHOTOS TO GROUP, then stabbed the next item with the point of my pen. CALL ETIENNE.

Feeling equal parts anticipation and dread, I punched up his number

"This is Miceli," he said in his steamy baritone. "Please leave a short message. I'll get back—"

I slammed the phone down, unwelcome tears blurring my eyes. He wanted to make amends? He wanted to make it up to me? Sure he did. That's why he was falling all over himself to answer the message I'd left on his machine two freaking days ago!

I swiped moisture from my cheeks with an angry

hand and scratched his name off my list. "Take that, Etienne Miceli," I sniffled, disguising my hurt as anger. But, hey, it was Halloween. Everything was parading around in costume. Even my emotions.

Proceeding to the last item on my list, I dried my eyes and punched up another number on the phone. "Are you through not being seasick?" I teased when Duncan answered.

"Completely." He lowered his voice seductively. "Are you through not pining over your no-account Swiss police inspector?"

Was I? Damn. It was time to stop waffling. I was old enough to be a ma'am, for God's sakes. I had to make a decis—"Yeah," I blurted out before I had a chance to change my mind. "I'm . . . I'm through."

I could hear him smile through the phone. "I could be at your cabin in five minutes."

"I'm scheduled to do the buffet bash with my group, so I'll be tied up for a while."

"No worries, I had plans to do the buffet myself. I'll find you in the dining room."

"I'll be in costume, but without a mask, so you shouldn't have any trouble spying me."

His voice sizzled like a low current through an electrical wire. "With a mask, without a mask. You could be dressed in a soup can and I'd still know it was you."

He said it with so much conviction, I almost believed him.

Relieved not to be dithering anymore, I raced into the bedroom and grabbed my costume from the closet, my heartbeat quickening inexplicably when the phone on the bedside table began ringing. I stared at it in trepidation for a moment before charging around the bed and ripping it off the hook. "Etienne?"

"It's Nana, dear. Since you're the one what's gonna tail that Jennifer, I thought I'd let you know that Tilly and me seen her in the elevator, and she's all dressed up in black rubber."

I tried to visualize that. "What's she supposed to be? A Michelin tire?"

"I think she's s'posed to be Catwoman, on account a she had a tail."

"She's kind of early for the buffet, isn't she?"

"She told someone on the elevator that she was headin' to the rental shop 'cause her zipper got stuck and she wanted 'em to fix it. She was afraid if she fiddled with it, she'd break it, and she didn't wanna get stuck payin' for no damages."

"Catwoman, huh? I owe you one, Nana. Thanks." I could picture Jennifer French as Catwoman—a self-absorbed, sharp-clawed creature with a poorly disguised vicious streak. But I was hoping that unlike your average feline, Jennifer would have a lot fewer than nine lives.

I strutted into the dining room at precisely seven o'clock in my thigh-high boots, French-cut blue satin shorts speckled with white stars, strapless red bustier trimmed in gold, wide metal belt, tasteful gold tiara, bracelets that fit like soda cans, and attitude. My face was painted, rouged, and dusted with shimmering powder. My eyes were lined, smudged, and mascaraed in a deep black. My lips were outlined, stained, and polished with candy apple gloss. As I watched heads turn and jaws drop at my entrance, I realized Margi hadn't been spinning idle yarns about taking on the personality of the character you're disguised as. With missile-deflecting bracelets hugging my forearms and a gold lasso strapped to my waist, I wasn't just *dressed* like Wonder Woman. I *was* Wonder Woman.

I had my fingers crossed that the uncontrollable sexual arousal part was true, too.

I felt glances sidling left and right to check me out as I cut a sassy path through the gathering crowd. I saw brows lift in shock. Heads tip with curiosity. Mouths curve in admiration. I heard throaty growls of approval. Conspicuous lip smacking. A few low whistles. And why not?

I was hot. Not only did my legs start at my throat, but my bustier was inset with a push-up bra that did for my chest what yeast did for bread dough—the only problem being, if I made the mistake of bending over, I'd probably knock myself out.

I surveyed the room with my superhero vision, assessing the guests, the food, the decorations. Paper skeletons and witches on broomsticks hung from the ceiling, dangling over tables that had been shifted to one side of the room. Carved jack-o'-lanterns perched in the center of each table. Cornstalks nestled in obvious corners. Food islands angled across the floor, tempting partygoers with aromas that were sweet and spicy, piquant and peppery. Guests huddled in scattered circles, masked and unmasked, everyone living out some alter ego fantasy. I eyed the Lone Ranger in his little black mask and white "good guy" outfit. Little Bo Beep encased in an igloo of ruffly pink flounces with a ribboned shepherd's staff. Count Dracula in his tuxedo, cape, widow's peak, and fake incisors. At least, I hoped they were fake. If not, he could forget about tearing into the corn on the cob I saw steaming under a nearby heat lamp.

"Emily?" a voice croaked close to my ear. "Holy crap! Look at you."

I pivoted to find a six-foot broccoli spear practically standing on top of me. "Jonathan?" His bespectacled green face poked out of an opening three-quarters of the way up his stalk, but his arms were hidden somewhere beneath his fibrous beta carotene layer. I looked him up and down, root to floret, reaching an unexpected conclusion. "You know something, Jonathan, that color green really accentuates your eyes. Are you fresh or frozen?"

"Fresh. If I was frozen, I'd be in a major thaw right now. Emily, wow, you're so—" His gaze dipped to the acre of exposed cleavage rising above my bustier. "I mean, I never realized you were so . . . so—" his tongue stuck to the roof of his mouth as he riffled through his vocabulary—"tan."

"Instant bronzer. My ex-husband swears by it." I circled around him, testing his stalk with my fingertip. "Hey, how'd you manage to get into this thing with two arms in a sling? There's a zipper back here."

"I had the rental shop hold it for me and went down there to dress. And guess who I ran into while I was there?"

"Mmm, the tattooed blonde who looks like your ex-wife?"

His eyes rounded in amazement. "How did you know that?"

I shrugged one naked shoulder. "Goes with the territory. Remember? I'm Wonder Woman."

"Yeah," he said, his voice soft and breathy. "You sure are."

"So did the costume rental people get Jennifer's zipper unstuck?"

He stood very still, his mouth gaping open like a knot hole. "Man, this is awesome. It's the belt, isn't it? Wonder Woman's belt is the source of her superpowers. Who would have thought this stuff was actually real?"

I cocked my hip and gave him a flirty wink. "You should see what I can do with my lasso. So Jonathan"—I poked his broccoli belly with my forefinger—"what about Jennifer?"

He gulped down a mouthful of oxygen, looking as if he were trying to prevent his florets from wilting. "Is that her name? Jennifer? What a whiner. I think someone should do the rest of the world a favor and put her out of her misery. She nearly took the clerk's head off when he told her the zipper was broken and he'd have to give her a new bodysuit. But you know what I overheard when she was jabbering with some of the female clerks?"

"Hello, dear," said a short passerby in a belted tunic, leggings, and floppy mushroom cap of a hat. She wore a half-face mask, carried a miner's pick, and sported a slash of embroidery over her breast that read HAPPY. She gave me a thumbs-up as she nodded toward one of the food islands. "Snow White and me are all over Bailey. But she's not in costume, so it's not too challengin'. Woulda been more excitin' followin' that Gjurd fella around. He's dressed like a Vikin', and you wouldn't believe the fine-lookin' gams he's got under that wolfskin skirt a his." Nana acknowledged Jonathan with a wink and a nod. "You better stay away from the appetizer table, dear. You look tasty enough to dip. Oops. There's Snow. Duty calls. We're gonna stalk Bailey while she gets her food."

I waved to Tilly, who stood pencil straight and shapeless in a low-cut, puffy-sleeved gown with a huge bow roosting atop her head of synthetic black hair. She waggled her cane at me as she flicked wisps of hair away from her face, but her wig was charged with so much static electricity, the hair kept flying back, attacking her cheeks like bats. That had to be annoying.

As I watched her and Nana trundle off, I blinked at the nearest food island, whipping around suddenly to stare at Jonathan.

"Like I was saying," Jonathan continued, "while I—"

"How are you planning to go through the buffet

line?" I cut him off, gesturing to the two empty sockets in his stem. "Have you seen yourself? You have no arms."

He looked down his nose at his stalk. "I thought maybe I could ask one of the waitstaff to help me. You suppose they do stuff like that?"

"Probably. But how is the food going to travel from the plate to your mouth?"

His florets bobbed in thought. "Don't know. I haven't thought that far ahead."

"Jonathan, Jonathan, Jonathan." I glanced beyond him to where a female in a black bodysuit with a Catwoman hood was edging into line at the salad island. Eh! Jennifer. "Tell you what. Sit down at this table—" I yanked out a chair and navigated him into it. "I'll get you some food and bring it back to you. Maybe I can even help you get it to your mouth."

He regarded me with puppy-dog eyes. "You'd do that for me, Emily?"

"I'm a tour escort," I said hurriedly. "It's one of the many functions I perform."

"But I don't get it. Why are you being so nice to me? No one's ever been this nice to me."

"I'm from the Midwest. We're all like this."

I strutted across the floor, dropping into line three people back from Jennifer and wondering if her agenda for the evening included a quick cut-and-run after the dessert course. She didn't look to be in too much of a hurry as she piled Caesar salad onto her plate, which meant my plan was working perfectly. She didn't have a clue I was onto her.

"Trick or treat," said a digitalized voice behind me. I spun around and nearly scraped my nose on the broad chest of Darth Vader, evil galactic lord of an empire that existed long ago and far, far away—like my love life. He towered miles above me, a striking figure in his floor-length cloak and hermetically sealed breathing mask. He curled a gloved hand around my bare shoulder and looked down at me through bulbous orbs of tinted glass that I suspected were the science fiction equivalent of Foster Grants. "Nice costume," he announced, sounding like the voice inside my answering machine.

"Duncan?"

He expelled a heavy breath through the vents of his mask and trailed a gloved finger down the nape of my neck. "Darth."

I smiled up at him, rapping a knuckle on his helmeted face mask. What was it with guys? Jonathan with no arms. Duncan with no face. Did their brains shut down completely when they crawled into a costume? "Tell me, Darth, will you be taking this thing off to dine, or are you planning to eat dinner through a straw?"

"I'll take it off for you. Later. In private."

If I got lucky, he might even take off more than just the mask. I tapped my finger on his tinted insect eyes. "Can you actually see through these things?"

"I was managing fine until I saw your costume." Air shot out of his mask like steam from a volcano. "Now I'm having a small problem with condensation."

"We've identified our mark," Alice Tjarks announced in a flurry as she seized my arm. Her dwarf's hat was so big it drooped over her head like a flaccid bucket, blinding her, but at least her mouth was still visible. "He's over there." She swung her pick-axe toward the back of the room, accidentally thwack-ing the Lone Ranger in the holster as he passed.

"Hey!" he warned. "Watch it."

"Oh, honestly," Alice scolded him. "As if that hurt you." She lifted my forearm and whacked it a few times with her miner's pick. "See? It's made of foam rubber." She grabbed Darth's arm. *Whap, whap, whap.* "The only way this pick can hurt you is if you eat it. So how about if you 'Hi ho Silver and away.' "

I blinked in surprise. Eh! This didn't sound like sweet, shy, demurring Alice. What was wrong with her? I glimpsed at the name embroidered on her tunic. *GRUMPY?* Oh, my God, it wasn't a fluke. It wasn't just me. Everyone was morphing into their Halloween character! Eh! I shuddered to think what this meant for Jonathan.

"Dumb dwawf," the masked man spat as he hitched up his holster and stomped off. I followed him with my eyes, suddenly privy to one of the Lone Ranger's best-kept secrets. He wasn't from the Old West. He was from New England!

Alice coaxed her hat off her nose and latched onto my arm again. "Listen, Emily, Gjurd is going through the meat buffet right now, dressed like Hagar the Horrible, and Osmond is hot on his trail. Or is that tail?"

"Trail," said Darth.

Alice squinted up at him from behind her mask. "Do I know you?"

He shot to attention and clicked his booted heels together. "Darth," he said, offering her his gloved hand.

Alice continued to squint. "Not Batman? You look a lot like Batman. Or Zorro. But Zorro's cape is shorter, and he has a sword."

Darth whipped a cylindrical rod off his belt. "I have a light saber," he said in a digitalized monotone.

Alice hovered over the weapon, nodding. "Does this have one of those new fluorescent bulbs in it? They're supposed to save you lots of money, but personally, I don't think they give off enough light. It's a scam, if you ask me."

"Alice," I asked, troubled by a sudden niggling concern. "Which dwarf is Osmond dressed as?"

"Sleepy."

SLEEPY? EHHH! If behavior patterns stayed true to form, that could spell disaster! I grabbed Alice by her shoulders and spun her in the right direction. "Look, Alice, you've gotta get back to the meat buffet right away. Stay close to Gjurd and, whatever you do, keep Osmond awake!"

"Who's Gjurd?" Darth asked, bending so close to my ear that I could feel his hot breath on my cheek.

"He's—" My attention got diverted as Catwoman sashayed away from me with a plate piled high with greens, her tail dragging on the floor behind her like a broken exhaust pipe. *Uff da.* There was too much happening all at once! "Would you save my place in line for a minute?" I asked Duncan, unwilling to lose sight of her.

I darted, bobbed, weaved, and threaded my way through the crowd after her, relieved when she finally sat down at a table that was within view of the table where I'd planted Jonathan. Scurrying back to Duncan, I hopped in front of him and within two minutes, filled an ice-cold plate with enough fresh fruit and salad to feed the state of Florida. When I exited the line, Duncan remained close on my heels, but unlike me, he wasn't carrying a plate. I stared at his empty hands. "What seems to be the problem? No straws or no appetite?"

A torrent of unsettled air swirled around him as he cradled the small of my back with his huge vinyl glove. "I have an appetite. But not for food."

Unh. I locked my knees to prevent them from buckling. Never having been hit on by an evil warlord with a retractable light saber before, I didn't realize how titillating it could be.

Removing his hand suddenly, he clicked his heels together again and bowed dramatically at the waist. "I've just remembered something I've forgotten to do, Emily. Will you excuse me? I'll rejoin you in a few minutes. Where will you be sitting?"

I nodded toward Jonathan. "Over there, with the broccoli spear. Don't be long, okay?" For some reason, the thought of that light saber was making me frisky.

"Holy cow," Jonathan exclaimed when I set his

plate down before him. "I don't know if I can eat all this."

I pulled out a chair and sat down beside him, shoving aside some orange flyers with spiders and skeletons and lots of writing on them. "Pace yourself. This is only the first course. Open wide." I forked a few leaves of spinach into his mouth, keeping one eye on Catwoman and one eye on the rest of the room while he chewed.

"Aren't you eating?" he mumbled around his spinach salad.

"I'm focusing on you first."

He sighed regretfully. "I wish Beth could have been more like you. I bet you'd never run off with another man, or get a tattoo, or sign up for gourmet-cooking lessons with a famous Indian chef whose name is long as my arm. I bet you don't even like Indian food."

Indian cooking? Hadn't someone else talked about Indian cooking recently? I shoveled a couple of supersized croutons into his mouth as I tried to recall the conversation. "I interrupted your story earlier, Jonathan. I'm sorry. What were you saying you overheard while Jennifer was being outfitted in a new costume?"

Crunch. Cruuunch. "Oh, yeah. Remember when I told you that the blonde's tattoo was just like Beth's? You want to know why they looked so much alike?" *Crunch, crunch.* "Because they had it done in the same tattoo parlor! Tattoos Unlimited, close to the Penn State campus. The same artist probably did it using the same pattern. Can you believe that? The blonde lives in University Park. We're probably neighbors and don't even know it." *Crunch, crunch.* "Could I try some of the avocado salad?"

I speared an avocado slice and fed it to him thoughtfully. "You never mentioned you live in University Park." And I wasn't exactly sure why the news bothered me.

"I don't actually live *in* University Park, just outside the city limits. And don't ask me what a Nittany Lion is. I've lived there for six years, and no one's ever been able to tell me."

"Well, you're on the right cruise ship to find out. The woman Jen confronted outside the infirmary the other night? I bet you anything she'd know. She's working on a Ph.D., so she probably knows everything. But you'd better hurry up and find her because she's getting ready to leav—"

My fork clattered to the plate as the conversation I'd forgotten lasered back into my brain. *Bailey!* That's who'd mentioned Indian cuisine. The day when we'd visited her in the infirmary. She'd informed us that Professor Smoker's only vices had been golf and Indian cuisine. I stared at Jonathan, my mental connect-the-dots picture suddenly exploding with an impossible notion.

"Jonathan, I don't mean to be insensitive, but I remember you telling us at dinner that Beth ran off with someone in her gourmet-cooking class. Was it the Indian cooking class you were just talking about?"

He waggled his florets. "Yeah. The campus union

offers minicourses to the staff and public every semester. Specialty cooking. Self-defense. Origami for dummies. They only last six weeks, but I guess six weeks was all it took for Romeo to lure Beth away from me."

Dorian Smoker, a beautiful, dissatisfied, gold-digging wife, and a shared love of exotic cuisine that was spicy enough to strip the enamel off your teeth? Was I grasping at straws, or had I just stumbled upon the ingredients of a toxic cocktail? "The man she ran off with, Jonathan. Did you ever learn his name?"

He averted his eyes. "She didn't stick around to tell me his name. Um, look, even though I was the one who mentioned Beth first, is it okay if we don't talk about her anymore tonight? I'd rather sit here with you and pretend that Beth and her boyfriend never happened. That's old history. I'm more into current events now." He slanted a ravenous look at the mounds of food on his plate. "Is that white stuff ambrosia? That looks pretty good. How about a bite of that?"

The white stuff on the plate was indeed ambrosia, but the more critical question was . . . Who was the guy in the broccoli suit? Was he an aggrieved husband who was finding ways to mend a broken heart? Or was he a not-so-mild-mannered computer geek who, like thousands of cuckolded husbands before him, had found an ingenious way to get even with the man who'd run off with his wife?

CHAPTER 15

NUTS! I didn't want Jonathan to be involved in this. I didn't even want to *consider* his being involved. I didn't need another last-minute suspect; I already had a full roster. Jonathan couldn't be guilty. I didn't even have his photo to hand around! Damn. I . . . I needed to prove myself wrong about this.

Yeah. That's what I'd do. I'd prove myself wrong. I smiled at the simplicity of my scheme, then frowned. How exactly would I go about doing that?

"I signed up for one of those minicourses a few years back," Jonathan chattered between bites of ambrosia. "I ended up being the only man in a whole roomful of women. Not that any of them ever noticed."

"What were you taking? Beginning macramé?"

"Self-defense," he mumbled around a couple of mandarin orange slices. "I don't want to brag, but by the end of the course, I could take down our instructor with one hand tied behind my back."

Proving that having a broken arm was no impediment to him? Ehh! I *so* did not want to hear this! I turned my head as someone tapped on my bare shoulder.

"If you're looking for Shelly Valentine, she's the one in the white tights over there dressed like the Sugar Plum Fairy." Bernice swung her pickaxe toward the nearest buffet island. "But you're gonna have to do something about those two dumb Dicks, Emily. You see them giggling over there at the end of the line? Well, they're supposed to be following those two Limeys around, not sniffing around that girl's tutu."

I executed an eye roll of epic proportions. "Bernice, would you please march over there and tell the Dicks that if they don't shape up, I'll . . . I'll . . ." I'd what? How did you threaten a dwarf? Revoke permission to whistle while he worked?

"I'd rather have you speak to them," Bernice demurred. "You're much better at handling disciplinary issues than I am. I don't want to give the appearance that I'm overstepping my authority or being pushy."

Whoa! This from the woman who delighted in being the thorn in everyone's side? The pain in everyone's neck? THE BANE OF MY PERSONAL EXISTENCE? I checked out the name on her costume.

Aha! *That* explained why she was being so nice. She wasn't Bernice Zwerg any longer; she was *BASHFUL!* Damn. What were the chances we could get her to wear that thing permanently? "Um, Bernice, do you know if the Dicks at least *found* Percy and Basil?"

"Yup. One of them's duded up like Sherlock Holmes, and the other one's got a really long scarf wrapped around his neck."

A really long scarf? That was a no-brainer, but a little odd. "One of them's dressed like Isadora Duncan?" Who knew that cross-dressing was as popular with the English as it was with New Yorkers?

"I'll give you another clue. He's accessorizing his scarf with a flight jacket, aviator goggles, and a leather helmet."

"Charles Lindbergh?"

"A good guess, dear, but his name tag says he's the Red Baron."

Dear? Bernice Zwerg called me dear? I snapped my mouth shut to prevent my jaw from dropping off the planet. No way was I ever going to let her out of that costume. I'd staple it to her body if I had to!

The floor suddenly quaked beneath us, causing Bernice and me to dart looks at the gigantic lug who was bounding past our table. He looked about twelve feet tall, broad-backed, and bare-chested, a gladiator's trident in one hand and a net in the other. Leather shin guards rose above his sandaled feet. A spiked helmet hugged his bearded face. And below the metal belt that girdled his waist was a loincloth of gold lamé that fit him like a diaper. He ate up the floor as if he owned the place, the quickness of his strides creating a definite problem for the Three Little Pigs who were chasing after him.

"Nils," I whispered to Bernice, indicating the gladiator.

"Helen, Grace, and Lucille," she whispered back, nodding toward the pigs.

I checked their names off my mental list. That accounted for just about everyone. I loved it when a good plan came together.

Bernice motioned toward the opposite end of the room with a head bob. "Sherlock and the Baron are slopping either mincemeat or lumpy grape jelly on crackers in the cold fish line. You can check them out if you want, but Doc is charting everyone's location and movements on her clipboard, so she'll be giving you the lowdown on what's happening every fifteen minutes or so. No need for you to run yourself ragged."

"Which one of you is Doc?"

"Margi. And she's taking our vital signs in her spare time. The person with the lowest average heart rate at the end of the evening wins a prize."

I stared at Bernice, realizing that I'd been transported to some weird parallel universe but not knowing how to react. I cast a long look across the room at Shelly and the Dicks, grappling with my next move. "Look, Bernice, would you mind taking over with Jonathan while I talk to Sneezy and Dopey? I'll only be a minute."

"But Emily," Jonathan whined.

"You go right ahead, dear." She plucked the fork gently from my fingers. "Take all the time you need. We'll be fine right here, won't we?" she asked Jonathan as she sat down beside him. "So what kind of tree are you anyway? Crab or apple?"

Eyes narrowed, boot heels pounding, I strutted across the floor, circling around the giggling Dicks to grab them by the scruff of their fat little necks. "What's this I hear about you deserting your posts?" I whispered as I herded them out of line and steered them toward an open space on the floor. I spun them around to face me. "Do you have anything to say for yourselves?"

Dick Stolee thundered out a sneeze. Dick Teig went curiously rigid. He parted his lips and pointed a pudgy forefinger at me, garbled sounds bubbling up from his throat as he looked me up and down.

"Balls," snarled Dick Stolee as he dried his eyes. "I think my allergies are kicking up a—" His mouth fell open as his gaze collided with mine. He seized Dopey's arm, leaning into him for support. "Geez, Emily, that's . . . that's some outfit." Dopey mouthed something into his ear.

"What's he saying?" I asked.

"Sounds like 'Gaaaaaaaa.' "

"Listen, you two: enough with the detours to follow Shelly. You're on Percy and Basil. Got it?"

Dick Stolee hitched his wide leather belt up over the round mound of his belly. "Say—uh, Emily, do you need anyone to follow you around? Bodyguards? We could change assignments with someone. You give the word, and we could be all over you, couldn't we, Dick?"

Dopey nodded enthusiastically before gasping out more sounds.

"Is he suffering a stroke?" I asked, concerned.

Dick Stolee shook his head. "Nope. He's volunteering to be a guinea pig for any demonstrations you'd like to give with your lasso."

"Come on, you two. Get going. I'm counting on you."

"Bernice sent you over here, didn't she?" Dick Stolee grumbled as he thundered out another sneeze. "Damned tattletale. Even when she's being nice she's a pain in the butt."

As they waddled off, I turned back to the buffet line, getting a bead on the Sugar Plum Fairy as she exited the queue, her tutu fluttering around her hips like a many-layered halo. "Shelly," I called, catching up to her.

"Awesome getup," she said from behind her feathered mask. She doubled her fist to butt knuckles with me. "Girl power. What's up? Were you as sick as I was last night? Man, I was just looking for the right hole to die in."

"I spent the night in the infirmary. Something in my eye. Say, I have a quick question. Do you happen to know if Professor Smoker ever signed up for an Indian-cooking course at your college union?"

"Oh, sure. He signed up for those things all the time. He was a real paragon of virtue. Golf and Indian cuisine were his only vices."

I guessed boinking a large percentage of the student population wasn't considered a vice. "Okay. Thanks." I turned on my boot heel, only to wheel around again. "One more question. Did you happen to speak to Bailey yesterday before you ran off to your manicure appointment?"

The eyes beneath her feathered mask went blank for a moment before refocusing. "I didn't see Bailey yesterday. In fact, I don't think I've seen her since Dori's lecture." She shrugged her flawlessly white shoulders. "It's a big ship." She twirled on her toe shoes, sizing up available seating. "Things are really starting to get crowded. Do you have room for me at your table, Emily?"

"Sure. The more the merrier." Could I make this any easier for Bernice?

"Oh, good. Where are you sitting?"

"The table at two o'clock."

She followed my gaze. "With the dwarf and the broccoli spear?" Her mouth turned down at the corners. "Mmm . . . I don't think so. Thanks anyway."

"She's a terrific little dwarf!" I called after her. "You'd really like her!" But Shelly kept walking until she found an empty spot at a table with a couple of pirates, a Roaring Twenties flapper, and a bald-headed Friar Tuck who was sporting a full beard. Marking the location of her table on my mental map, I directed my gaze back to Jonathan, disheartened by my own success.

This was just great. All the puzzle pieces were there. Time. Place. Location. Opportunity. All I had to do was nudge them together. So why was it that the one time I wanted to be wrong about something, I was dead on? Except for figuring out what happened to the treasure. Was that Jonathan's work, too? Had he offed Professor Smoker *and* stolen Tilly's box? Was he the one who'd Maced me? Could he do that with two arms in a sling, or had he enlisted someone else to help him with his dirty work?

I heaved a frustrated sigh. How come all my answers were only producing more questions?

"I'm fetching Jonathan course number two," Bernice announced as she crab-walked around me, bent beneath the weight of her dowager's hump. "He's the nicest fella. If he was a half century older, I'd take him home with me. I've always wanted to know what it'd be like dating a younger man."

Oh, no, they were bonding. This was terrible! "Thanks, Bernice," I said distractedly. "I owe you."

She paused before scuttling back to me, looking up at me with her grizzled little ex-smoker's face. "You got anything on you for general malaise, Emily? I don't know what's wrong with me tonight, but I'm not feeling quite myself."

I should have seen this coming—being agreeable was making her sick. "I don't have anything on me, Bernice, but I could run back to the cabin. I have lots of over-the-counter stuff."

She waved off the suggestion. "I don't want to take you away from anything, dear. Never mind. I'll survive."

As I bolstered my courage to head back to the table, I looked toward the entrance to find Darth making his way back to me, cloak flying, shoulders squared, looking like an evil lord with an agenda. I gave him a little finger wave, feeling an inexplicable thrill when he cupped his gloved hands around my head and droned, "You're so beautiful. You should be illegal." I suspected he might have kissed me then if his mouth hadn't been trapped behind the grill of a Dodge Ram truck. "Have I given you time enough to think about my question, Emily? Will you give me your answer?"

His question? Oh, my God. It was *Duncan* who'd popped the question? But . . . but how could I give him an answer? I was in the middle of a criminal investigation! I was on the trail of a killer! Was he completely blind to the fact that I was a little preoccupied at the moment?

"We've had a little incident at our table," Nana said as she scampered breathlessly toward me. "We done just what you said, Emily. Snow and me come right out and asked Bailey if we could join her for dinner, and she seemed real pleased to have us, so all of us was sittin' there eatin' when it happened."

I blinked numbly. "When what happened?"

"When a little chain she was wearin' slid right down her bosom. She had a devil of a time findin' it 'cause she wasn't wearin' no push-up bra, but she eventually fished it out. It was the little ring on the clasp what come apart. She was so upset, I offered to fetch her some tweezers so she could fix it, but then Margi come along, so I didn't need to. It was real strange though, Emily. It was like Bailey didn't want no one touchin' it."

"Margi had tweezers?"

"Forceps. Trust me. That ring'll never come apart

again. Oh, look, dear. Isn't that Shelly, dressed like the Sugar Plum Fairy? Looks like she's callin' it a night."

Shelly? I poked my head around Darth just in time to see her tutu disappear behind a small swarm of killer bees. *Oh, no!* No one was tailing her! Where was Bernice?

"Emily," implored Darth, in his answering machine monotone.

Nana squinted up at him. "Are you s'posed to sound like that, or is your mask defective?"

"I'm supposed to sound like this." He paused. "Why? Do you think I'm too nasally?"

"Where's Bernice?" I ranted, standing on tiptoe to scan the nearest buffet islands. When I couldn't find her, I grabbed Nana's arm. "Follow Shelly. I'll send Bernice to take over as soon as I find her."

"Roger that," she said, saluting me with her axe handle.

Darth stepped in front of me, blocking my view with eight towering feet of *Made in China* polyester and plastic. "*WHAT* . . . is going on?"

"Wait! There she is. S'cuse me." I raced after Bernice, breathless when I reached her. "Shelly's gone. Nana's tailing her. If you hurry, you can catch both of them."

She shoved a plate of hot entrées at me. "Give this to Jonathan. Which way did they go?"

Which way did they go? People actually said that? "Out the main entrance. Hurry." I took a deep breath as Sherlock Holmes and the Red Baron sauntered casually past me—"A—CHOOOO!"—with Sneezy and Dopey nipping at their heels.

I rushed back to Darth, my heart leaping into my mouth when I saw Catwoman prance idly by him, she and her overlong tail looking to be headed for the nearest exit. *Uff da!* What was going on? Why were people leaving so early? What was I supposed to do? Follow Jennifer? Stay with Jonathan? DAMN!

I dished off the plate to Darth and nodded in the direction of my table. "Please. Would you deliver this to the broccoli spear over there?"

"Over where?"

"There!" I cried, thrusting my hand toward the table . . . that was now unoccupied. I looked left. I looked right. Oh, my God! No one was sitting at the table. It was empty! NOOOO! WHERE DID HE GO? Geez, I HATED it when a good plan fell apart. "I don't mean to ditch you, Darth, but . . . I'm sorry, I've gotta run."

I sprinted across the room on the lookout for Jonathan's florets, weaving through the crowded tables in my kick-butt Wonder boots.

"Did you happen to see a broccoli spear pass by here within the last few minutes?" I asked a table of Crayola crayons close to the exit.

"I noticed a green vegetable on its way to the door," said a woman whose golden hue was labeled *BANANA MANIA*. "But I can't swear it was broccoli. It looked more like asparagus."

I charged to the other side of the room, running into Margi, who was making her rounds. "Did you hear the news?" she asked as she scribbled a notation on her clipboard. "We're arriving in Maui ahead of schedule. I heard someone say we picked up a tail wind."

I slanted a look out the dining room's glass-paneled wall to discover we were so close to land, I could see onshore lights winking in the twilight. "We're there?" How could we be there? I hadn't even found time to eat yet!

"We dropped anchor about a half hour ago. And have you noticed how people are leaving in droves? I bet it's because of the freebies at that Lahaina resort."

I frowned. "What freebies?"

Margi snatched a familiar orange flyer off the nearest table and handed it to me. "These freebies."

I skimmed the paper to discover that one of the big beach hotels in Lahaina was offering free booze to anyone who showed up in costume before 9:00 P.M. Damn! This changed everything. Were my suspects going ashore to get lost, or get tanked?

"Margi, you need to rally the troops. Tell them this isn't a drill. Whatever's going to happen is about to happen right now. Man your posts!"

"Ten-four." She dipped her head close to mine. "You want me to take your pulse before I leave? You could be eligible for the grand prize."

"NO!" I dashed out the exit and ran through the foyer at the speed of light. I passed the Guest Relations Desk like a human blur, and when I reached the atrium, I skidded to a stop, sucking in air as I heeded the mob of revelers yukking it up around me. I looked up, and up, and up, at the guests hanging over the endless tiers of balconies, brandishing tommy guns, plastic sickles, and oversized cocktail glasses that were brimming with booze. I spied Antony and Cleopatra, Scarlett and Rhett, Bonnie and Clyde, but nowhere did I see Catwoman and a broccoli spear . . . until I glanced at the elevator shaft and saw a slender green vegetable shoehorned into the car, his stalk crushed against the interior glass. That was him! Jonathan!

In the next moment, the glass tube swooped belowdecks and disappeared.

He was going down, which meant he was definitely leaving the ship.

"Gjurd up and left!" snapped Grumpy as she beat a path through the crowd toward me, dragging Sleepy behind her. "We think he's on his way back to his cabin. But don't worry; we're on him like ugly on an ape. Isn't that right?" She whacked Sleepy in the gut, prompting him to nod sluggishly.

"You bet," Osmond said, yawning into my face.

"What about Nils?"

"He left, too, but the pigs are trotting right after him. See? There's one of them now."

I followed Grumpy's gaze to find one of the little pigs signaling a greeting to me with her hoof. I flashed her a thumbs-up, then watched in bewilderment as she waddled around, wiggled her corkscrew tail at me, and oinked.

I hoped that wasn't a secret code, because I had no

idea what it meant. "I'm on my way to the disembarkation deck," I told Grumpy. "I'll probably see you down there."

I snaked through the noisy crowd toward the central staircase, my descent slowed by streams of people who were swimming against the tide and incapable of figuring out how to get out of each other's way. And to think I'd considered Times Square on New Year's Eve a zoo! I fought my way through the foot traffic, wasting precious minutes as I waited behind revelers who stopped to converse on the stairs. When I reached the end of the line, I put a bead on the bulkhead door that was opened to the darkening sky. "Did a broccoli spear just leave the ship?" I asked the crewman who was standing by the door.

"Just barely. He nearly got deflowered heading out the door. He better remember to duck when he climbs into the tender."

I narrowed my gaze at him. "Tender?"

Grinning, he guided me onto a metal ramp beyond the bulkhead door. "The tender," he said, indicating a large boat that bobbed in the water below us. "That's how guests get transported over to Lahaina. It's not a deep-water port, so the *Princess* has to anchor in the bay."

I looked from the boat, to the harbor, to the crewman again. "We can't just dock and walk over?"

"You're Wonder Woman." He flashed a cocky smile. "If you don't want to take the boat, why don't you fly?"

I drilled him with a withering look. "Wonder

Woman doesn't fly. She just moves really, really fast." I clomped down the metal stairs, across the length of a wobbly float, and up the gangway of the ship's launch, where I ran headlong into the Sugar Plum Fairy, who was trying to look inconspicuous as she lingered outside the men's head.

"Emily!" she asked when she saw me. "Are you going into Lahaina?"

Not wanting to give anything away, I did my best to muddy the issue. "Um, I haven't actually decided yet."

"Look, I hate to sound paranoid, but there's something really weird going on here."

From the tail of my eye I caught sight of Nana and Bernice, looking enormously pleased with themselves as they aimed fingers at Shelly and flashed victory signs at me. Uh-oh. I wondered if Shelly's paranoia had anything to do with dwarfs.

Shelly lowered her voice and spoke to me from behind her hand. "I can't go in there to check it out, but there's a guy in the john who—"

The door swung open at that moment, ejecting the rotund form of Friar Tuck. "Get him!" shouted Shelly as she grabbed him by his cassock, kneed him in the groin, and kicked his legs out from beneath him. He crashed onto his face like a felled tree, bellowing out an agonized wail as she straddled his back and forced his arms behind his shoulder blades.

Hunh. Pretty slick moves for a fairy. I stared down at my boots and bustier. Maybe she was the one who should be wearing the Wonder Woman outfit.

"You're busted!" she screamed at the fallen friar. "You're a dead man! You hear me? A dead man!"

"I think you'd have to hit him way harder to incur death," Bernice said helpfully.

Passengers rushed toward the commotion, emptying out the bow and stern. Jonathan in his broccoli stalk. The Red Baron in his scarf and aviator goggles. Sherlock Holmes with his signature pipe and cloak. Dopey and—"A-CHOOO!"—Sneezy. Nils in his gold diaper and trident. Grumpy and Sleepy. Gjurd in his wolfskin skirt and horned helmut. Two of the Three Little Pigs. A butcher, a baker, a candlestick maker, and the whole table of Crayola crayons.

A wave of panic choked me. One or two I could handle, but did the whole freaking suspect list have to show up for the showdown? I stared dumbly at Dopey. "How did you all get down here so fast?"

"Elevator. We thought about the stairs, but did you see them? They were way too jammed."

"Talk!" Shelly yelled, bouncing the monk's head off the floor like a Wiffle ball.

"A fairy taking down a friar," Sneezy marveled. "How would you score that? A sin or a sacrilege?"

"Excuse me." Nana waved her pick axe at Shelly. "If you keep thumpin' his head on the floor like that, I'm afraid you might hurt him. Wouldn't be so bad if he had hair, but he's got no cushion."

"You are *sooo* dead!" Shelly blasted the back of his head. "You're—"

A lifeguard's whistle blared behind us, piping out with a long, shrill tone. "Make way!" shouted a uniformed seaman as he muscled through the crowded passageway. "What's going on down here?"

As we shuffled back to let him through, Friar Tuck boomed out a roar that could have raised hackles on a cue ball. Imbued with superhuman strength, he shambled to his feet with Shelly still on his back, whirled around like a dervish, and with adrenaline-crazed power, drove her hard into the wall, clocking her. He stepped away from the wall and shook her off him, causing a collective intake of breath as the lifeless fairy fell on her tutu.

"She attacked me!" he explained to onlookers in a finely cultured British accent. "You saw what happened. She's a madwoman! Tell the bloke."

"A clear case of self-defense," Bernice announced.

"She's right," Nana agreed. "It was one a them unprovoked attacks."

"I vote he's innocent," yawned Sleepy.

Nodding his appreciation for their support, Friar Tuck hobbled toward the bow and slid into a bench while the seaman knelt over Shelly, checking for vitals. Within a minute, three more crewmen joined the first, rolled her onto a stretcher, and carted her off, leaving the rest of us to buzz about what we'd just witnessed.

"Who am I supposed to tail now?" Bernice asked, as she and Nana joined me. "Is there anyone good left?"

Hearing a familiar thump, I glanced right to find Snow White hustling down the gangplank, leading with her walking stick. "I would have gotten here sooner," she whispered in a breathy, conspiratorial tone, "but I made the mistake of taking the stairs."

"Where's Bailey?" Nana asked.

Snow angled her walking stick to starboard. "Pulling up the rear."

Bailey appeared in the door, weighed down by a backpack, a soft-sided briefcase, and an over-the-shoulder bag. "Ladies," she said, stopping beside us. "I guess this is good-bye. Again." She scanned the tender from fore to aft. "Look at all the people. I didn't think there'd be this many guests heading into Lahaina tonight."

I sighed with dismay. "Neither did I."

"I guess the prospect of free alcohol has all the rats abandoning ship. Which resort is it again?"

I stared at her vacuously as Catwoman sashayed on deck, dragging her tail past us as if we weren't there. I'd read the announcement only a few minutes ago, so how come I couldn't remember? "Umm, I'm not going ashore for the free booze, I'm . . . I'm going ashore for the"— I glommed onto the half-hidden chain around Bailey's neck—"for the jewelry. One of the hotels is having a special Halloween sale on coral and . . . and pearls, and maybe . . . abalone."

"Bailey's got a real pretty necklace," Nana piped up. "Why don't you show Emily and Bernice?"

Bailey shrugged self-consciously. "It's nothing, really. Just a cheap trinket."

"Cheap?" Snow protested. "It looked like fourteen-karat gold to me. Don't be modest. Show them."

Cheeks reddening, Bailey fished the chain out

from beneath her blouse, using her palm as a back-drop to display the charm that was attached. "See, it's just a trinket."

"Cute," I said as I perused the little gold rowboat. Actually, charms weren't my thing. I was more into shoes.

"But take a real good look," Nana instructed. "It's got real fine detail. Little oars. A fishin' rod. A tackle box. Your grampa woulda loved that boat."

Yeah, Grampa Sippel had always been fond of well-appointed fishing boats and ice shanties.

Bailey dropped the chain back under her blouse. "You think we'll be leaving anytime soon? Seems like everything around here is always hurry up and wait." She looked around the cabin once more. "Would you excuse me? I'm going to stake out a seat while there are still some available."

"Us, too," said Nana, grabbing Bashful and Snow and heading off behind her.

I leaned against the wall by the men's head, com-pletely flummoxed. So now what? Throw in the towel?

I shook my head and tried to think of the kinder, gentler days of my youth, when my responsibilities included nothing more than playing, daydreaming, and netting fish for Grampa Sippel when he'd nose his boat out into Gull Lake. Only Grampa never called it a fishing boat. He'd always called it a—

Bailey's fourteen-karat gold charm flashed in my brain. I pushed away from the wall, trembling at what I was thinking. I scrubbed my face with my hands, puzzling together all the pieces of the jigsaw, until the whole picture revealed itself to me—the lies, the illusions, the chance meetings, the deceit. Holy shit! Shelly had been right! Something weird *had* been going on!

Unlooping my lasso from my waist, I coiled the rope into two large circles. Targeting my prey, I strutted toward the bow, and with Wonder Woman stealth, slid into the bench behind Friar Tuck. "GET HIM!" I yelled as I threw the lasso over his head.

"Are we doing that again?" Dopey asked behind me.

I jumped onto Tuck's back, clobbering him with my fists. "You fake!"

"GET OFF!" he barked, twisting his body to detach me.

"Leave her alone!" shouted Jonathan, steamrolling across the aisle to head butt Tuck in his round little belly. *WOOF!* "Let her go!"

"She has *me!*" Tuck spat, batting Jonathan's florets out of his face.

"Emily, dear!" I heard Nana yell over the din. "Do you know that man?"

"YES!" I screamed, sinking my fingers into his beard and ripping it off. "IT'S DORIAN SMOKER! Shelly recognized him even in his beard and fat suit. She called him a dead man because, guess what? He's supposed to be dead!"

"Owww!" he hissed, clapping a hand to his naked jaw.

"Who's Dorian Smoker?" asked one of the crayons.

"DORI?" screeched Catwoman, pouncing up onto

a bench. "You're alive? You scumbag! You rat! I'm going to kill you myself!"

In the next moment Smoker jackknifed his body and catapulted me over his head, propelling me into Jonathan's stalk like a misfired rocket. *BOOM!* We crashed to the deck in a heap of limbs, my head woozy as Smoker jerked me onto my feet and collared his arm around my throat. "No one is going to move, or I swear, I'll snap her neck like a twig."

Catwoman clawed the air hard enough to draw blood. "I don't care what you do to her. I don't like her anyway." She leaped onto the deck, her eyes spitting venom as she took a step toward us. "Shelly's right. You're so dead, Smoker. *Meooow!*" She scratched the air again, making me cringe to think what she might have done if there'd been chalkboards handy.

"Not so fast," Nana said, seizing her tail as if it were the end of a tug-of-war rope. "Sneezy! Dopey! Lucille!"

Jennifer shot a glance behind her shoulder as her forward motion suddenly switched to a backward slide across the deck, compliments of three dwarfs and a pig.

"That's my granddaughter," Nana scolded Jennifer. "So we're not gonna make no waves. Understand?"

"Let go my tail!" Jennifer twisted her body around, swatting at Sneezy and Dopey. "So help me, Granny, when I get my paws on you, I'll—" THUNK! *BOOM*.

Snow White stood over Catwoman's body, all satisfied smiles and innocence. "Whoops. My walking stick must have slipped."

The green Crayola elbowed the brown one. "Help me out here. Are those guys dwarfs or elves?"

"Step away from her bódy!" Smoker snarled at the dwarfs. "Nice and slow. That's it. Now, everyone over to the port side of the boat."

People shuffled left. People shuffled right. The undecideds stood in the center aisle looking desperately confused.

"TO THE LEFT!" Smoker bellowed.

Everyone shuffled left while Jonathan rolled around on the floor like an upended tortoise.

"I'll save you, Emily!" he vowed as he tried to get his legs beneath himself. "Any minute now!"

Nana raised her hand. "Excuse me, Professor, but I seen on a Travel Channel special where too many people crowded onto one side of a boat wasn't a good idea, on account a it could make the boat capsize and sink."

"I'll make a note of that, Mrs. Sippel." He exerted pressure on my throat as he wrenched me into the aisle. "Anything else?"

Nana gave her mushroom cap hat a little scratch. "I can't figure somethin' out. If you're still alive, who was it what got throwed over the side?"

"No one!" I croaked within his hammerlock. "It was a sham! He—!" I gasped in panic as he tightened the circle of his arm.

"No one died?" Nana enthused. "Did you hear that, Emily? Isn't that nice?"

"You're a thief, sir," Tilly accused. "What have you done with my journal?"

"And a sweeter journal I have never seen, Professor Hovick. You're going to make me a very rich man. Thank you for the windfall. Where would we be without the unmitigated trust of Midwesterners like you? No need to worry about the book's whereabouts; it's safe. In a place where you'll never find it, I might add. Can you believe the damned thing was authentic?"

I squirmed futilely in his grip, nearly breaking out in song when Darth Vader swept menacingly into the cabin, boots pounding, cloak flying. Thank God! Duncan would know what to do. Duncan wouldn't let my neck be snapped like a twig. Duncan would—

"If you'll kindly join the others," Smoker instructed calmly, "I won't be forced to break this young woman's neck."

Duncan joined the rest of the group without a word of protest. A little disappointing, considering he could have protested in *five freaking languages!* On the up side, at least Smoker hadn't called me ma'am.

"Hold on, Emily," Jonathan wailed, his feet flopping around like fish. "I've almost mastered it."

Smoker made a point of kicking Jonathan's stalk as he steered me around him. "Who would have thought that a lowlife like Griffin Ring could change my fortunes so radically two centuries later? Finding his journal was like winning the lottery."

"I won the lottery," Nana piped up. "If you let Emily go, I'll write you a check. I got twelve million."

"Twelve million?" said Dopey. "Last time I heard it was eight."

"Tech stocks," she explained. "I made a killin' before I bailed."

Tilly's expression hardened. "Since you have the journal, Professor, I assume you also have the treasure?"

"A logical assumption. You were quite lucky to uncover it the way you did. I was absolutely certain it was buried somewhere on the grounds of the Secret Falls; that's why I scavenged the place on my own after all of you cleared out. Unfortunately, someone else had the same idea, and much to his detriment, he recognized me." He jerked my body around in the direction of Nils and Gjurd. "Sorry about your companion, gentleman, but it couldn't be helped. Prime example of wrong place, wrong time."

Nils seemed to expand to twice his size. "It was *you* who killed Ansgar?" His voice thundered like that of the Great Oz.

"Not my fault. He forced my hand."

Color stained Nils's cheeks. "You killed him? You stole his wallet? You boarded the ship using his identification?"

Smoker nodded. "It couldn't have worked out better if I'd planned it myself."

Roaring in anguish, Nils hurled his trident through the air, scoring a direct hit in the center of Smoker's forehead—a blow that could have killed him if we'd been talking steel instead of styrofoam.

Smoker kicked the trident out of the way as Tilly's voice grew more stern. "You forced your way into my cabin last night and stole the puzzle box."

His manner grew short, his calm rapidly deterio-
rating. "Aren't you the academic genius? Thanks for
leaving it in the open the way you did. You made my
job much easier. Ransacking a cabin isn't my idea of
fun."

My eyelids flew up into my head at his admission.
Smoker was the one who'd stolen the treasure from
Nana's cabin? *Smoker* was the one who'd shot pepper
spray into my face? *Smoker was the one who'd
slammed me into the wall?* SMOKER WAS THE ONE
WHO WOULD HAVE DONE THE SAME THING
TO NANA IF SHE'D ANSWERED THE DOOR?

I inhaled a deep breath, clearing my mind, expand-
ing my lungs, energizing my will, igniting a hot, inner
fire that turned me into the justice seeking Amazon
known as WONDER WOMAN!

"AAARH!" I screamed, hammering my boot heel
into the instep of his sandaled foot. He yowled in
pain, dropping his arm from around my throat to
hop backward on one foot. I spun around and
slammed my palm upward into his nose. CLONK! I
dropkicked his kneecap. THUNK! He stumbled
backward over Jonathan, falling onto his fat suit in an
awkward heap.

"I've got him!" cried Jonathan, rolling on top of
him like a giant rolling pin.

I pivoted on my heel. "Grab Bail—"

She was smiling at me from the far end of the aisle,
a can of pepper spray in each hand, fingers on the
nozzles. "You are *such* a pain," she said patiently. "Get
the broccoli off Dori, then step aside."

NUTS! Would nobody give me a break here?

"You've got some good moves for an escort," she said begrudingly. "Self-defense lessons?"

"It's the costume," I said, panting. I stood my ground, matching her stare for stare. "You fell in love with the wrong man, Bailey."

"Says you. I know he's the right man."

"He's slept with half the student population of Penn State!"

"So? He's a man. He has needs."

"Does he need condoms?" Nana interjected. "Margi's got extra."

I shook my head. "So if he was sleeping with the immediate world, why keep your relationship with him a secret? What difference would it make to anyone?"

Bailey stared at me as if I'd suddenly sprouted a spare head. "Hel-looo? I can't afford to have any hint of scandal appear in my personal records. I want to teach in the Ivy League! You think I'd stand a snowball's chance in hell if word got out that I was shagging my major professor? If I don't maintain the appearance of being intellectually superior and morally upright, I end up at East Podunk University with all the other academic losers. Do I strike you as the kind of person who'd let that happen?"

"I've heard a East Podunk," said Nana. "Where's that at? New Jersey?"

Bailey threw an irritated look at Nana and Tilly before circling back to me. "You put two and two together, didn't you? Dori thought he was being so clever by giving me that necklace. No one ever made the connection. He loved it that we were pulling the wool over everyone's eyes."

I shrugged. "People in Pennsylvania might say rowboat, or fishing boat, or dinghy, but in the land of ten thousand lakes where my grampa lived, a lot of people say *dory*. So if you're wearing a fourteen-karat gold *dory* around your neck, and the people in Professor Smoker's inner circle are the only ones allowed to call him by his pet name, I'm thinking that makes you about as inner circle as they come."

She smiled with quiet respect. *"Touché."* Nils hedged slightly toward her. *Pssssssst!* She blasted him with her pepper spray.

"Uff da!" he cried in a spate of rabid Norwegian, driving his fists into his eyes. I winced in sympathy.

"Anyone else?" she offered. "There's plenty where that came from."

"Nice job playing the aggrieved graduate student," I complimented her.

"Thanks. I minored in theater as an undergrad."

"So how was this supposed to work?" I prodded. "Smoker dies, then the two of you rendezvous on some remote Carribean island where you divide the proceeds from the sale of the journal and treasure?" I tried not to react as Darth Vader materialized by the men's head behind her. Wait a minute. Darth was already there. I shifted my gaze from the evil lord on my right to the one standing straight ahead. *Holy crap*. There were two of them?

"Orkney Islands," Bailey corrected. "Not so much

tourism there. A change of identity for Dori. A fake passport. It was rather an ingenious plan, considering how quickly we had to hatch it. Dori gets to escape the censure of school administration for his sexual practices, and I get to spend the rest of my life with a man who has placed me in the center of his universe."

"You and everyone else," I fired at her. "Not to mention, he killed a man!"

"That wasn't part of the plan. What do you want me to do? He said he was sorry! Look, enough with the chitchat. Help him onto his feet. We have a boat we need to sink."

Halfway up the aisle, Jennifer French stirred back into consciousness, coiled her body around to regard Bailey, and before I could blink, charged at her like an offensive tackle.

"EHH!" cried Bailey, as the pepper spray flew out of her hands and rolled out of reach.

"Catfight!" cried Dopey, leaping onto a bench for a ringside seat as the two women crashed to the deck with a reverberating BOOM! The two Darths swept forward, one yanking Jennifer to her feet, the other hoisting Bailey off the floor.

"Leave me alone!" Jennifer shrieked at Darth Number One, swinging her fist at his mask. "Daaaamn!" she cried, cradling her hand against her black feline chest. "Bastards! You're all bastards!"

I shook my head. Was anyone besides me noticing that Jennifer might have a few unresolved issues with anger management?

"Give it up," Darth Number One ordered Jennifer, forcing her onto an empty bench.

"You, too," ordered Darth Number Two, cuffing Bailey to an upright pole.

He had handcuffs? I looked on curiously. Was that part of Vader's official equipment, or were cuffs only included in the superdeluxe version of the costume?

"Emily!" Jonathan beckoned from atop Smoker, his florets fluttering wildly. "I could use a little help over here!"

The dwarfs and crayons rallied, coaxing him to his feet and standing him upright, while two little pigs replaced him on top of Smoker, paralyzing the professor beneath six hundred pounds of pork on the hoof. "Would somebody get a picture of this?" yelled one of the pigs. "Emily might be able to use it in her newsletter."

I brushed off Jonathan's stalk, embarrassed that I could have ever thought him capable of murder.

"Did I do good?" he asked shyly.

"You did great." I flashed him a face-cracking smile, my mouth dropping open as I looked beyond him to the two Darths who stood before me, minus their breathing masks. EH! "Duncan?" I rasped, touched by the desire playing on his handsome face. "Etienne?" I whispered, warmed by the passion smoldering in his electric blue eyes. "You're both here." I forced the smile to remain on my lips. "Imagine that." And one of them had asked me to marry him.

Euw, boy. This was a little awkward. "About my cabin upgrade." I darted a desperate look between them. "That was so generous and . . . and romantic of you!"

"It was nothing," said Jonathan.

I swiveled my head, drilling his little green face with a horrified look. "*Excuse me?*"

"Your upgrade. I wanted to thank you for saving my life."

"*You?*" I stabbed my finger at his stalk. "You paid for the upgrade?"

"I was happy to pay for it."

"But you have no money, Jonathan. You don't even have a job!"

"So? I have an American Express card. That's just as good as money."

Oh, hell! "Was it you who sent the flowers?"

"That was me," said Duncan.

"And me," said Etienne.

I exchanged frustrated looks with both of them before turning to Duncan. "You knew about my new cabin the day it happened. How?"

He shrugged. "The clerk in the florist shop pulled up all that information on the computer when I placed my order. She mentioned you'd been upgraded to a suite with a great balcony."

I threw my hands into the air. "WHO SENT THE MARRIAGE PROPOSAL?"

"That would be me," Etienne whispered, in a voice that vibrated down my breastbone. "I love you, Emily."

"I love her, too," objected Duncan. "And the only thing that kept me from proposing earlier was that I was heaving into a barf bag!"

"Don't listen to them," Jonathan cried, dropping to his knees in front of me. "You're the only girl in the world for me, Emily. Will you marry me?"

Oh, yeah. This was going well.

CHAPTER 16

At ten o'clock the following morning, while other passengers were bicycling down Mount Haleakala, snorkeling, or touring a tropical plantation to learn of Hawaii's rich agricultural heritage, I sat at the dining table in my stateroom, staring at the puzzle box that security had removed from Bailey's backpack the night before and returned to Tilly, along with her missing journal.

"How much longer are we gonna gawk at this thing before we get down to business?" Bernice sniped. "I say we set the dang thing on a chair and let one of the Dicks sit on it. That should be enough to bust it into smithereens."

All the Halloween costumes had been returned to the rental shop, so everyone was pretty much back to normal again.

"How come you're singling the Dicks out?" Lucille

objected. "I'm just as big as they are. Why should they have all the fun?"

"You can't sit on it," Tilly reprimanded. "It's not a whoopie cushion. It's an historic artifact."

"I think Bernice has a point," Margi spoke up. "What good has come of that box? It played a part in getting the little Norwegian killed. It nearly got Emily killed. I think it's bad luck. We should get rid of it before anything else happens."

Knock knock knock. We all swiveled our heads toward the door before I gave Alice the okay to pop up and answer it. Nana and Helen Teig straggled into the room, their faces long with disappointment.

"I was so sure I was gonna win," Nana lamented, as she and Helen dragged chairs to the table to join the rest of us. "I come up with everythin'. The business card. The map with no advertisin'. The blue M&M." She shot a glance at Helen. "A *real* M&M, too. Not one a them doctored-up things."

Helen elevated her chin to a haughty angle. "I don't want to hear it, Marion. Scavenger hunts are like love and war. Everything is fair."

"What do you mean, doctored-up?" asked Margi.

Nana gave her lips a "well, let me tell you" smack. "Helen couldn't find no blue M&M, so she colored one a her Skittles to look like an M&M."

"I would have won, too, if the ink hadn't rubbed off on the judge's fingers."

"I *told* you to use your Magic Marker," her husband chided. "But *nooo*, you had to go with the ballpoint."

"The Magic Marker was dark blue," Helen barked. "I needed peacock blue. Besides, I was glad I lost when they showed us the prize. An ugly chunk of rock from the Volcanoes National Park. Can you believe that? They tried to dress it up by sticking it in a little acrylic box with a brass label, but it was still ugly."

"They actually gave away some of the island's volcanic rock?" I questioned. "But isn't that supposed to rain bad luck down on the recipient?"

"That only applies to folks what steal the rock," Nana explained. "If the State Parks Department makes a gift a the stuff, you don't got nothin' to worry about. At least, that's the line they give us before they announced the winner."

"And the winner was none too happy with the prize, either," Helen stated. "You could tell by the way he ran screaming from the room."

"What's the big deal about that?" asked Bernice. "They do that on *The Price Is Right* all the time."

"So who won?" I asked. "Anyone I know?"

"A fella with two broken arms," said Helen.

I stared at Nana, wide-eyed. "Jonathan won the scavenger hunt?"

"Beat me out by two minutes and thirty-three seconds."

"Wow, his luck really is changing. I'll have to congratulate him."

"I'm sure he'd like that, dear. But you won't find him in his cabin on account a he's in the infirmary."

Uh-oh. "Please tell me he's only visiting a friend."

"Nope. He run outta that room so fast, he didn't see the 'wet floor' cones outside the potties until he was airborne. But they was sayin' he only broke one leg, so that was real good news."

Tap, tap, tap. Our heads pivoted to the door again. Osmond got up to answer it and returned with Duncan.

"Good morning, all," he said to the room at large before directing a meaningful look my way. "Would you believe I was stupid enough to think I might actually catch you alone?"

"Group meeting," I said, shrugging. "We're trying to decide what we should do with Tilly's treasure."

He sauntered toward the table, peering at the oblong box in the middle. "So this is the infamous Ring treasure?"

"Some treasure," fussed Bernice. "If we don't know what's inside, it's nothing but a piece of junk."

"Did you have a chance to talk to Percy and Basil?" I asked Duncan.

"This morning. It took a while, but they finally coughed up the information. They put marbles into the ship's vault, pure glass ones that were manufactured years ago. I guess collectors consider them on a par with Superman comic books and old Coke bottles."

I regarded him skeptically. "Marbles? That's what they dug up at the Secret Falls and were being so secretive about? Marbles?"

"Basil's family owns the Broomhead Gallery and Museum in Pudsey, England, so he's always looking for articles to replace the ones he destroyed when he accidentally burned the place down when he was a little nipper. I guess it's been a terrible burden for him to bear all these years. His relatives have never let him live it down."

Marbles? I shook my head. "So did you convince them to explain about the list of names on the back of Percy's business card?"

"Your hit parade?" He laughed. "The town of Harrogate in Yorkshire sponsors a parade every year to commemorate Captain James Cook's birthday, and each year the board of tourism tries to find people who have some relationship to Cook to ride in the main float. Next year's selections were going to be two James Cook scholars: Dorian Smoker and Bailey Howard—the first two choices of the Harrogate Institute of Tourism. Otherwise known as H. I. T."

I made a small O of my mouth as warmth crawled up my throat. "It was a real parade? Not . . . a hit list?"

"An honest mistake," Duncan soothed. "And very creative, I might add."

"But I don't get it. If Percy was so anti-Cook, why was he carrying around the names of people who were candidates for a pro-Cook celebration?"

"He and Basil intended to convince Smoker and Bailey *not* to participate in the parade. Their real beef is with the tourism board, and their long-term goal is to bring an end to the festivities entirely."

Knock. Knock, knock.

Groans. Hissing. Eye rolling.

"Why don't you just leave the door open and stick

an Open House sign on it?" Bernice suggested. "Save us from having to get up so much."

"I'll get it," said Duncan, returning in a half minute with Etienne at his side. EH! Just what I needed. All the competition in the same room again. I gave Etienne a little finger wave and wondered how many Tums I'd have to swallow to calm my stomach. He gave me a long, lingering look that would have caused internal combustion if I'd been sitting closer.

"I'm glad you're all here," he said, in his beautiful French/German/Italian accent. "I believe I have some information that might be of interest to you. Do you mind, Emily?"

"Please." I allowed him the floor with a sweeping gesture.

"As a professional courtesy, the Maui police shared some of their findings with me this morning, so I have answers to a few of the questions that were still bothering Emily last night after the professor and Miss Howard had been taken into custody."

"What kind of questions?" asked Bernice.

"Questions about Nils Nilsson," he responded. "He was not the Nils Nilsson who was arrested on charges of assault with a baseball bat. That was another Nils Nilsson, one of sixteen former presidents of the World Navigators Club with the same name. Nilsson is apparently as common a name in Norway as Bucherer is in Switzerland, or Smith is in the United States."

So how was I supposed to know that? Heat crept from my throat to my cheeks. "Did Nils or Gjurd tell the police what they found at the Secret Falls?"

"Coins," said Etienne. "Or what they thought were coins. Upon closer examination, they discovered they were actually old tokens from the New York subway system. Still, if presented to the right collector, they could be worth something."

"I wanna know how Jennifer French got hold a our treasure map without buyin' it from Bernice like everyone else done," said Nana.

Etienne smiled. "When she was questioned about her attack on Miss Howard, she mentioned how a significant archaeological find might have worked in her favor at the university. As to how she came by the map, she said someone had forgotten to remove it from the photocopier in the business center, so she simply took it."

Oh, this was cute. *Everyone* had forgotten to remove the map from the photocopier, even Bernice. That had to make Tilly feel better about her own mental health. But I was still curious about one *teensy* point.

"Can you explain something to me?" I asked Etienne. "Professor Smoker obviously jumped ship in Kauai. But what did he do until he left? Stay holed up in Bailey's cabin? He couldn't have stayed there the entire time because he would have been found out by the cabin steward, wouldn't he?"

Etienne nodded. "Bailey had a duplicate key made

for her cabin so they could both come and go as they pleased, then she shaved his head and rented a disguise for him in the costume shop. A fat suit. Facial hair. Bought him a Hawaiian shirt. I believe you might have run into him the night of the storm in the Anchor Bar."

Oh, my God! The guy in the bar had been Professor Smoker?

"I believe the professor was feeling rather full of himself by then, skulking about the ship incognito. His original plan had been to lie low in Kauai until Bailey sent him his falsified travel documents, but when she contacted him about your grandmother's friends finding the treasure, he decided he needed to help her steal the thing, so he used Ansgar's ship ID card to reboard. He probably would have gotten away with murder if not for Shelly Valentine's and Emily's keen eyes." Etienne glanced at the box in the middle of the table for the first time. "Is this the piece that has been causing all the trouble?"

"You bet," said Nana.

"It's a piece of junk," snapped Bernice.

"It's an item of inestimable worth," pledged Tilly as she opened her journal to the proper page. "Griffin Ring himself says it's priceless. It's right here in black and white."

"You haven't opened it yet?" Etienne asked.

"We don't know how," said Nana. "It's one a them puzzle boxes."

"Do you mind if I try?"

Tilly handed him the box. "Be my guest."

He held it above his head, checking all the angles,

then lowered it to his waist and with pressure from his thumbs and forefingers, eased the lid effortlessly off the box.

Oohs. Ahhs. Gasps.

"How'd you do that?" asked Nana.

"My grandmother has one much like it. They're very European."

When he set the box back down in the middle of the table, we peered into the interior, agog.

"What is it?" asked Dick Teig. "A pocket watch?"

"It's too big for a pocket watch," said Dick Stolee. "The thing's big as a saucer. My money's on an antique stopwatch."

"You're both very close," said Tilly as she lifted it into the palm of her hand. "Do you know what this is?"

"Piece of junk," said Bernice.

"It's a chronometer," Tilly marveled. "A device to measure the longitude of a ship. This must be one of the original chronometers designed by John Harrison. Oh, my goodness. This is incredible! Captain Cook must have enlisted Griffin Ring to bury it so that if the other devices were stolen, they'd still have one to use on the return voyage to England. The Sandwich Islanders were notorious for stealing everything they could get their hands on, so this chronometer must have been their backup. After Cook was killed, the crew obviously never bothered to retrieve it. Do you know what this means?"

"I'm hoping it means we're all filthy rich," said Dick Teig.

"It means we can make a noteworthy contribution to the National Maritime Museum in Greenwich, England! We'll be greeted like conquering heroes!"

Dick Teig rolled his eyes. "I'd rather be filthy rich."

"I can't thank you enough, Inspector Miceli," Tilly enthused as she boosted herself to her feet. "Come along, people. We're going to have this secured in the vault straightaway."

Grumbling. Pouting. Groaning. But in the time it took to blink, they were out of their seats and through the door, leaving me alone for the first time with the two men in my life.

I smiled at Etienne. I smiled at Duncan. I tried to think of something profound to say. "Would you like to sit down?"

They sat on either side of me, bookending me like a couple of pumped up Chippendales. "Do you have an answer for me this morning?" asked Etienne, cradling my right hand.

"I was about to ask the same thing," said Duncan, cradling my left.

"I asked her first," announced Etienne.

"So what?" countered Duncan.

Etienne narrowed his eyes at Duncan. "Who the hell are you, anyway?"

Duncan clenched his fist. "You want to take it outside, bud? I'll be glad to show you."

Oh, this was nice. I looked from one to the other, thinking that you really did need to watch what you prayed for, because sometimes you actually got it. In spades. "Um—" I bobbed my head toward Etienne. "I'm a bit curious. When did you board ship?"

"In Kauai."

"So why did you wait until last night to pop up?"

His face darkened with embarrassment. "The storm. I—uh—I was a bit seasick."

"You, too?" asked Duncan, softening. "Was that the absolute worst feeling you've ever experienced, or what?"

"Absolutely the worst. I didn't think I'd make it through the night. I was *praying* I wouldn't make it through the night. Sorry, darling," he apologized.

"They say Admiral Nelson was seasick his entire career," Duncan went on. "I don't know how he stood it. You ever been to Portsmouth, Miceli? If you tour the *HMS Victory,* you can stand on the very spot where Nelson bought the farm. It's pretty awe-inspiring. I know the guy who leads those Portsmouth tours. If you're interested, I could put you in touch with him."

"Thanks, I appreciate the offer. By the way, I don't believe we've been formally introduced." He reached his hand across my chest toward Duncan. "Etienne Miceli."

Duncan clasped his hand and grinned. "Duncan Lazarus. Glad to meet you."

That's what I loved about guys. They were so basic, it didn't take much for them to become fast friends. But if I was to give either one of them an answer, I needed to see their true colors at work, and there was only one way I knew to do that.

"I have a great idea, guys. I know it's a little early in the morning, but why don't we continue this discussion at the ice-cream bar on deck eleven? They always have the makings for great sundaes. Hot fudge. Pecans. Whipped cream. And of course, my personal favorite." I looked from one to the other and smiled brightly. "Maraschino cherries."

Pocket Books
proudly presents

G'DAY TO DIE

Maddy Hunter

Coming soon in paperback
from Pocket Books

Turn the page for a preview
of *G'Day to Die* . . .

CHAPTER 1

If you were to ask your average American to locate the west coast on a map, he'd rap a knuckle on California. If you were to ask your average Australian the same question, he'd slap his hand over the lower right-hand corner of his country to indicate Victoria—a state whose southern border flanks the sea, but whose landlocked western border is a whopping fifteen hundred miles away from Australia's *actual* west coast. Which, comparatively speaking, makes it the geographical equivalent of Iowa.

There's a simple explanation for this anomaly.

It's Australia. It's complicated.

We'd spent our first full day Down Under motoring along Victoria's Great Ocean Road, a one-hundred-sixty-mile, two-lane roller-coaster of a highway with panoramic views of the Southern Ocean's golden beaches, pounding surf and craggy bluffs. In the late afternoon we'd arrived at Port Campbell National Park so we could ooh and ahh over windswept cliffs, fjord-like coves, and chimney stacks of rock that jut up from the sea. Our travel brochure refers to these limestone monoliths as "The Twelve Apostles," and they were spectacular. With the fearsome Southern Ocean gnawing at their base and the sun gilding them with blinding light, they were the most dazzling natural wonder I'd seen in my fifteen-month stint as a tour escort.

"What a gyp," Bernice Zwerg grated in her ex-smoker's voice as we gathered at the visitor center, waiting to reboard our tour bus.

"Why is it a gyp?" I wasn't surprised by her negative reaction to one of Australia's most popular landmarks; Bernice hated everything.

She held up her travel brochure and squinted at me down her orange-zinc-oxide-covered nose. It was January, the height of summer in Australia, so all the seniors in my group were taking measures to prevent sunburn, but the orange nose was pretty distracting.

"Twelve Apostles? Did anyone bother to count them? There's only eight. I paid to see twelve, so I'm thinking refund."

"Maybe the Aussies have a different numbering system," offered Helen Teig as she dragged her three-hundred-pound frame toward us. She used her travel brochure to fan her face, which had turned candy apple red in the hundred degree heat and body-battering wind. "Maybe 'twelve' to them is 'eight' to us."

Bernice rolled her eyes. "That's the dumbest thing I ever heard. Hey, you." She thwacked the arm of a ruggedly good-looking man whose pale green bush outfit and wide-brimmed Akubra hat hinted that he was either a home-grown Aussie or a seasoned *Travelsmith* shopper. She flashed three fingers before his face. "How many fingers am I holding up?"

"Wot's she want to know?" shrieked the grizzled gnome of a woman who clung to his arm.

"She wants to know how mini fingahs she's holding up!" he hollered in a Crocodile Dundee twang that labeled him as a local.

"Why? Can't she count?" The little woman fixed Bernice with an impatient look. "Three fingers. Wot are you? Stupid?" The woman's hair was a wild, windblown cotton ball, and her eyes were pinpricks of brilliant blue in a face so deeply seamed with wrinkles that she looked a thousand years old. I was on a two-week tour of Australia with the world's oldest living human.

"Excuse me. There used to be twelve," said a tall, chestnut-haired, middle-aged man in neatly pressed walking shorts and sandals. "Unfortunately, time hasn't treated them kindly. Four of them have collapsed into the sea, and there's another that looks to be on the verge." He punched a button on the fancy digital camera that hung around his neck and angled the display screen toward us, poking the screen with his forefinger. "This one here. Did you notice? The base has been all but eroded away. In another few years, there may only be seven."

"The Magnificent Seven," said Helen, hand splayed over her ample bosom. "I loved that movie. Yul Brynner was so . . . so . . ."

"Bald," snapped the thousand-year-old woman.

"As a bowling ball," agreed Helen. "Yul was a real trend-setter when it came to hairstyles."

"Those are some great pictures," Bernice allowed as she hovered over the man's camera. "I've got a digital camera. How come my shots don't look like yours?"

Whoa! Had an actual compliment just escaped Bernice's mouth? Grab your bobsleds; hell had officially frozen over.

"I'd better be a halfway decent photographer," the man said, laughing. "It's how I make my living. Guy Madelyn." He gave her a smile that animated his face. "Weddings are my specialty, so if you're ever in the market for a high-priced wedding photographer, I'm your guy. Pun intended."

Bernice peered up at him, doe-eyed. She gave her name tag a demure touch and her stubby eyelashes a seductive flutter. "I'm Bernice. Did I mention I'm a widow?"

She was twice his age, half his height, with a dowager's hump that rivaled Ayer's Rock. Oh, yeah. That was gonna fly.

"I got pictures, too." Nana shuffled toward me in her size five sneakers. She was wearing a duckbill visor, white capri pants, and a shell pink T-shirt embroidered with flowers, songbirds, and the words Iowa's No. 1 Gramma. My brother Steve's family had splurged last Christmas and bought her one in every color, which had aroused some envy among her friends. T-shirts bearing the words Best, Greatest, or No. 1 were all the rage at the senior center.

"You wanna see, dear?" She handed me a fistful of Polaroids, narrating as I flipped through them. "That's the wooden walkway leadin' to the lookout points. And there's them scrubby bushes growin' beside it. Don't know how that pink flower ever managed to sprout up in the middle of all them brambles, but it sure is pretty. That's Dick Stolee after the wind blew his baseball cap off his head." She lowered her voice to a whisper. "I was waitin' to shoot the expression on his face when his toupee flew off, but it just sat there. He must be springin' for better glue than what he was usin' in Switzerland."

Guy Madelyn craned his neck to peek at Nana's shots. "Have you tried a digital camera? I'm sold on mine."

"Already got one," Nana said, "but it's too much fuss. Pricey batteries. Pricey memory cartridges. Pricey photo paper. Monkeyin' with every picture you download. So I'm back to my Polaroid. Pixels might be the in thing, but I'll take instant gratification any day."

I flipped to a photo of a towering stack of limestone that vaguely resembled a T. rex.

"Can you guess which apostle that is, dear? I think it's a real good likeness."

Bernice burst into laughter. "The rocks don't have names, Marion. Someone called them the Twelve Apostles as a marketing gimmick."

Nana ignored her. "That's St. Peter, and the puny one in the next shot is Judas. You can tell 'cause it looks more sneaky than them others."

"Which one's Dopey?" asked eighty-eight-year-old Osmond Chelsvig, hobbling over to us on his spindly white legs.

Osmond's inability to distinguish dwarfs from apostles wasn't surprising, considering he hailed from a long line of agnostics.

"Excuse me." Guy Madelyn was suddenly at Nana's elbow. "Would you mind if I take a closer look at your photos? You seem to have captured some unique angles that I missed entirely."

"No kiddin'?" She handed the stack over, smiling broadly as he examined every snapshot. "They look pretty ordinary to me, but the light here's real bright, so it makes everything look good."

"You're being modest. The Australian light isn't what makes your shots so outstanding. It's your composition. Your contrast. Look at this shot." He flashed it at the handful of guests circled around us. "You've turned an ordinary pink flower into something extraordinary. I've never seen anything like it. And on a Polaroid camera, no less. You have an incredible eye." He lowered his gaze to her name tag. "Marion Sippel, eh? I'm not familiar with your name or your work, but tell me I'm right in assuming you're a professional."

Nana gave a little suck on her dentures. "I do have some professional trainin'."

"I knew it. Where did you study? The Royal College of Art? The Brooks Institute?"

"Windsor City Senior Center. They ran a two-hour minicourse last November. It was real in-depth."

He let out a belly laugh. "You took pictures like *this* with only two hours of training?"

"It was s'posed to be four, but we run into a schedulin' conflict with the low-vision group's Christmas cookie exchange."

He shook his head, awe in his voice. "Mrs. Sippel, if you'll allow me an unbiased opinion, these photos are nothing short of Ansel Adams caliber. I'm speechless."

"Lemme see those," said Bernice, snatching the stack from his hand.

"Me, too," said Helen Teig, grabbing a fistful from Bernice.

"Careful!" Guy shouted as Nana's photos made the circuit, passing from hand to hand. "Don't get your fingerprints on them. Have a quick look, then give them back."

Amid the buzz of enthusiasm, he turned back to Nana. "Have you ever thought of turning professional, Mrs. Sippel? Hollywood glitterati are willing to pay ridiculous amounts for wedding photos these days, and the photographer they're clamoring for is me. But I'm having trouble going solo. Too many remarriages to keep up with. I've been looking to hire another photographer, but I haven't found anyone suitable—until today. Are you available? I'd start you out as an apprentice, but with your talent, I could probably guarantee you a six-figure salary."

A hush descended over the crowd for a nanosecond. Limbs froze. Mouths fell open.

Then Bernice hit a button on her digital camera and

shoved it in Guy's face. "I take some pretty good pictures myself. See here? What do you think of that contrast? And look at this one. Have you ever seen better composition?"

"My Dick takes better pictures than that," Helen claimed. "DICK! WHERE ARE YOU? GET OVER HERE!"

"I've taken some mighty fine pictures," said Osmond, elbowing Bernice out of the way. He angled his camcorder display screen in front of Guy. "My scenery's moving, but if you see anything you like, I'd be happy to freeze-frame it for you."

"This is Mushroom!" cried Margi Swanson, waving a snapshot of her cat in the air. "I took it myself. You think I have potential?"

"Get out of the way!" snarled the thousand-year-old woman as she pushed toward Guy. "I've got a photo for you."

I stood on tiptoes to peek at the sepia-toned picture she handed him. The print might once have been glossy, but time and touch had dog-eared the corners and dulled the finish so much that all I could see was an irregular pattern of creases cobwebbing an image that was no longer clear.

Guy studied it for a long moment in the manner of one accustomed to handling other people's photographic treasures. "A lovely picture," he said kindly. "But if you want to preserve it, I'd suggest a frame rather than a wallet. Or perhaps a photo restoration process. They'd have this looking good as new in no time."

"Come along, lovey," said the young man in the bush outfit, tugging on the crone's arm. He retrieved the print from Guy and gave him an appreciative wink. "Photo of her mum. You know how that goes, mate. She shows it to everyone."

"Certainly. Would everyone please start handing Mrs. Sippel's photos back? I don't want to lose track of any."

Bodies shifted. Elbows flew. I got jostled left and right and suddenly found myself ejected from the crowd like a stray pinball. I skidded to a stop on my new ankle-strap wedges and looked back at the melee. Geesch! Who'd have guessed that one teensy compliment could start such a feeding frenzy?

"Emily!"

I looked across the room to find a man beckoning to me. This was no ordinary man. This was Etienne Miceli, the Swiss police inspector I wanted to marry.

"Come join us!" shouted his companion.

And this was not any ordinary companion. This was Duncan Lazarus, the doggedly persistent tour director who wanted to marry *me*. The two men had become "buds" since they'd met two months ago, and seemed to be enjoying the kind of intense male friendship that's so ballyhooed among Marines, college athletes, and belching contest finalists.

"Be there in a sec," I called back, still unnerved by the prospect of juggling both of them for the next fourteen days. But this had been their idea. They insisted on going head-to-head on a level playing field, like players in a *Survivor* challenge, and no arguments on my part could change their minds. So here they were, in the same room, vying for me as if I were the lone bucket of chicken wings on an island whose only other food source was sand flies.

As I marshaled my courage to join my two suitors, the crowd encircling Guy spat out another guest who came hurtling straight toward me. "Eh!" I cried, sidestepping her before her sturdy Birkenstocks creamed my open-toed wedges.

"Oops! Sorry." She paused for a breath, shivering as she stared back at the mob. "I didn't mean to get caught in the middle of that." She patted down her five-pocket blouse and hiking shorts as if taking inventory, before flashing me a smile. "I've never seen people get so maniacal over photographs. I specialize in chopping off heads, so I don't even own a camera. I learned long ago that postcards are the way to go. I'm Claire Bellows, and you're obviously not part of the Aussie Adventures tour since you're not wearing a name tag."

I returned her smile. "Emily Andrew. I'm part of the tour, I just don't do name tags."

"I like that idea." She removed her ID from around her neck and stuffed it into her breast pocket. "We're not school kids, right? I hate name tags, and I'll be stuck wearing one for a whole week after the tour is over."

"Conference?"

"Yeah. Scientific meeting in Melbourne. How 'bout you?"

"I'm on the job as we speak. Official escort for a group of Iowa seniors who are in the middle of that mob over there."

"So you're not alone?" Claire Bellows reminded me a little of Rosie O'Donnell—dark-haired and chunky, with a directness that oozed confidence. "I always travel alone. When you're by yourself, other tourists feel sorry for you, so they adopt you. It's a great way to meet new people. If I keep at it, I figure I'm bound to run into Mr. Right one of these days. Are you married?"

"I used to be." I let out a sigh. "It's a long story."

"I've never been married. I'm thirty-seven years-old, on a career track that has my head pressed against a ceiling made of three-foot glass, and unless I can reinvent the wheel and wow my company's CEO, that's where I'll be stuck until I'm ready to hang up my lab coat. So I've entered the marriage market. Husband, two point three kids, dog, gas-guzzling SUV—I want it all. I hit the snooze button on my biological clock when I started work and the alarm is about to go off, so I'm pulling out all the stops. Guaranteed, I'll be walking down the aisle in the next few months." She glanced around the room as if scouting out likely prospects. "Do you have time to date much?"

"Um . . . dating is a problem."

"Well, don't be surprised by what you find when you get back into the dating scene. If you don't have good instincts, you're going to end up disappointed." She bobbed her head toward Etienne and Duncan. "You see those two hunks over there by the window? Case in point. The two best-looking men on the tour, and they're taken."

My neck grew warm with self-conscious guilt, but in my own defense, *this wasn't my fault!* I wasn't flaunting them like trophies. I hadn't even invited them to join me on the tour!

Claire let out a moan. "It never fails. The gorgeous guys are always gay."

I jerked my head around to stare at her. "What?"

A gust of wind whistled through the room as our guide banged through the main entrance, his navy blue uniform putting him in danger of being mistaken for a United States Postal Service worker. His name was Henry, and in addition to narrating our travelogue, he drove the bus, prepared and served mid-morning tea and cakes, directed us to the restrooms, counted heads, snapped guest photos, maintained our vehicle, treated minor injuries, exchanged currency, and could belt out a rendition of *Waltzing Mathilda* that made your teeth vibrate. I was dying to see what he'd do for an encore.

"If I can trouble you for your attention!" he called out. "I apologize to those of you waiting to board the Aussie Adventures bus, but one of our tires has blown, so I'm waiting on a mechanic from Port Campbell for assistance.

No worries, though; we'll only be delayed an hour or two. Sorry for the inconvenience."

Groans. Hissing. "What are we supposed to do for two hours?" a disgruntled guest yelled.

"Introduce yourself to your mates!" Henry suggested. "You're in this for two weeks together. Give it a go."

Claire gave my arm a squeeze. "I'm heading outside. Something I want to check out. See you on the bus."

"But wait—" I sputtered as she broke for the door. I had to set her straight about Etienne and Duncan before her imaginings became grist for the rumor mill. If there was one thing I'd learned in Ireland, it was to nip a vicious rumor in the bud before it had a chance to blossom.

Tying a bandanna around my head to keep my hair out of my eyes, I signaled Etienne and Duncan that I had to leave, then exited the building, bracing myself against the force of the wind.

The sky was electric blue, the sun so hot that it blurred the air. I shivered at the hostile acres of briars and brush that stubbled the cliff top, then stepped onto the slatted walkway that knifed through them, noting the frequent signs that cautioned visitors to PLEASE REMAIN ON THE WALKWAY. Like there was someone on the planet who'd willingly stray *off* it?

I spied Claire and the other guests a city block away, hustling full-speed ahead in spite of the heat and headwind. I couldn't chase her down in my five-inch stacked heels, so I trudged behind her for an exhausting ten minutes, cursing when I reached the brow of the cliff, where the walkway split into a T.

I squinted east and west, wondering which way she and everyone else had gone. Nuts! *Eenie, meenie, meinie, moe . . .*

Interrupted by the sudden clatter of footsteps behind me, I turned to find Guy Madelyn coming my way. "The wind's a pain," he called out, his shirt tails flapping around him, "but at least it keeps the flies from tunneling up your nose." He stopped beside me and nodded seaward. "Did you know that if you leaped off this cliff and started swimming south, you wouldn't run into another land mass until you reached Antarctica?"

"Assuming you leaped at high tide."

He raised his forefinger in an "Excelsior!" kind of gesture. "Timing is everything. I'm sorry, I didn't catch your name in the visitor's center."

"Emily Andrew. You want to hire my grandmother as your new photographer."

"Mrs. Sippel is your grandmother? Damn, she has some fine photographic genes. Did she pass them on to you?"

"No, I got the shoe and makeup genes." I regarded him soberly as he opened the lens of his camera. "Were you serious about wanting to hire Nana?"

"I'll say! And I'd like to sign her up before the competition finds out about her." He scanned the horizon through his viewfinder before motioning me toward the guardrail. "Could I get a shot of you with the great Southern Ocean as a backdrop? I don't charge for my services when I'm on holiday."

Was I about to be discovered? Oh, wow. I might not have made it as an actress, but could Guy Madelyn make me look like a cover model?

I struck a pose against the guardrail and emoted like a *Sports Illustrated* swimsuit model. Sexy. Sultry. Windblown.

"Can you open your eyes?"

I tried again. Sexy. Surprised. Windblown.

"Maybe we should try this from one of the lookout points. We're getting too much light here."

Which I interpreted to mean it was a good thing I was employed, because I had no future as a cover model.

"So you're not here to shoot a wedding?" I asked as I walked double-time to keep up with his long strides.

"Family reunion. It seems the Madelyn side of my family played as important a role in Australian history as the *Mayflower* passengers played in American history, so when my wife and kids fly out from Vancouver in a couple of weeks, we're planning to meet all the Aussie relatives for the first time. The kids are really fired up, which is remarkable since they're at the age where nothing impresses them. I think they're finding the idea of celebrity status for a few days 'way cool.'"

"Because they're related to a famous photographer?"

He laughed. "Because the town is planning to honor us with an award to recognize the contribution my ancestors made toward populating this part of Victoria. We've dubbed it the Breeder's Cup. The kids figure we'll be the only family in British Columbia with a commemorative plaque for inveterate shagging, so that gives them bragging rights. Kids, eh?"

Noticing a discarded candy wrapper littering the wayside, I switched to good citizen mode and ducked beneath the guardrail to pick it up, frowning when I realized what I was holding. "This is one of Nana's photos. What's it doing out here?" It was bent and a little scratched, but in good shape otherwise. I showed it to Guy, who threw a curious look around us.

"I was positive all your grandmother's photos found their way back to her. People are so careless. I hope this is the only one she's missing."

I shrugged and slipped it into my shoulder bag. "It probably fell out of someone's hand and blew out the door. I'm glad I found it; she'll be thrilled to get it back. So, where did your ancestors emigrate from? England?" I knew everyone in Australia was an import, except for the

Aborigines, who'd been roaming the continent for either four centuries or sixty thousand years, depending upon which scholarly study you believed. Yup, the scientific community had really nailed that one.

"Portsmouth. They set sail in the early eighteen hundreds on a ship called the *Meridia,* and fifteen thousand miles later wrecked on a submerged reef along this stretch of coast. My relatives were among the lucky few who survived." He bobbed his head toward the open sea. "Over twelve hundred sunken vessels lie out there—more than anywhere else on earth. This whole stretch of ocean is a graveyard, which hammers home a point I've held for a long time."

"What's that?"

"Air travel is a wonderful thing."

We followed the walkway through a stand of trees that were as stunted and gnarled as Halloween ghouls, then descended a short flight of stairs to a lower level that afforded sweeping views of the apostles, the deeply scalloped coastline, and—

Guy suddenly ducked beneath the guardrail and charged through the underbrush, heading straight for the cliff's edge. Eh! Were Iowans the only people who ever observed the rules?

"What are you doing?" I screamed after him. "Didn't you read the signs? You're supposed to stay on the walkway!"

He dropped to his knees twenty feet away, and rolled something over.

Oh, God. It was a body.